What Night Brings

Brings

a novel by

Carla Trujillo

CURBSTONE PRESS

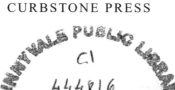

FIRST EDITION, 2003
Copyright © 2003 by Carla Trujillo
1st printing: March 2003; 2nd printing: July 2003; 3rd printing:
    February 2005.

Printed in the U.S. on acid-free paper by Bang Printing
Cover design: Susan Shapiro
Cover art: "The Dream" by Patssi Valdez, acrylic on canvas, 2000,
6'x8'; courtesy of Patricia Correia Gallery, www.correiagallery.com.

The publishers want to thank Jane Blanshard for her help in the copy-
editing of this book.

Portions of this novel were previously published in *TBC* and *TBCII*
(*To Be Continued* and *To Be Continued II*).

Connecticut Commission
on the Arts

This book was published with the support of
the Connecticut Commission on the Arts,
National Endowment for the Arts,
NATIONAL
ENDOWMENT
FOR THE ARTS
and donations from many individuals.
We are very grateful for all of this support.

Library of Congress Cataloging-in-Publication Data

Trujillo, Carla Mari.
  What night brings / by Carla Trujillo.—1st U.S. ed.
     p. cm.
  ISBN 1-880684-94-2 (alk. paper)
     1. Mexican American families—Fiction. 2. Mexican American
women—Fiction. 3. Working class families—Fiction. 4. Young
women—Fiction. 5. California—Fiction. I. Title.
  PS3620.R855 W48 2003
  813'.6—dc21
                                                    2002151447

published by
CURBSTONE PRESS
321 Jackson Street, Willimantic, CT 06226
e-mail: info@curbstone.org / www.curbstone.org

Acknowledgements

Mucho mil thank-you's to the following people who made writing this book possible:
Sandra Cisneros for her generosity, guidance, and insight. Tommi A. Mecca, who didn't know he kindled a flame. Margaret Cecchetti, for being la gran checker de Espanol. Katherine Forrest for reading my manuscript when *I know* she had her own to finish. Bryce Milligan for his support and feedback. Tey Diana Rebolledo, for her New Mexican smiles of recognition. Thaisa Frank and Mary Webb—teachers extraordinaire. Cherrie Moraga, Gloria Anzaldua, and Dorothy Allison, who told me my stories mattered. My family in New Mexico, who inspire me greatly. Michele Karlsberg for making it fun. Mimi Wheatwind and Janice Gould for the long talks. Caroline Kane and Mike Chamberlin for letting me work in your gorgeous place of peace. Jae Treesinger for Bay Area history. Jack Agüeros for selecting this book for the Mármol Prize. Curbstone Press, for all that you do, and for what you believe. And lastly, to Leslie Larson—with me through every word.

*This Book is Dedicated to
Those Who Couldn't Get Away*

What Night Brings

"The Revolution Begins at Home."

—Cherrie Moraga & Gloria Anzaldua

EVERY SINGLE DAY of my life I went to bed asking God to make my dad disappear. I didn't pray for him to die, just to leave. If I really wanted him dead, I didn't say it because that would be a sin. A big one. And I couldn't have big sins because I wanted something else from God. Something special.

The easiest thing would be for my dad to meet another lady and go away with her because my mom goes crazy whenever he looks at anyone else. The minute Mom catches him sneaking a look, she cusses in Spanish, tells him she's leaving, then walks across town to buy a pack of cigarettes. When she comes back, she sits in the living room smoking every one of them till the pack is gone.

My dad likes looking at girls—all kinds, all the time. If a girl he likes has big chiches, he smiles and looks at her like he's about to eat pudding. Nothing makes him happier, though, than a lady with big nalgas. The bigger, the better. If a lady like that walks by, he'll stare at her butt till he practically drills a hole in it. Then he'll turn and tell whoever's standing around how much he loves big women and how he'd like to get his hands on one. "Marci," he'd say jerking his head toward a lady twice his size. "If I could have just one night with something like that."

I don't even know what my dad would do with a lady with big nalgas. He's so little he'd probably get crushed if one sat on him. He likes to talk like he's big and tough. But to me, he's just little and mean. And he's always saying how good-looking he is, like, "Did you know that people stop me all the time and ask if I'm Tony Curtis?"

My dad's from Colorado. Born in '35 and raised with five brothers in Hermosa, a little town outside of Durango. Grandpa Santos was a cement layer, but he died when Dad was sixteen. After that, my dad had to help out and ended up doing cement, too—on highways mostly. He said he made all kinds of roads, even big freeways, all over Colorado, New Mexico, and some parts of Utah. He hated working Utah. Said it was because "the beer there's like drinking a goddamn can of water."

Dad's a lot darker than Mom. Probably because he's been out in the sun so much. His hair is black and his eyes are light green like a cat's. They stand out against his face, so you can always see him watching you, even in a room full of people. His arms are little, but hard. And he can whip off his belt faster than you can say son-of-bitch because that's what you're usually saying when you're about to get it from him.

Mom was born in Gallup, New Mexico and started working behind a bar when she was "tall enough to reach the sink." The Coronado was Grandma Flor's bar. Mom's the baby in the family and all the other kids moved out when they got married. When Grandpa Chon ran off with that gabacha, there was no one else to help except Mom, who got up early every morning to clean and put beer in the cooler. Later, after school, she went back to the bar, did her homework, and helped Grandma whenever she got busy. Mom liked being the waitress, but Grandma only let her do it for people she knew.

"One day," my mom said, "your daddy was working on a road close by and came into The Coronado for a beer. I was old enough so I poured the drink myself. The second I saw him with his dimpled chin, little butt, and sparkly green eyes, se acabó. That was it. Your daddy was so damn cute I practically knocked your grandma over running up to give him his beer. He quit his job that very day. And in two weeks I became Mrs. Eddie Cruz."

They moved to California where Dad got a job making cars at the Chevy plant. He tells everyone he's "making cars no Mexicans will buy." Why not, people ask. "Because their name is Nova, *No Va*. Get it?" Then he starts laughing like it's the first time he ever heard the joke.

We've been living here in San Lorenzo ever since. A lot of people on our street work at Chevy. It might be because our town is close to the factory. My dad drives an Impala, and in five minutes he's at work. On the other side of us, not far from where you get on the freeway, is the refinery. Some of my friend's dads work there, too. When the wind comes our way it can smell bad, like rotten eggs. Most of the time we're lucky because it blows toward the bay. Dad's been working at Chevy for thirteen years, but Mom doesn't work because he won't let her. She doesn't drive either. It's been that way as long as I can remember. Except for Tía Leti, Mom doesn't have any friends. She spends the day cleaning house, doing Jack LaLane, and watching *Dialing for Dollars*.

People might not think eyes talk, but Mom's eyes do. They're two different colors; one's blue and the other's brown. Whenever she sits still and looks like she's thinking, the brown one crinkles up like she's looking into the sun. Mom acts like she's afraid to see anything for herself. I don't know if she does it on purpose, but whatever she sees or thinks seems seen or thought by my dad first. Anything she says is only what he's said, and that goes for what's inside of her, too. Except for getting mad at my dad about other ladies, I never know what she's really feeling.

Mom's tall. Tall enough to kiss my dad without him having to bend over. When they do kiss, Dad tells her to close her eyes. Maybe it's because of the colors. You can't look at brown and blue at the same time because your head gets mixed up. You lose your balance. And if you look at just one eye, you won't see what the other one's doing. It wasn't that way with Grandma Flor's dog, Jaime. He had eyes like that, too, but his fur was different colors, so everything matched.

A lot of people think my mom is pretty, including me. She looks like she could be part Sophia Loren and part Rita Moreno. Her skin is soft, and her hair is brown; that is until Tía Leti comes to dye it. Tía Leti is Grandma Flor's baby sister. She comes over all the time with her cigarettes and her grouchy dog, Pepito. Tía can't afford the beauty parlor, but she can afford my mom. So every month, the doorbell rings and there she is with her little box of Revlon "Autumn Evening." Then she sits in the kitchen smoking cigarettes and jabbering away while Mom goes to work. Pepito sits in her lap the whole time sneezing from the smell. When they're done, the kitchen looks like a bomb hit it, with all the stained bowls, gloves, towels, and combs lying around. To pay Mom back, Tía dyes her hair "Copper Sunset." And after everything's finished, she has to listen to Dad squawk like a jaybird about the "goddamn puta hairdo" his wife's got.

I have a little sister but no brothers. My name's Marcía Cruz, and my sister's name is Corin. Dad named her after a song. It goes: "Corinna, Corinna; Corinna, Corinna; Corinna, Corinna, I love you so." I never heard it, but that's how my dad sings it. Corinna's her real name, but we just call her Corin. When I look at her, the first thing I think of is Wile E. Coyote, because she's sneaky and sad like him. I wish I could read her mind, just so I could be ready for all the crazy things that come out of it. Sometimes those things get us into trouble. I don't know how it happens. We could be playing, yelling, having fun, and the next thing you know, she does something wrong, and there goes my dad.

My dad can't go through a single day without worrying. He's nervous, just like Tía Leti's dog. Pepíto's different than most dogs because he's mean. Even if you petted him nice, he'd bite you if he felt like it. Pepíto's part Chihuahua. And my dad, just like Pepito, walks around listening and looking for something to happen, something that will probably make him mad.

Dad doesn't smoke. He should, though. Maybe if he did he wouldn't hit me and Corin so much. I've tried leaving cigarettes around the house that I borrow from Tía Leti, since my mom smokes only when she's mad. But it's no use, because Mom just picks them up and throws them away. Once, I left one under his pillow, hoping he'd dream about it, then start wanting to smoke when he woke up. But all that happened was loud screaming when Mom made the bed. Then she threw me and Corin out of the house, yelling about smashed cigarettes, and a mal ojo. Next thing you know, Tía Leti had to come over and scare away the evil eye with her velas and hierbas that she gets from a botánica in San Francisco.

Mom likes to do things the old way. You know, using stuff she learned from her grandma to make you better, like soaking sliced potatoes in vinegar, then putting them on a rag and tying it to your head for fevers, or grinding up roots to make a tea that smells like pee if you get diarrhea. But it's Tía Leti who uses the hierbas, and it isn't just when you're sick either. I'm not supposed to know this, but I like to sneak and listen to my tía talk to Mom about her polvos, candles, and hierbas. She uses them, she says, "to give me fuerza to deal with my husband, claridad to deal with work, and suerte when I go to Reno to play the slots." I was going to tell Mom that it was me who left the cigarette underneath the pillow that day, not a mal ojo, but I figured I was better off keeping quiet. Like I do when it comes to asking Tía if she can find me a polvo to get rid of my dad.

※

When night comes, that's when everything is best. Right before I go to sleep, I turn into Supergirl. Don't be surprised. It feels good to be her. When I'm Supergirl I can fly over people's heads, and San Lorenzo, where I live. On TV, George Reeves plays Superman, but he's a fake because he's soft and doughy. Plus, if you look at him sideways, you'll swear his head looks like a ham. I'd make a better Superman because I'm stronger and smarter. They ought to put *me* on that show. Girls could be on it. They could make me Superman's sister.

I watch lots of *Superman* but I've only seen one girl: Lois Lane. On top of that, she's old and white. If you look at her face hard, though, you can see she might be part Mexican like Rita Hayworth. My dad said Rita Hayworth was really Margarita Carmen Cansino. She changed her name so she could make it in Hollywood. Movie stars are always changing their names, which means they can't sound real, and for sure not Mexican.

After my dad told me about Rita Hayworth, I spent the next week thinking of a Hollywood name for myself and nothing I came up with sounded good: Mary Cross, Marci Christa, or maybe Margi Cress. But those names were stupid, so I told my mom and Tía Leti I was dyeing my hair blonde and calling myself Linda Ledoux, since I like both names. Boy, did they laugh. Tía Leti, who has a really big butt (one of the few my dad doesn't look at), was sitting next to my mom and laughed so hard she peed her pants. The spot went right through her dress onto the couch. They were laughing so much they didn't care.

I didn't think it was *that* funny. When Mom could finally talk, she said, "Ay, no. You look too much like one of the Indians from the *Texas Rangers*. Y, también, being named *Linda* means you have to *be* pretty."

Tía Leti said I was "too goddamn dark to be running around with blonde hair," which made them laugh again.

I held my arm up to the light and looked at it. Who needs blonde hair anyway when it's easier being Supergirl? Every night I dreamed I saved beautiful girls. Usually, a mean man was hurting the girl. I'd beat the man up, then carry her away. She would be so happy I saved her, she'd want to marry me. I'd say yes and the dream would end with me kissing her neck and feeling her chiches.

✳

I love going to bed, but the nights aren't always quiet. There are lots of times me and Corin wake up hearing Mom and Dad yelling.

"Eddie, por favor!"

Me and my sister ran to the living room to find Dad crying and pulling the rifle out of its case.

"Que chinga, Delia. I've had it with these fucked-up assholes trying to run my life."

He was crying while he talked. There was a box of bullets on the table and we watched him take out four. His hands were shaking but he could still load all the bullets—fast.

"They got a goddamn boot on my neck every fucking day." He rubbed his hand softly across the barrel of the rifle. "And I'm just tired of it." He hung his head down and looked at the rifle.

Mom grabbed his arm. "Eddie, por favor, hombre. I need you here. The kids need you."

'No we don't,' I wanted to say.

Mom sounded scared. She looked like she believed my dad. Corin, too. Not me. I looked at how long that rifle was and how long his arms were. Dad was strong, but like I said, he was short. When he had his cowboy boots on he was maybe five-six. At least that's what Mom said.

"He can't do it," I whispered to Corin. Mom sent us back to our bedroom where we stood in the doorway watching.

"He can't?" Corin asked, her eyes big.

"No. That rifle's too long, and his arms are too short to point it to his head."

"He could put it in his mouth."

"But that would only add maybe two inches. He can't put it in too far, otherwise, he'd throw up." I looked at my dad's arms again. "Uh-uh. He can't do it."

My sister turned to go back to bed.

"Aren't you coming?" she asked.

I sat down on the floor. "No, not yet."

"Why not? What about what you just said?"

"He can't pull the trigger," I whispered, "on him." I looked at my dad again. He had the rifle in his lap with one hand on the trigger. All of a sudden, he jumped up, still holding the gun.

"Delia! Tell Him to come get me!" he cried out, yelling at the ceiling.

The muscles on his arms rippled like a rope as he held the gun tight.

"Who's he talking to?" Corin asked sitting down next to me.

"God, I think."

"Estoy listo, Señor! Papá, come get me!"

"How come Dad is talking to a señor?"

"I think Señor means God. He's talking to both Grandpa Santos and God."

"But Grandpa Santos is dead?"

"If Dad dies, he can go be with him."

"He can't," Corin started laughing like it was the best joke in the world. "Grandpa's in heaven."

"Yeah." I laughed, too.

But I was worried.

"Corin, he can't use the rifle on himself," I whispered. "But he can still use it on Mom."

"Oh," she said, and stayed next to me where we both kept watch until he put the gun away.

When we woke up Mom was singing and making eggs, same as always. She likes to sing while she cooks, but she never knows all the words.

"Mama, looka, booboo...hmmm, hmmm...that is your daddy...Oh, no! My daddy can't be ugly so. Shut your mouth. Go away. Mama looka boo boo day. Huh! Shut your mouth, go away, da da da da, boo boo day."

"Mom, what're you singing?"

"No sé, some song I heard."

Dad was outside changing the oil in the car.

"What was wrong with Dad last night?"

"Quién sabe?" she said as she dropped two more eggs in the skillet. "You know how your daddy gets. I just wish that menso would find some other way to do himself in. That damn rifle scares me."

Scares me, too. If he wants to die, fine. But how do I know he doesn't want to take us with him? Every time that rifle comes out he sticks in four bullets. It's not like I want to ask him why. He has the rifle for hunting, but I never see any dead elks or deer brought into this house. Instead, all I see is him bringing that gun out every time he wants to kill himself. I never know the reason. It can be anything. But it doesn't matter, because it's always the same. First, he cries while the rifle's still in its case. Then, after crying for a while, something happens and he pulls it out fast; so fast, you almost thought he *had* seen a deer. Then he loads four bullets, undoes the safety latch, and waves the gun around for the rest of the night till Mom begs him enough to live and he puts it away.

Mom turns her eyes from me and keeps cooking.

"Shut your mouth, go away, Mama looka boo boo day. Huh! Shut your mouth, go away!"

✳

I have to tell you what I need from God. I have to change into a boy. This is what I want and it's not an easy thing to ask for. Not like wanting a new bike or a football. This takes special powers, and let me tell you, I've been wanting it a long time. It's not because I think I'm a boy, though sometimes it sure seems like I am. It's because I like girls. I don't know how or when it happened. Maybe I was born this way, but the second I saw chiches, I wanted them. I couldn't stop thinking of girls, during the day at school, at night in my dreams, and especially when I watched TV. Now, *I* know you can't be with a girl if you *are* a girl. So that's why I have to change into a boy. And it needs to happen by the time I'm fourteen since my science books say that's when a boy's birdy gets bigger. Anyone can see I needed help. And I had to be good. That way, God or Baby Jesus would hear my wish. I had to think, say, and do the right things. Because I know if I messed up, that would be it. And my wish, just like my life, would be dust.

This wish was what I want for *myself*. I already told you my other wish was for my dad to go away. That one was for me, my sister, and my mom. Me and Corin want our dad to go away but not our mom. I'm wishing it for her anyway because, like Tía Leti says, "She can't even think straight when it comes to that man."

My mom's smart. She can do math fast, plan every dime we spend on food, and know when someone's pulling her leg. But when it's about my dad, she's practically retarded. I swear, I sometimes think she's taking drugs because she never remembers what he does to her, or Corin and me. And she doesn't listen either, even when other people tell her how much my dad looks at other girls. "She don't hear shit, she don't see shit, and she don't do shit." That's what Grandma Flor says when she comes to visit. Grandma Flor says she sometimes can't believe my mom is her own flesh and blood. I told Grandma, "Mom's wearing ear muffs and blinders." Grandma looked at me, squinted up her eyes, blew out cigarette smoke, then cracked up so hard she cried.

✳

At a quarter past five, the hands on my watch called me home. It was one of Dad's rules that me and Corin had to be there before he was. After five, I looked at my watch every two minutes. I wondered what kind of mood he'd be in. I rode my bike into the shed and said a silent prayer to the Virgin Mary. "Please let him be nice." I don't even know why I said those prayers, habit I guess. They never made a difference.

But you never know, it might be an easy night, maybe a "chinga" here or a "joda" there, thrown in between complaining about whatever we were eating for supper. I walked into the kitchen and saw Mom frying to death some pork-chops she got on sale that were cut so skinny you could practically see through them. Already, I knew my dad would use his fingers to throw the dried-up meat on his plate with that same old "this makes me sick" look he always had when he hated my mom's cooking. It's not that the pork-chops tasted bad, though Corin said they looked like one of Pepito's rawhide chews. It's just that I felt sorry for Mom because she was always trying to make Dad happy. She'd look at him like a scared pup, hoping he'd eat anyway. I hated that look. I wanted her to tell him to "eat shit," or "get up and fix it yourself." I practiced those words for her, but she never said them. Instead, she'd say "What's wrong with it?" or, "Can I fry you some eggs?"

✳

There's different ways to be scared. Like when you bike down a hill, or ride The Hammer at the fair, or when the teacher catches you stealing art paper to take home. These I could handle. But nothing is as scary as my dad getting mad. I can't remember the first time he hit me, only the sound of mad feet. I'd be so scared I didn't know who I was. It was like I was across the room watching him come after me, chase me, then catch me.

It was Friday, a payday. He was happy and brought home hamburgers from McDonalds. "Hey you guys! Look what I got!" he yelled as he walked in the door. It was our favorite, and we ate everything, clear down to the burnt-up french-fries.

Dad loved paydays, and after a beer or two, he play-wrestled with me and Corin, then tickled us till we screamed. But the problem was you never knew what would make him mad. One minute he was laughing and playing. Next thing you know, bam! He's lashing across our legs with a doubled belt. I don't even remember what started it.

"Qué chinga! Son-na-va biche! Marci, I - am - *sick* - and - *tired* - of -*you* - and *Corin* - and your - *pinche* - mierda!"

He liked to yell at us while he hit us.

"I've - *told* -you - time- and - *again* - not to do this!"

It could've been funny if it didn't hurt so much. Each time he hit me it felt like he was slapping every bone inside me. The first one knocked me to the floor. I tried to get up, but he grabbed my arm and held me down by twisting it. I looked at his face; trying to make his eyes see mine. *Look at me! Look!* My eyes begged him. But it was like he'd turned into a monster, a werewolf with eyes that couldn't see. My mouth felt full of sand. I couldn't say or do anything; couldn't even scream. When he finished with me he turned to Corin. She was sitting pressed against a corner, her knees up to her neck, looking like she was melting into the crack.

"No, Daddy! Please Daddy! I promise I'll be good. I promise!" she yelled.

If my dad didn't have eyes, he sure didn't have ears. It was like he saw, heard, and felt nothing. It was a hot night and we had on shorts. The belt left thick, red marks on our legs. I watched my dad hit Corin the same way he hit me. Only it was harder to watch since she was littler and skinnier.

Corin tried to get away from him, but that only made him madder. He caught her by the hair.

"Cabrona! Get over here!"

He dragged her back into the room, picked her up by her neck and threw her against the wall. He started choking her.

"Goddammit, I'll teach you to run away from me!"

"Eddie, stop! You're gonna kill her!"

My mom, the watchdog of the whippings, stood in the doorway. She must have felt my dad really *was* going to kill Corin, because that was the only time she said anything.

Most of the time when he hit us I didn't think he was going to kill us, but on that day, I thought he might.

"Hail Mary, full of grace..."

He picked her up again. "You little bitch, I'll show you this time!" He held her neck with his left hand, then slapped her face.

"Eddie, déjalo! You're being too rough!"

"The Lord is with thee..."

I was kneeling in a corner.

"Blessed art thou among women..."

This time when she fell, she closed her eyes and sunk to the floor.

"And blessed is the fruit of thy womb, Jesus."

"Eddie!!!" Mom screamed out his name.

"Holy Mary, Mother of God..."

He stopped. He could hardly breath. The room was hot from all the sweat and crying. The belt fell to the floor. His chest was going up and down like he'd just run a race. He looked at Corin, then he picked up the belt.

"Pray for us sinners..."

Mom rushed past my father to see if Corin was okay.

"Shut the goddamn hell up, Marci."

"Now and at the hour of our death."

He took the belt, brought it up over his shoulder, and swung it across my mouth. Then without looking at anyone, he turned and walked out of the room. My lips swelled up like inner-tubes. I licked them and swallowed the metal taste of blood.

Now, you see what I mean about saying prayers?

Corin opened her eyes. I was glad, but I could only lie on the floor and cry. My mom, after she saw that Corin was okay, went to my dad who was sitting with his head in his hands in the dining room. Corin sat up and stared at her legs. Pearls of blood were forming across the marks left from the belt. The pink shorts she had on were dirty and smeared with snot. One of her shoes lay upside down in the corner. The other was halfway on her foot. Bruises were already glowing around her neck. We were both crying. I looked at her, but her eyes were far away. For the longest time, we weren't even in the same room.

We sat there crying, and then we heard him.

"Mijitas. Mijitas, come here."

We looked at each other.

"Mijitas, come here. I want to talk to you."

It felt like the Devil himself was calling us. I didn't want to talk to him now, or ever, but fear's stronger than hate, and I found myself standing with Corin in front of him. Corin's arms had purple dots all over where his fingers had squeezed her. Her nose was bloody and her eyes were flat like glass. He grabbed our hands.

"Mijitas. I'm sorry. I'm sorry I hit you. You know I don't like doing this." He looked at both of us. "You think I like doing this?"

I thought he must, otherwise he wouldn't do it so much.

"Answer me. Do you think I like to hit you guys?"

"I don't know," I lied.

"You know I don't. Venga aquí." He moved his hands like he wanted us closer. "Turn around. Let me look at you."

He twirled each of us around, slowly going over our legs, arms and faces. He spent an extra second on Corin's face. Wetting his fingers with spit, he rubbed them across the bloody marks, then started to cry.

"I'm sorry, mijitas. I'm so sorry."

He hugged us and I hated it; the sweat on his arms, the feel of his skin, every hair of his that touched me.

"I love you both so much. You know I do. I just wish you wouldn't get me so mad."

He wiped his eyes, then let us go. When I turned to walk back to our room, I saw Mom reach out and touch his hand. He looked at her and shook his head. I promised myself I'd always hate him and that I'd never forget what he did to us. But I knew it wouldn't be forever. It never was. He always said he was sorry, and even though I hated myself for doing it, I forgave him.

✳

Did I tell you that part of the reason I wanted to be a boy, besides loving girls, was so I could grow big muscles like the men in my Uncle Tommy's muscle magazines? Then, I'd be able to beat up my dad.

I knew me and Baby Jesus would think of some kind of plan. The next part was to work out so I could build the muscles. I had to get a set of weights. I knew weights would make me stronger faster than riding my bike, or throwing a ball around. I asked my dad if he would buy me some, knowing what he'd say as soon as I asked it.

"Why do you want weights?"

"I need them." I had to be careful here. I looked down, my eyes zeroing in on a crack in the floor. "I need them so I can get stronger."

"Delia! Marci wants me to buy her some weights." He started laughing. Mom came into the room looking at me with her brown eye crinkled up into a slit.

"Some weights?" she asked. "Why do you want weights?"

I let out a big breath of air because I knew my mom would never understand.

"To get stronger."

"I don't think it's a good idea, qué no?" she said looking over at my dad.

"Why not?" I asked.

"We can't afford it," said my dad. "Go ask your Uncle Tommy if he's got any lying around that he can loan you." Then he laughed since he knew Uncle Tommy wouldn't, even if he did.

We went over to Uncle Tommy's house that week and I asked him if I could borrow his weights. He didn't act like it was weird, but he said he didn't have anything extra to loan me. He said I could use his while I was there. So each time we visited I went down to the basement and did sit-ups on his slant-board, and arm curls with his dumbbells. I never told my parents what I was doing down there. I think it was better that way.

✳

Our town is so little I can walk from our house to downtown. We have a grocery store, library, drug store, two bars, a gas station, and a bakery. Shakey's Pizza, McDonalds, Woolworth's, and the bus station are down the road a ways. I don't mind walking everywhere, because I have to walk to school, so I'm used to it. Mom doesn't like walking (except when she's mad) so she never goes anywhere unless Dad takes her.

Mom wanted to drive once, but she was scared. Plus, every time she got behind the wheel my dad would start yelling: "Ponga la pata on the clutch! The clutch! The clutch! Not the goddamn brake! Pendeja!" I told her later that maybe she should hitchhike. At least there wouldn't be anyone yelling at her.

When I was littler, I had this picture of how my mom and dad were supposed to be from watching TV. I'd see a man in a suit leave for work, and asked my dad how come he didn't wear one. Mom said it was because he didn't need to. Then, I'd see two people kissing in a way I never saw my mom and dad kiss, so I asked them "how come you don't kiss like that?" They looked at each other like they couldn't tell me something. Then they laughed and said people only kiss like that on TV. My parents must have thought I was the stupidest person in the world. Finally, I saw this lady on TV having a baby, but they didn't show anything, just the "before picture" of her with a big panza and lots of sweating. Then, the "after picture," which showed her still sweaty, but happy, with a gigantic baby next to her. One day, my cousin Berta and her husband, Lalo, were over the house, and Berta had a really big belly, which meant she was having a baby. Now, I thought, was the perfect time to learn the truth.

I knelt down in front of Berta with my hands on her knees. I wanted to get close so that she couldn't squirm out of it. I also thought Berta was cute, so I took every chance I could to touch her. This time I'd get her to tell me the truth, right to my face.

"Berta, where do babies come from?"

I saw Mom look over at Dad, but no one said anything.

"From my stomach," Berta said, matter of fact.

"I know they come from your stomach, but how do you make 'em?" I really *didn't* know how babies were made, but I was beginning to think that Lalo had something to do with it. I didn't want to think about it, but I hoped it had nothing to do with his birdy. I didn't think I could stomach him touching her anywhere with that.

"We pray very hard."

"You *pray* hard?" I couldn't believe she gave me the old first-grade catechism reason.

"Yes we do, don't we, Lalo?"

Lalo was watching *Bewitched*, so he wasn't paying any attention to us.

"Qué?"

Berta pointed to her stomach. "We prayed for this baby, didn't we?" She looked at him while nodding her head in my direction.

"We sure did. Every damn night."

They all started laughing, which told me I was right.

✳

Just once, I'd like to read a story where Jesus kicks everybody's butt. Plus, have you ever heard of Jesus yelling at people? Maybe *my dad* should take some lessons from him.

I can't remember hardly anything about Jesus though, since I stopped listening to the nuns when they wouldn't answer my questions about dinosaurs. They told me I needed to be quiet and "rely on faith." Can't they see I'm a scientist? I already read every kid's book on dinosaurs and knew how the earth was *really* made. Plus, I knew tons about volcanoes. Catechism was boring. Sister 'Lizabeth didn't like to call on me, since I always asked questions like "What do you think of Cro-Magnons? Did God plan Pterodactyls? Or how 'bout those saber-tooth tigers?"

I was in fourth grade when I started catechism. Mom and Dad said we're supposed to start it young, like first grade. I don't know what made them the experts. The only time *they* ever went to church was on Christmas and Easter. They kept saying they were going to send me to catechism, but it never happened. That is, not until my dad stopped being mad from a fight he had with Monsignor Hullihan. My dad was mad because the Monsignor wouldn't let me into Catholic school, even when I got straight A's. When I asked why, Dad said, it was "because we didn't give those assholes enough money." I thought about how much we did give. Every Sunday at Mass, I'd take the dollar my mom gave me, stuff it in the envelope, and write "Cruz" on the outside. Then I'd put it in the basket when the man with the blind eye came around to collect. I guess when you thought about it, he was probably right.

So me and Corin finally got to go to catechism, but there were two classes, so they stuck her in the other one to keep us apart. I don't know why they wouldn't let us be together. It was awful being in there with all those little kids. Sometimes, when I got really bored, I'd stare at the nun's head. Did all that stuff around her face give her a headache? I'd look at her and wonder what her hair was like underneath. Bettina Bepler, who was in my class, told me nuns didn't have hair, that the priests shaved their heads for them once a week. I think I spent the first six weeks of catechism looking for any sign of a crew-cut. Then I started wondering what was underneath their robes. Were they naked, or in their underwear? Did they even wear underwear? Maybe they wore shorts like I did when I wanted to twirl on the monkey bars.

I noticed Sister 'Lizabeth wore a wedding band so I asked her who her husband was. She looked surprised, then she started getting weird splotches all over her face. My mom told me her husband was Jesus, and that I shouldn't have asked her that because "it wasn't nice."

"How are all the nuns on this planet supposed to share one man who isn't even alive anymore?"

"They make do."

My mom was cooking beans for supper.

"How?" I asked. "Who kisses them and sleeps with them at night?"

"Ay! Marcía. Malcriada! You and your nasty questions." Then she stopped and thought about it for a second. "Well, they don't really get to be with Jesus...like a man, you know." Her brown eye was screwed up so tight it was nothing more than an eyelash.

"It's just pretend?"

"Sí," she said slowly. "Pues, sí."

I asked Sister 'Lizabeth if we had any proof that Jesus was ever alive.

"Yes," she said.

"What?"

"Well, the Bible, of course."

"The Bible? But who wrote that?"

"Oh, Marci, you know it was written by a group of different holy men."

"You mean God didn't even write it?"

"Dummy, how can God write it if He's up in heaven?" Anna Rodríguez, always talked like she knew more about God than Sister 'Lizabeth.

"Gee, I don't know, Anna. Sister 'Lizabeth says 'you

never know what God can do.' Maybe he threw the book down from heaven."

"Anna and Marci, that will be enough."

I turned back toward the nun. "Sister 'Lizabeth, you have to explain to me why the Bible is proof that Jesus was alive"

"Well, Marci, I can't." She looked around the room as if she hoped God would come down and help her. "Pray to God, so that you understand His wisdom and power. Ask Him for guidance. Read your catechism book. Then," she paused and looked me right in the eye, "if that doesn't work, rely on faith. That's what everyone else does."

"But Sister, I'm still trying to figure out how the dinosaurs fit into everything."

The nun took a deep breath and let it out real slow.

Sister 'Lizabeth must have told on me because she had a talk with the Mother Superior that same afternoon. They were standing outside the classroom while we wrote in our catechism books. Then they called me out in the middle of class and walked me to the Mother Superior's office.

Mother Superior was somebody no one (unless you were out of your mind), would spend time with. She had long, gray whiskers on one side of her chin and eyes that looked like somebody had just stuck them on. The more she talked to me, the more she reminded me of a giant tree sloth. And her breath—just like an aquarium. Sister 'Lizabeth, who could've been cute if she wasn't a nun, stared at me with her eyebrows knotted up so high they touched the white part of her outfit. I didn't know how she could stand being so close to Mother Superior. I looked at Sister 'Lizabeth. She must be really happy with her ghost husband to want to stick around that face.

The inside of Mother Superior's office smelled like cigarettes, and the pictures on the wall were of Jesus as man and as a baby. Sister 'Lizabeth motioned me toward a chair and I sat down with my feet swinging back and forth. Mother Superior sat down. Then, with her hands folded together, told me I wasn't allowed to ask any more questions in class, of any kind. Ever.

"Why not?" I asked.

"Marci, you're older than the other children, and your questions tend to be a bit...disruptive."

"They do? I only want to find out why you're saying I have to believe in these things when my science books say something else."

"Marci," Mother Superior talked sweetly like a robin. "Your questions do no one any good. They only make the other children doubt what we teach them, which makes it much harder for Sister Elizabeth to get through the lesson."

Sister 'Lizabeth looked at me with that same scrunched-up eyebrow face. I felt sorry for her, but not sorry enough to stop asking questions.

"And, furthermore," she continued, "if you truly believed in God, you wouldn't be asking these kinds of questions."

"That's easy to say if it was just a year or two, and dogs and ponies, but we're talking millions of years with mammoths and dinosaurs!"

"That will be enough!" Mother Superior might've talked like a robin but she looked ready to kill me, so I decided to get the hell out.

"Okay," I said.

"So you understand our little agreement?" She finally seemed happy. "No more questions in class, of any kind, ever?"

"Ever?" I asked.

"Ever," she said. "Do you think you can honor this agreement? It's a contract with God and you know He'll be watching." She squinted one eye and cocked her head like a dog hearing a squeaky noise.

I nodded and smiled. I saw Sister 'Lizabeth let out a giant breath of air.

"Very well then, you and Sister Elizabeth may go back to class."

As we walked back I looked at the Sister's outfit. She was wearing one of those big black dresses and it was a really hot day. As we walked down the hallway I asked her who made her clothes. She said she didn't know who made them, but that the "habit" came from a very old tradition. I couldn't believe they had to wear those dresses on hot days. I wondered what they wore when they got off work.

"What's the white thing around your face?" I asked, knowing I didn't have many more chances to ask questions.

"This?" She touched the white band across her forehead. "This is called a wimple."

"A what?"

She started laughing, "A wimple. I know it's a funny name, but that's what they're called."

"Do you ever take it off?"

"Only at night, when I go to bed."

"Do you take everything off?"

"Well, y-yes," she stuttered. Her face was getting those splotches again.

We were almost to the door.

"Sister 'Lizabeth, do you have any hair on your head, or do the priests really shave it off once a week?"

She started laughing so hard she had to grab her legs to hold herself up.

"Marci, you do ask the funniest questions. Of course I have hair! Look." She pulled up her wimple and showed me some short, brown hair.

"Uh-huh," I said. "You still keep it pretty short, though."

"Yes, we have to keep it this way."

"Cause you'd sweat too much?"

"Uh, yeah, sort of," she said, still chuckling. "Something like that. Now get inside."

"Wait, can I ask you one more question? Remember, it's my last."

"Okay, what is it?"

"Do you like that Mother Superior?"

"Yes, of course. She's the Mother Superior. I love her like all the other sisters. Now scoot. Get inside. Class is waiting."

I sat at my desk and stared at Sister 'Lizabeth. Her cheeks were red and she wouldn't look at me. What a weird day. I saw two things I never thought I'd see: hair underneath a habit, and a nun lie.

✳

"—and she says it's fun." Andrea stopped to lick her sucker. "She's done it before."

"Who'd she do it for?"

"My four sisters. I'm the last."

"She's not tired of doing it?"

"Nope."

"What kind of things do you do in Girl Scouts?"

"Fun stuff."

"Like what?"

"Like crafts, field trips, songs and dances. Things like that." She took another long lick off her sucker. "Best of all," she stopped and looked at me closely. "It's just for girls."

"Sign me up," I said.

We went to the Salvation Army to search for a uniform, and I was in luck because I found one that fit me. I put it on and my dad started laughing the second he saw me. My mom told him "cállate," and that I "looked cute." Corin started crying because she wanted to join, too.

The first meeting was a total let-down from the build-up Andrea gave me. All we did during that meeting was say our names and what animal we wanted to be. There were fifteen girls there; seven said they wanted to be a cat, five a bird, one a snake, with Andrea saying she wanted to be a fish. "Oh, brother," I thought. I told everyone I wanted to be a saber-tooth tiger. They looked at me like I'd lost my mind. That is, except for the girl who wanted to be a snake. She smiled. Miss Dibble, the Girl Scout leader, said I was "creative."

After we did the dumb animal game, we went around the room and said where we were born. I was so bored I looked over at Andrea. She saw me look at her, so she crossed her legs and pretended to smoke. I started smoking, too. Andrea pretended to drink a martini, like the ricos do on TV. Miss Dibble didn't see us smoking but she heard me giggling. She jerked her head around to see what I was laughing at. In a heartbeat I had my hands down. Andrea was caught red-handed and tried to pretend she was rubbing something off her lips. This made me laugh more.

"Marci and Andrea, if you two don't settle down, I'm going to ask you both to leave." Boy, Miss Dibble sure didn't play around.

"Yes, Mom," Andrea said.

I didn't say anything.

After that we learned this dumb song called "Silver and Gold," which was about making new friends and keeping your old ones. "Big deal," I thought. "Who doesn't know that?" Girl Scouts sure didn't seem what everyone said. I needed to find out if it was going to be fun or not.

"Miss Dibble," I interrupted her as she started a new song about "walking around a corner to a donut shop."

"Miss Dibble! Can I ask you a question?"

"Marci, if you don't mind, we are singing now. Join in. Questions will be answered at the end of our meeting."

I don't know who I was beginning to hate more, Miss Dibble or Mother Superior. I sat on my hands till the end of the meeting when I finally got to ask what we were gonna do this year. Miss Dibble cleared her throat and told me it was "up to us."

"Up to us? What does that mean?" I asked.

"Well, Marci, it means we'll do whatever everyone decides they want to do."

She turned away from me to face the rest of the group.

"Ladies! Can I have your attention please? Marci's asked me what our plans are for the year. I have a little checklist I'd like to read to you. Please raise your hands whenever you hear something you'd like to do."

Miss Dibble read off a bunch of things. Most of them sounded about as fun as dusting the house, but there were four that might be good. I raised my hand to 1) BBQ at her house (Andrea said they had a swimming pool), 2) field trip on the Bay, 3) camping at Tilden Park, and 4) trip to the Oakland baby zoo. We sang "Silver and Gold" one more time before we finally got to go home.

*

Anything can happen. It happened to my cousin, right here in my own backyard. Raylene is a girl. But when she was born, she was a boy. Her parents named her Ray, after her daddy and dressed her in baby overalls and a little Oakland A's baseball cap. After one year, though, the doctors found out she wasn't a boy. She was really a girl. Mom didn't tell me until now.

"What happened?" I asked.

"Quíen sabe. I guess the doctors made a mistake."

"How do you make that kind of mistake? You're either a boy, or a girl. Couldn't they tell it was a boy? Didn't she have a birdy?"

"Marci, I don't know!"

"Didn't you ask?"

"No." My mom was ironing clothes. She dipped her fingers in a pot of melted Niagara starch and flicked the drops over my dad's blue work shirt.

"How come?" I stood next to the ironing board and tried to get her to look at me, but she'd only stare at the shirt.

"Porque it's not polite to ask those kinds of questions, that's why." She stood with her legs spread like a soldier, holding the steaming iron like a smoking gun.

"Mom, if they named her Ray, then she must have had a birdy. So what happened to it?"

"Marcía, no sé. Entremetida! You ask too many questions! Now go play!" She was mad so I gave up and went to my bedroom.

My cousin is two now. She moved to Montana three months ago with her mom and dad. We never go there so I didn't know how I was going to find out the truth about how she changed into a girl. I wanted to see what she looked like, and if she still acted like a boy. I wondered if she was going to like girls like me. It's not fair, they should have let her keep her birdy. She might want it later.

The one thing my mom told me after she finished ironing was that my cousins didn't want to change Ray's name to something totally different. How would you like it if that happened to you? Anyway, Ray's name was changed to Raylene, and he became a she.

Just like Raylene, it could happen to me.

The next week, my dad came home, called up his cousin Inez and after talking to her for practically an hour, hung up and said we were moving to her old apartment up the street because she bought a house in Oakland and put in a good word to her landlord for us. At the end of the month we moved in and I was happy because the new room me and Corin shared was bigger. But the most important reason I was happy, was that I found the girl of my dreams.

I was playing football by myself outside when I saw a girl who looked like a model getting out of a car. She had on a skirt, white go-go boots, and long hair bubbled up on top. She seemed to flow from place to place like the mercury Miss Dibble used in a science project. I felt all melty and good when I looked at her, like I'd just eaten two packs of Reese's Peanut Butter Cups. She saw me and waved. Then she started walking toward me and I had to kneel down because my legs felt like they couldn't hold me up anymore. As she got closer I could see her lips were big and poofy, like

Halloween wax lips and she had lots of black eyeliner around her eyes like my cousin Berta.

"Hi," she said. "You new here?" She sounded nice—like fresh picked flower petals.

"Yes."

"What's your name?"

"Marcía—but all my friends call me Marci."

"Oh, okay, Marci. I hope it's okay for me to call you that, too."

"Yeah, sure." I took the football and twirled it in my hands. "If you ever want to play sometime, let me know."

"Okay," she giggled, then turned to walk toward her house.

"Uh, hey!" I yelled out.

"Yeah?"

"What's your name?"

"Raquel."

"Oh, that's—that's a nice name."

She stood there waiting. I guess she thought I would keep talking, but no words would come out, at least not the words I wanted to say. I could only kneel and look up her face.

"Well, I gotta go," she said as the flower petals began floating away.

"Okay, see ya later."

"Ba-bye!"

I watched her walk up the steps to her house. She looked like the Holy Spirit floating toward the front door. I found out later she was 16, but knew in my heart it didn't matter.

I liked lots of girls, but not like this. Well, except for Audra Barkley from *The Big Valley*. I was in love with her, too, but it would be hard to meet her. Audra was a movie star who lived in Beverly Hills, and I was a kid who lived in San Lorenzo with no money, no car, and no way of even getting a chance to *see* her.

But I had a chance with Raquel. She lived next door and already knew my name. I was starting to get worried, though, about the fact that I was still a girl. I wondered if God was going to come through with his part of the deal.

The next day, after school, I went to the city library. Miss Buck, the librarian, was squinting through her glasses at a bunch of checkout cards. I waited till there was no one around.

"Miss Buck," I whispered. "Have you ever read anything about a girl changing into a boy?" I tried to ask the question in my best scientific voice.

Miss Buck, tall, in a sort of giraffey kind of way, wrinkled her nose, and stared at me over the top of her glasses.

"Marci, you ask the oddest questions."

"Uh-huh. Well...have you?"

"Don't you think that's an unusual question for someone to ask?"

"No," I said it like it was the most normal thing in the world.

"Why do you want to know this?"

"It's a science question. I just want to know, that's all."

I was getting really scared, but was still trying not to show it.

She folded her arms across her chest.

"Well actually, no. I've been a librarian for seventeen years and I've never heard of that happening. Nor have I come across it in any books."

"Okay. Thanks, Miss Buck." I walked away losing hope.

I went to the "fiction for young adults." Lately, I was into books about Indians. I found one on Cochise, and another on Geronimo. Then I picked out a new book on volcanoes and another on the Hardy Boys. When I had all my books and was checking them out, I turned and saw Miss Buck walking toward me fast, like a Green Beret on a special mission. She was holding a big book in her hands like she was carrying special orders from the president.

"Oh, Marci, I was a bit mistaken. I don't think I should be showing you this book, because it's more for adults, but we do have this story of a man who decided he was living in the wrong body and got an operation to become a woman. It's called *The Christine Jorgensen Story*."

Miss Buck is really great. It makes me happy that she truly respects science. But she also has one of the loudest whispers I've ever heard. There were five people standing behind me waiting to check out their books. When she whispered, "Christine Jorgensen," I turned slightly around and saw ten eyes all staring at me. Even Miss Pierce, the snotty old lady who never looks at anyone when she checks out books, couldn't keep her eyes off me and made squishy noises with her lips that seemed almost ready to swallow themselves.

I looked at the cover of the book. It had two pictures on it. One was of a beach ball headed guy with a thick neck and a crew cut. The other was the same beach ball head, but this time the he was a she, with blue eye shadow, eyeliner, and a hairdo like Dusty Springfield. She was wearing a dress and pearls, but you could still see the same thick neck. You'd think that if they could do something with that birdy, they could at least do something about the neck.

I had to get out of there. "Uh, thanks, Miss Buck," I whispered. "I got enough books for right now. I'll check it out next time."

Like in about a hundred years. I could really see myself bringing that book home. Besides, it wasn't me. I didn't want to go to the hospital and have an operation. I didn't even really want a birdy. I just wanted Raquel. Why was everything so hard? I decided me and Baby Jesus had better have another talk.

I started saying my prayers to Jesus that night. Then I figured I'd better talk to God. He had the most power. Baby Jesus and Mary had powers, but I knew it was God who handled the big wishes. So that night, after regular prayers, I said a special prayer. I did this only after I said one "Our Father," and one "Hail Mary," and after I blessed everyone.

My mom liked to sit on the bed while me and Corin knelt to say our prayers.

"Bless my mom and my dad, and my sister." I squinted my eyes open to see if she was looking at me. She wasn't. "Bless Grandma, and everybody up in heaven that I don't know."

"All right, get in bed," Mom said. She said good night and walked out of the room.

My sister closed her eyes while I read for a while. Then I turned off the light and folded my hands way down by my cuca.

"Okay, God," I whispered. "Are you listening? I need you to hurry up and change me into a boy." I looked over at my sister to see if she looked like she could hear me. Her breathing was already deep.

"I know you probably don't get asked this very much, but I need some help. I like this girl named Raquel who lives next door. She's like a model, and really nice. I want to marry her, but I think she'll want to marry a boy. This is why I need to get going on this change. I also need a penis (I thought it was more polite to say this word) and no chiches. Do you think you could do this? If you need more help, could you ask The Virgin Mary, and your son, Baby Jesus, to help you? I'll say a prayer to them, too, so you can all work on this together. I don't usually ask very much from you, but I have to change into a boy. Otherwise, how else can I be with Raquel? Thank you. Amen."

I turned on my side, and was almost asleep when I suddenly remembered I forgot to ask for one more thing.

"Oh, can you do it before I turn fourteen? On second thought, can you make it twelve? Thanks. Amen." I thought it was better to change earlier so people could get used to the fact that I was a boy while I was still little.

I said this prayer every night. The next Sunday, before Mass, I went to the chapel and stood under the statue of The Virgin Mary holding Baby Jesus. There were lots of lit candles by her toes that smelled like old smoke and ear wax. I put a nickel in the slot, which was a lot of money for me, but I was glad I could pray to both of them for one price. I lit a candle and started praying. "Mother Mary, please help me be a boy. I love girls so much and I need you and Baby Jesus to help God change me. Only you guys can do it. I promise to be good so please don't forget me."

I didn't want to think about it, but I was starting to get a little worried.

✳

Every day I woke up, peeked into my pajamas and looked at my cuca. Nothing was happening. Nothing was growing. It was always the same. I wanted to believe that if I wanted something bad enough, God, Baby Jesus, or Mary would help me. I'd been told to trust in God so many times that I *had* to believe it. I couldn't think about staying a girl. It'd make me sad since girls were always in my head. *I* was the one who rescued Judy in *Lost in Space*, or rode with Audra Barkley on horseback rides. And it was *me* who saved other girls from mean men. And, on top of everything, there's a dream girl who lives next door who I know won't give me the time of day unless I turn into a boy. Look at me, God. Are you listening? If you're all-knowing, like everyone says you are, then how come you don't know about me?

I felt really mad when I looked at Randy Torres. He was a big sissy kid who lived down the street. He didn't like baseball or football, even though he would have been good as a tackle. He liked to watch old movies, and read books about other countries. His father was mean to him. Sometimes, when I was riding my bike past his house, I'd see his dad trying to get him to play catch. Randy told me he thought playing catch was the biggest waste of time. Every time his dad threw the ball he dropped it.

"Catch the goddamn ball. How the hell did I ever end up with a kid like you?"

Randy looked sad, and I felt sorry for him for about a second. How did Randy end up a boy and me a girl? I knew I could throw a ball so hard it would've made his dad's hand sting. But, if Randy ever wanted to be with Raquel, he'd have a better chance than me. Randy dropped a ball that was perfectly thrown into his mitt. I wondered who got to make the choice of what you were when you were born. I memorized this question to ask Miss Buck later.

Even though I didn't think life was fair making me a girl and Randy a boy, me and Corin sometimes had lots of fun with him, especially in the summer. He liked the water, and already knew how to swim. Our other next-door neighbors, the MacCormacks, had a big doughboy swimming pool. We were friends with them, even though Randy's mom and my mom both called them "dirty Okies." I could never figure out why my mom called some people dirty Okies. When I asked her, she said it was because "they weren't very clean." I knew lots of people who weren't very clean. Like Ricky O'Riley, who was in my class and always smelled like poop. We complained to Miss Stevens, our teacher, who acted like she didn't believe us when we told her Ricky poops his pants. One time, he walked past my desk, and a nannyberry of poop fell out of his pants. Andrea Dibble screamed, and called Miss Stevens who told Ricky to get a Kleenex and pick it up. Ricky, who was always saying how proud he was that he was Irish, smelled bad and his pants and shirts were dirty. Did this make him a "dirty Okie?" When I asked my mom, she said, "probably."

The other thing Mom was weird about was saying she was Spanish and not Mexican. I got the story from Dad when I asked him what we were. He told me we were Mexican-American, which he said "is half Indian and half Spanish." I asked him what kind of Indian we were and he said Comanche on his side, and Navajo on my mom's. Mom was in the room reading the paper when he said this. She put the paper down and looked at him like he'd just said she was part Martian.

"Éste, mira, your mom likes to think she's just Spanish," my dad said in a voice that made fun of her. "Bueno, Delia, tus ancestors son de España, qué no?"

My mom stuck her nose up a little bit. "Tú sabes."

"Pero, old Miss Hispañola there hasn't figured out that her asshole is as black as mine."

"Eddie! My God, do you have to be so nasty!"

"Pues, mujer, you know it's the truth! You just don't want to admit that your mother is a full-fledged member of that special New Mexican tribe of corner-bar Navajos."

Mom started laughing. We really didn't know if Grandma was Navajo because she never said so. We think she was. First, because she looked it, and second, because she never answered us when we asked her. But no matter how many times you asked Mom what she was, she'd always say Spanish.

"Your mother, con la nariz de los Indios, doesn't like to say she's a Mexican."

"I'm pure Spanish, and you know it," she said looking over at him.

When my mom's hair is not dyed red, it's straight and dark. On top of that, she has a big nose.

"You have an Indian nose, so why don't you admit it?" I asked her.

"My nose comes from the conquistadores."

It was no use trying to talk to her.

The thing about the MacCormacks was that their mom was mean and their Dad was nice. "Mr. MacCormack *never* yells at his kids, even when he's mad," I said one day after swimming at their pool.

"Yeah," Corin said, looking down at the grass. "Suzy says their dad doesn't hit 'em."

"He doesn't?" Randy asked.

"No."

Even though I was there when Suzy told us this, it was hard for me to think of her dad not hitting them. "Their dad sounds super nice," I said.

"But Mrs. MacCormack is a hell of a sea bass bitch," said Randy.

"A sea bass bitch," Corin said it again, then laughed.

"And your mom is a, a halibut booty bitch," I said. Randy's mom could be mean, too.

Randy scrunched up his face for a second like he was thinking hard, then started laughing.

"Yeah, she is a big-o-halibut butt." Then he got up and started imitating his mother. "Now Randall, look at this mess! Get in here and clean it up immediately." He wiggled his butt to copy his mom's way of walking. "And furthermore, I would really like it if you didn't associate with the MacCormacks down the street. They're just a bunch of Okies who *I know* never saw a pair of shoes till they came to California." Then he sniffed hard and farted.

All three of us burst out laughing.

"Yeah, we can call your mom halibooty bitch for her secret code name," I said.

"Okay, but what'll we call your mom?" he asked.

"How about raisin booty bitch?" Corin said.

We laughed again.

"Raisin booty. That's good. She does have a shriveled up ol' booty," I said.

"Who has a shriveled up old booty?" My mom had her head out the window. I don't know how long she'd been listening.

"Miss MacCormack," I lied, which I knew was a mistake, since Miss MacCormack had a fat booty.

"Yeah, she just told us to go home," said Randy.

"Uh-huh," my mom said. She didn't look like she believed anything we were saying. "Don't forget, your daddy comes home at five thirty." She shut the window.

Things got quiet.

"Well, I guess I'd better get going," said Randy.

"Yeah. We need to change out of our suits. It's ten after five." I looked over at Corin.

She nodded and the three of us got up, finished drying off, and walked to our houses. Randy put one hand on his hip and pointed his finger like he was yelling at us, then turned and ran down the street.

✳

My dad didn't come home from work on time. In fact, it was time for bed and he still wasn't home. At first Mom was worried. Then when my dad called to tell her he was "having a few beers with the guys," she got mad.

"I fix your daddy a nice supper, then he stays out till all hours of the night, gets drunk, and expects la comida to be there for him when he gets home. On top of that, everything gets dried out." She said this, nodding her chin toward the food. I heard her say "cabrón" quietly under her breath.

"Why do you put up with it?" I asked.

"Yeah, Mom?" asked Corin.

She didn't answer and I thought she wasn't going to until she said "It's not so easy," like she was serving a life sentence in prison. "I'll show him tonight though. You wait and see."

My stomach started getting tight. Mom never talked like that. She seemed mad, and I didn't know what she was going to do, but it probably wouldn't be good.

She let us play outside till dark, then read to Corin from one of her school books. I was still scared so I couldn't pay much attention to anything.

When it was time for bed, Mom said we had to sleep on the floor.

"Okay. Now get your blankets and pongalo in the middle aquí." She pointed to the floor between our beds, then helped us pull the blankets off the beds and put them on the floor.

I thought this was the stupidest thing I ever heard of. "This is dumb," I said.

"How come you want us to sleep here?" Corin asked, pointing to the floor.

"Because I want your daddy to think we left him. When he comes in to say goodnight, I want him to think we're gone." Mom looked proud of her idea.

"He's going to see us. Plus, what about you? What are *you* going to do?" I asked, still not believing this was really happening.

"Me? I'm going to hide, too."

"Where?" We asked at the same time.

"I don't know. I'll think of somewhere."

"Mom, don't you think we should be hiding for real instead of lying here?" asked Corin, pointing between the beds.

She sat on the bed and let out a big breath of air. "Maybe we should just call your Uncle Tommy like we did before, and have him come get us."

"Yeah. We can hide at his house. Then Dad won't know where we are." You could tell Corin liked that idea.

"He'll find us anyway. He knew where to find us the last time we ran away." I thought either way it was a waste of time. If we really wanted to leave, then we should go someplace for good.

"I know, let's go down to the bus station and catch a bus to San Francisco. Then we can ask Uncle Rudy and Aunt Idene to take us to their house. Dad won't think of looking there." I thought my idea was the best.

"Yeah, Mom. Can we?" Corin was getting happy.

"No. Not now. It's too late," she said, looking at her watch. Then she grabbed each of our pillows and put them next to the blankets. "Come on, get in. "

36

"Ahh, Mom. This is stupid." Corin sadly slid between the blankets.

"Sí, sí, it's gonna work. Now get in."

I slid in at the opposite end from my sister. There wasn't enough room for us to sleep side by side, so we laid down with our feet touching and our heads out at each end.

"Bueno, remember, when your daddy comes in, be real quiet. Don't say nothing. Okay? Buenas noches."

With that, she got up and left. I heard noise in the dining room. I didn't know what she was doing and I was getting too tired to think about it.

Later, I heard my dad walk into the house. I looked at the clock, twelve thirty. He was loud and kept bumping into walls.

"Delia! Where the hell are you?" he yelled out.

Corin giggled.

"Shhh! Be quiet," I whispered.

He opened up the door to our room. I could see his shape from the hall light behind him. I held my breath. He stood there a long time. Then I heard him start to laugh, slowly, soft and low.

"Your mother is crazy, that's all I got to say. What the hell she doing thinking she could hide you guys." He came into the bedroom. "Come on, get in bed."

"Hi, Dad," Corin mumbled.

"Hey, why'd she put you on the floor?"

"'Cause she's mad at you. You stayed out all night drinking," I said, but he seemed too drunk to care.

"Delia! Pendeja! Get your skinny roach ass over here!"

I heard Mom get up from her hiding place, walk past my dad and head for the bedroom. Dad turned and started walking toward their room.

"Delia, 'stás loca? Why in the hell—" he shut the door, "did you put the girls on the floor? What the hell were you thinking? That I wouldn't see 'em?"

"I got nothing to say to you," I heard her say.

"You are one goofy-ass woman. If you're gonna leave, then leave for Chrissakes. Don't be pussy footin' around with your dumb games. A guy can't have a few beers without you getting pissed off. Next time, tell you what—*I'll leave.* How's that?"

✳

Dad was gone when I got up the next morning. After last night I asked Mom to leave him and take us to New Mexico to live with Grandma Flor. I loved my Grandma. She was nice to me and Corin and always gave us free Cokes and gum from The Coronado. She didn't even get mad when we stole more gum and got caught. Even though her house was little, I knew she wouldn't care if we stayed with her. When I asked Mom if she was going to divorce Dad she never said anything. I guess it was good she didn't, otherwise I'd get my hopes up. Sister 'Lizabeth said "Catholics aren't supposed to divorce. It's what the Pope says." I told her if the Pope had to live with my dad, he'd change that rule fast.

But no matter how mad Mom got at Dad, she always stopped being mad by the next day. "No ulcers for your mom," said Tía Leti. Sometimes even I didn't want to leave him. There were things I liked about him, especially when he was happy. My favorite was when he'd play-wrestle with me and Corin, rolling around with us on the rug, laughing and tickling us. That's when I liked him. That's how I wish he could always be.

But it didn't happen very much. He liked to tease me because I was dark by asking me what reservation I came from. Then he would mix me up by saying he was proud of being "part Indian." I never knew what he was thinking, or what was gonna come out of his mouth.

I sometimes wondered what Dad would do if he knew I liked girls. I almost didn't care because I liked Raquel so much. In my house, I was a hawk, listening and looking for

38

any sign of her. I could tell when it was her talking, even if she was in the same room with her mom and sister. I thought of ways to get her to look at me. I played football by myself, pitched tennis balls against the wall, skate-boarded, anything so I could hopefully see her, or better yet, get her to come over and talk to me. I wanted her to look at me, but not like I was just some girl next door. I wanted her to think I was tough or cute; someone she could like. All she ever said when she saw me though, was "hi," or "having fun?"

One day I saw Raquel come home with this boy who drove an old Chevy. My dad was watering the grass so he saw them too.

"Fifty-five. Nice car. Who's that asshole she's got with her?"

I didn't like my dad looking at her.

"All's I can say is she better watch herself. That guy probably wants some hootchie-cootchie and she'll get knocked-up fast, if she don't watch out."

I didn't know what "knocked-up" meant, but I could tell it was something bad. I didn't like him talking about her like that. And I didn't like that boy driving her in his car and dropping her off like she was already his. I guess I never thought there would be anyone else but me who could love Raquel. No one else who would be as nice to her as I would. Now my dad and this dumb boy were wanting her. You could tell by their eyes. Every time my dad looked at her, it was as if he had x-ray vision, like he was seeing through her clothes. Then he'd practically glue his eyes to her butt. And that dumb boy who dropped her off would look at her face for so long I thought he was going to drill her head to the garage door. I hated it.

My dad kept staring at Raquel like she was the star of a dirty movie. Even though I loved watching her every chance I got, I couldn't stand him watching her.

"Hijo! She sure has a nice ass," he spoke it low, under his breath.

"You don't even know her." I practically hissed the words.

"Qué hombre! There ain't nothing wrong with looking at something good." Then he laughed and gave me a funny look.

I cut my eyes at him and walked away.

I went into our backyard to my garden. Our backyard was all cement and I wanted to grow things, so I asked Mom if I could make a garden. I dug up some dirt from the front and put it in a box that I nailed together from some old boards that were stacked against the back fence. It wasn't very big, but there was enough room to plant lots of things, except maybe pumpkins. I asked my mom what she wanted and she said radishes. I learned to plant things from Miss Scott, in third grade. She let us grow bean plants and geraniums in milk cartons.

But I didn't want radishes. I wanted corn. I liked the way it looked. Its smell. And how fast it grew. So I planted it. I got seeds when I went to the hardware store with my dad. In seven days six plants came up and I gave them houseplant fertilizer. Mom said that wasn't good for corn, but what did she know? She grew up in a bar. I watered my garden, pulled out the weeds, and looked at it every day. It made me happy.

"Hey Marci, I like your corn. When's it gonna be ready?"

I couldn't see who was talking to me. Then I looked up and saw Raquel. She was standing on her back porch with a big smile. I didn't know how long she'd been watching. I was so surprised I fell backwards and almost tripped over the garden box.

"I don't know," I said. "Not for a while."

"They haven't been growing long, right?"

"'Bout five weeks."

"Thought so."

I was shocked she noticed.

"Um, well I think it'll be probably two more months before you can eat it," she said. Then smiled again. "Hey. Want to come over and see mine?"

"You have a garden?" They had a really high fence. "The fortress," my dad calls it. I wasn't tall enough to see over, so I didn't know what she had back there.

"Yeah, come on back and I'll show you."

Raquel came down the steps and let me in at their side gate. There were plants and fruit trees everywhere.

"Wow!"

I saw a garden that took up most of their backyard. There was a table and chairs in the corner and a small pond in the shadier part of the yard.

"Come on." Raquel showed me the whole yard, starting with the popcorn.

"Looks like regular corn to me," I said, studying the stalks and leaves.

"I know, that's what everybody thinks, but it's not."

"Well, how does it grow into popcorn?"

"After it forms corns, you let them dry and twist the kernels off. That's it."

Raquel showed me everything: beans, peas, tomatoes, and onions.

"Hey, and look at this," she said all proud.

She pointed to two rows of peppers.

"Anaheims, bananas, and even red bells."

"My mom told me peppers were hard to grow out here." I bent down and looked at her plants. "She said it wasn't hot enough."

"Yeah, it is. Ya just gotta know how." She tapped her finger to her head.

"Your garden is cool," I said after Raquel showed me everything. "Did you plant everything by yourself?"

"Mostly. My sister Sandra helped a little. I like growing things. That's why I saw your corn. I've been watching it every day, just like you."

"I guess you see a lot from that porch up there."

I pointed to the porch, where it seemed like she could see a lot more than corn.

"Yeah," she said. "You can." Then she looked at me with eyes that went straight into mine, and down in my stomach. It felt like *I* was the one now being drilled into a wall.

"What else can you see?" I asked, feeling like she was peeling everything away that I kept hidden.

"Um, well stars, mostly. I like to come out at night and watch the sky. My mom and dad don't like it when I come out here after they go to bed, but I can usually sneak past 'em and come out for a little while."

"You like stars, huh?"

"Uh-huh, don't you?"

"I guess I never paid much attention to them. My dad doesn't let me out at night, so the only thing I know is what I read."

Raquel went over to the bottom of the porch steps.

"Come over here and sit down for a minute. Can you?"

I walked over, and sat next to her. My belly was starting to make noise, like some kind of animal was trying to get out. Raquel looked up at the sky, which was just starting to get dark. I knew I had to get home or I'd be in trouble, but right now I didn't care.

Her voice got soft, and clouds of it started falling around me.

"Stars are magic. They come out every night, some together, you know, like the Milky Way. Some alone, like the North Star."

I nodded, paying more attention to how pretty she was, than what she was actually saying.

"I guess they give me a feeling there's more out there than we'll ever know. A place where man hasn't gone and—." She stopped talking. She tilted her head and glanced at me out of the corner of her eye.

"You haven't been before."

Laughing, Raquel grabbed both of my hands.

"Yeah! Kinda like that!" She was excited. "So you know what I'm talking about?"

"Yeah," I was feeling funny and excited because she was touching me. "I guess I feel that way, too." To tell the truth, I never thought about it before.

"Marci, I think me and you are gonna go somewhere." She jumped up and spun around, looking up at the sky. "I don't even know where I'm going or what I'm going to do, but I ain't staying here. I'm leaving just as soon as I can save up enough money to take off on my own."

"Yeah, I want to go someplace, too, but I can't now.

"Yeah. Too bad you'll have to wait. But look at me. I felt the same as you when I was eleven, and I'm sixteen! Now me and you have a secret. You have to promise you won't say anything to anybody."

I smiled. "Don't worry," I said.

"Okay, come on then, I'm gonna give you some stuff from my garden."

"But—"

"Hey girl, no buts. I'll give you something and when your corn is ready you give me some, okay? I planted popcorn, remember?" She touched my shoulder softly.

"Okay," I said. "But you don't have to give me anything because I planted too much. And, I—I would give you some anyway." My face felt hot.

She started laughing. "Marci, uh-uh. Come on." Her eyes were shiny and black. "I'll give you some lettuce and spinach. We'll have to wait on the other stuff because it's too early." She walked around the garden, then stopped at the part that was close to the steps. "Does your mom like oregano? I got extra."

"Yeah," I said, "she does."

I followed Raquel while we stopped at different parts of the garden to pick. Each time she put something in my arms, I wanted to grab and kiss her just like the people on TV. But all I could do was look at her and smile like an idiot.

I left Raquel's house happy. And I felt good because I got to be with her.

43

Mom's eyes got big when she saw me walk in the door. I told her where I was. I was lucky because my dad was asleep and didn't even know I'd been over Raquel's.

"Hmmmm," was all Mom said when I told her Raquel only wanted some of my corn as a trade.

"Raquel's nice, isn't she?" I asked, as I carefully put the lettuce, spinach, and oregano in the sink to wash. It was so green that it almost sparkled in the light.

✳

My mom never hugs or kisses me. She used to but not anymore. When I was little she used to kiss me and let me put my head on her whenever I wanted. But not now. I remember the exact day she stopped letting me touch her. I was eight and we were in church. It was Christmas and crowded so we had to sit in the back because we didn't get there early. That made my dad mad, because he likes to sit closer to the front, don't ask me why. Maybe so he could pay better attention. Or maybe he thought it gave him a better chance for the priest to see him.

The Mass went on forever. I had a hard time sitting still. There was a tall white lady next to us with white gloves and a hat. She stood with her legs spread holding her prayer book in one hand. She sang loud, but her voice wasn't on the same note like everyone else's. I nudged my sister and looked over at the lady. Corin looked at her, then covered her mouth with her hand to keep from laughing. While everyone was singing "Hail Holy Queen," I picked up the missal and held it the same way as the lady. I opened my mouth real wide, copying her. Corin started laughing harder, which caught my mom's eye. She grabbed the book from me, whispered "behave!" and pinched me hard. That pinch hurt so bad it made my eyes water. I looked at Corin who pretended to sing. The song was finally over and I got to sit down, only now the priest had to talk.

The priest's talk that day was called: "thinking of others besides yourself." I hoped Dad was listening, but he had his arms crossed with his head down, sound asleep. I was sitting next to my mom, and Corin was next to me coloring in a book.

It was hard listening to the priest. First, he was old so he sometimes forgot what he was saying. Second, when he talked, he spoke the way Mother Superior did to our catechism class. She talked to everyone as if we didn't have brains. The priest was talking just like her, except he kept losing track of everything. It got harder and harder to listen.

After a while I think the priest forgot what he was supposed to be talking about. So he said whatever came to his mind. Dad was snoring and I was getting tired. Even the lady with the bad singing voice had closed her eyes. I thought it would be easier to listen if I could lean against Mom. I put my head against her arm. She didn't look at me, or say anything. Instead, she shook her shoulder and used her elbow to push me away. Hard. Then she just stared at the dumb priest. It made me feel bad, like I was shriveling up inside. My eyes started to burn, like when chile gets in them. I didn't want to cry, so I tried to listen to the priest. All I could think about though, was what my mom did.

My sister, still coloring in her book, didn't see what happened. With an orange crayon, she carefully filled in Bugs Bunny's carrot. The priest was talking about the power of love, but I didn't feel any, not from him, not from my dad and now, not even from Mom. I looked at my sister coloring happily. Somehow I knew she'd be in for the same.

*

Any chance I got I practiced shaving. I'd get my dad's shaving cream and squirt it in my hands, and spread it from the bottom of my eyes down. I'd fill the sink with water just like Dad, then get a bobby pin and shave, slow-like around my lips and nose. Then I'd stick my tongue on the inside of my bottom lip so the little patch in the middle would stick out. When I finished, I rinsed off my face and put on Dad's Old Spice cologne. It made me feel fresh and handsome.

It was Saturday morning and Mom was cooking breakfast. She always made fresh tortillas on Saturdays even though she made them every night for supper. I loved them. They were thick and puffy, and so big you had to cut a piece off because a whole one was too much. Then you put some butter on it and ate it up like a happy pig. Dad came in. He'd just shaved, too, so his face was shiny and smooth. I could smell the Old Spice on him. I got scared, thinking he might know I'd been using his shaving stuff, but he never said a thing.

Dad was in a happy mood. He was laughing about my cousin, Danny. I don't know what it was, maybe it was something funny Danny did as a kid. I was hardly listening because I was trying to keep the melted butter on the tortilla from dripping on my pants. Dad was talking about the dances they used to go to when they were in high school. He pulled the greasy spatula out of Mom's hands and grabbed her close to him while he sang, "Put your little foot, put your little foot, put your little foot right here." Then he pulled my mom even closer, rubbed his face up against hers, and made the song Spanish. "Dingo dingo doy, dingo dingo doy, dingo dingo doy, right here." Mom giggled, and told my dad to let her go, but I could tell she wanted him to keep doing it. I liked it when she laughed.

Later that day, we heard from Tía Leti that Danny was coming home from Vietnam. I guess that was why my dad was talking about him. I liked Danny. His dad, Tío Esteban, lives in Colorado. He's my dad's uncle. Danny's the baby in the family, and they had him when they were old. Danny left home when he was 16, and came out to California. That's when he got to know Tía Leti, who took him in like he was part of her family, even though he was from Dad's side.

Sometimes, when my mom and dad had enough money, they'd let Danny baby-sit us when they went out. He was fun because he'd play fight with us, and let us stay up as late as we wanted.

Danny was big. His fingers were fat like sausages and his belly stuck out over his pants. He had a little beard on his chin, and smelled like paint thinner since painting is what he did to make money. I guess when you're big, you're hungry, because Danny was always looking for something to eat. I told him good luck because Mom never had anything extra. We couldn't even invite friends over for supper, because she planned everything we ate down to the last pinto bean. There was always enough, but some of the stuff she fixed I hated, which is probably why I was so skinny. Uncle Tommy felt sorry for us and gave my mom a huge jar of protein powder to put in our milk because he thought me and Corin needed to gain weight.

Danny could never find anything to eat except leftover beans, chile, and tortillas, which I guess was fine with him, since he ate it all up. The next day, I'd hear the refrigerator open, then a low "Cabrón" come from my dad when he saw his chile and beans gone.

"Well, babysitters need to eat," I said.

When Danny left for Vietnam I got worried. I didn't want him to die. The news said everyone was dying there. I said a special prayer each Sunday to The Virgin Mary to watch over him. Danny was gone a whole year. I didn't think about him every day, but I thought about him a lot because of the news.

Tía Leti called and said she'd talked to Tío Esteban, who told her Danny was in Okinawa, on his way home. I was so happy he was alive. "He got a purple heart," my mom said. I didn't know what that was. I thought it meant something was wrong with his heart.

"No, mensa," she said as she ironed clothes in the dining room. "It's an award you get when you get hurt."

"But why is it a purple heart?" I didn't understand any of this.

"No sé. Go ask your daddy."

"But, why would someone get an award for getting hurt? I thought men only got awards for being brave."

"Pues, pienso que, they get one when they get hurt, too."

"They must have a lot of those to give out."

"Uh-huh."

I walked over to the table and sat down closer.

"What happened to Danny?"

"I think it was his eye."

"Oh," I said, wondering how bad his eye was. "Is he blind in it?"

"I don't know, Marci. Preguntalo a tú Tía Leti. She knows more than us. Pero, when he comes home, do not, I repeat, *do not* ask him how many men he killed."

"How come?" I said. "Isn't that what he went over to do?"

"It doesn't matter if that's what he went over to do. It's not polite to ask it." Mom sounded like she meant business.

"But, why?"

"Because I said so! Just don't do it. Entiendes?"

Dang! And that was the first thing I was going to ask him, too. Three days later he flew in from Okinawa, and I finally got to see him. He had a patch over one eye, and his two front teeth were gone. I asked him if he could see out of the bad eye and he said no. Me and Corin sat on his lap and studied his face. He smiled, but right away, I could tell he didn't look the same. Even though his good eye was smiling, it seemed different, like there was something inside. Corin asked him if he had to wear the patch all the time. He said yes, even when he was sleeping. Corin wanted to know what it looked like underneath, so she grabbed it and started to lift it.

"Corin, no!!" Mom had just walked into the living room with some coffee. Corin looked afraid. I never heard our mom yell like that before. Luckily, Danny caught her hand before too much of the patch was lifted. I saw it, though. I did. It was a hole with no eye in it. I wanted to scream. Even though it was hard not to, I held it back. I got off his lap and went over to the couch.

"Reponosa! Shame on you! That wasn't nice. Now get off him and go sit next to your sister." Mom's voice sounded more sorry than mad.

"Hey, don't worry, Delia," Danny said and patted my sister's leg. "All the kids have been trying to see underneath it. I'm used to it. Kids like to know these things." Danny looked over at me. "Hey! Marci! Did it scare you? Come back over here! My eye won't bite." He started laughing, reminding me of an unlit jack-o-lantern.

Something felt weird, but I wasn't sure of what. I did feel afraid of Danny's eye. And I felt bad for being scared of him, but I couldn't get my mouth to say anything. If I said the wrong thing, he would know that I'd seen it. Mom looked like she wanted to hide behind the couch.

"That's okay," I finally said. "I'm giving your legs a rest since I got really big while you were gone." That lie came out of me easy.

"Oh you did, eh?"

"Yeah, I probably weigh too much for you now, too. Look how big my muscle got." I flexed my right arm for him. It looked like a little brown cue ball.

"Com'ere and let me feel it."

I walked over and flexed it again. He squeezed it hard. I pulled my arm back fast, rubbing the sore muscle.

"Yep, you've gotten a lot bigger since I left." He laughed again, then leaned back and drank his coffee.

Corin must've not seen his eye since she stayed on his lap. I was glad that he couldn't tell I was afraid of him. I wanted him to be like how he was before he left. I felt bad now for even thinking of asking him how many men he killed.

Danny was still funny. He laughed a lot, especially when

49

my dad came home. Dad shook his hand, then hugged him. We had supper with Danny happily eating Mom's tortillas. After a while, me and Corin had to go to bed. We heard them all laughing. They were drinking beers and must have been talking about old times in Colorado. My dad sounded drunk. I could always tell because he talked louder than normal. When Danny finally left I laid in bed with my eyes closed but with my brain on fire. Mom and Dad were talking. Then I heard my dad say, "pobrecito." And that was it. I knew what was bothering me. It was his other eye, the one that *could* see. That eye was a hole, too. Like it didn't want to see nothing no matter what was in front of it.

✳

Aren't other people's religions weird? Our neighbors, the MacCormacks, were Baptists. They went to the Calvary Baptist Church which was painted the same color as bubble-gum. It had a big sign in front saying what the sermon of the week was, like "Abide With Me," "Look to the Light," and "What a Friend We Have in Jesus." Me and Corin asked Suzy and Debbie what they did on Sundays since we thought we were better than them, especially after we heard Baptists do lots of weird things like yelling, crying, rolling on the floor, and getting baptized in giant fish tanks. I got the shivers just thinking how cold that must be. But when Suzy and Debbie talked about their church it sounded more fun than weird. They went to Sunday School where they got to sing fun songs and do arts and crafts. All we got to do was listen to a boring priest and sing songs that were so bad they made plaster crack. I told Mom I wanted to go to Suzy and Debbie's church and she said "over my dead body," so that was the end of that.

One day Suzy and Debbie's little brother, Beaver, came over with Randy Torres to see if we wanted to go over their house next Thursday to have a meeting with a lady from their church. I asked Beaver what it was for, and he said it was this nice lady who came over to talk about God.

"But," he said. "It won't be nothing new. Nothing we ain't heard before. Best of all," he said, pointing his finger at me, "is at the end of the meeting she gives out candy."

"What kind?" asked Corin.

"Good candy. You know, red licorice, life savers, suckers." He looked at Randy. "Ask him."

Randy nodded fast. "Yeah, it's good. It's why I go," he said with a big smile.

I wasn't ready to say yes yet, so I gave Beaver my best FBI look. "Is your mom there?"

"Nope. She leaves."

I was sold. Corin wanted to go, too. That Thursday after school, we went over to the MacCormacks'. We walked in and saw a lady in a skirt with scraggly gray hair and a gazillion wrinkles on her neck. She had those eyes that go in different directions from each other so you could never tell which one's really looking at you.

"Just make yourselves at home, girls. My name is Miss Patt. Can you tell me your names?"

I was a little ashamed since Miss Patt seemed nice and I didn't want her to know that we were just going there to eat her candy. I stared at the carpet and said my name. Corin said her name was Sally which made everyone laugh, but no one told.

"Well, Sally and Marcía, now that sounds a little Spanish. Are you girls Spanish?"

I nodded and Corin said no.

"Well, you never mind. Jesus loves everybody. Come on in and join the group. We're just getting ready to sing a new song, 'Jesus loves the little Children.' All right now, everyone repeat after me, 'Jesus Loves the Little children, all the children of the world.'"

I never heard this song before. I liked it, but it sure sounded different from the songs we sang in our church.

"Red and yellow, black and white, they are precious in his sight, Jesus loves the little children of the world."

The song was easy to learn. Miss Patt spoke next about the time when Jesus decided he'd had enough of bad men running around the temple. When Miss Patt spoke, she had a sparkle in one of her eyes that I never saw in Sister 'Lizabeth's.

"And he chased those bad men out of the temple, re-establishing it as the holy place it's supposed to be." Miss Patt acted proud when she said this.

I checked my watch. Half an hour more and we'd get our candy. I could hardly wait. Miss Patt talked a lot. She kept talking about Jesus in a way that made him sound cool, like he could be your big brother. I looked around to see if the other kids were listening. Beaver and Debbie were. Suzy kept staring out the window and Corin was playing with her bubble gum. Randy was humming a song to himself. He had his hands folded together in his lap.

Miss Patt stopped talking for a second and closed her eyes real tight. I hoped she wasn't going to start crying or barking like a dog, which is what my dad said Baptists did when they were feeling the Lord inside them. I started to get a knot in my stomach, but then felt better when I decided I didn't have to stay at the MacCormacks' house if I didn't want to. That made me feel free. *I* could decide whether I wanted to stay or go. If I left, though, it meant I wouldn't get any candy, which made me sad since I felt by then that I really deserved it.

But the prayer session didn't last long. Miss Patt asked everyone to stand up.

"Those of you," she looked around the room, "who have never accepted Jesus into your heart, might want to think about it real hard. Think about what Jesus has done for you, for all of us, so that we can go to heaven." One of her eyes tried to catch mine. "Now in case you were wondering, heaven is where all of God's children, and that's me and you, can go, but not everyone can go to heaven. Only those who have accepted Jesus can go. And the reason I'm talking about heaven so much is it's because it's God's home. A place where there is no sadness and no tears. A place where only love"—she said "love" like she was eating a fudgesicle—"exists. A place where everyone is happy, where"—

"Where we can eat all the candy we want?" Randy asked, all excited.

"Yes, dear. A place where the candy is piled high as a mountain."

"And it never runs out?" Randy couldn't get the candy thing out of his head.

"Nope, it never runs out. There is no sickness, no hardship, no evil in heaven. Heaven is the happiest place in the universe. She looked at all of us like a mother hen. So those of you who want to go to heaven must come up to me now and accept Jesus in your heart. For without Jesus, there can be no heaven."

Miss Patt sounded like she really believed what she was saying. I knew that the stuff about the mountain of candy was a lie, but I felt sorry for the lady since no kids were going up to accept Jesus. I checked to see if anyone was moving. Randy and Beaver wouldn't go because they told me they accepted Jesus last week. Corin was looking out the window and everyone else was studying the carpet. That left it up to me.

"Okay, Miss Patt," I said as I slowly walked up to the strange white lady's side.

"Are you ready to accept Jesus?"

I felt stupid, but not as bad as I felt for Miss Patt. She had just spent all this time talking about Jesus and heaven and everything, and no one was going up to accept him, which didn't sound like that big of a deal since I had done it in catechism. I figured accepting Jesus like a Baptist was the same thing as accepting him like a Catholic. It didn't make any difference to me, but it sure would make Miss Patt happy.

So I walked up to the lady, who smiled big and proud. She put her arm around me, and pulled me close to her side. It felt weird to have a lady I didn't know touch me like that. My own mom didn't even hug me that close. I let Miss Patt do it, since I guessed hugging was normal for Baptists. It sure wasn't for Catholics. They could barely look at each other in my church. Miss Patt asked me again if I was ready to accept Jesus. I nodded yes.

She yelled out "Marsha wants to accept Jesus in her heart, dear Lord. She wants to be one of God's angels on earth."

Corin started giggling because Miss Patt called me Marsha.

"Now Sally," she looked over at my sister. "You got something you want to share with the group? This is a very special moment for Marsha, and I want to see everyone paying special attention." Everyone started laughing again.

Miss Patt still had her arm around me and I was dying for it to be over so I could get the heck away from her. I gave my sister a dirty look. The room finally quieted down.

"Okay." Miss Patt turned to me. "Now repeat what I tell you: I Marsha,"

"I Marsha," The room busted up again.

"Children! Quiet down, please!" She turned back to me. "I Marsha, do solemnly accept Jesus into my heart. Repeat it, now." Her left eye looked deep into mine. The other seemed to be looking over my right shoulder. "Marsha, honey, can you repeat that?"

"I Marsha, do solemnly accept Jesus in my heart." The words came out slow, for some reason, as if Jujubes were holding my teeth together.

"And you, Miss Marsha, agree to love, cherish, and serve the Lord Jesus for the rest of your life?"

"Yeah, I guess so." I felt like I was in a ceremony that was a combination of "fly up" in Girl Scouts and getting married.

"Halleluia! Little Miss Marsha has now accepted Jesus!

You are a very special person, Marsha! Let's all close this session with one of our favorite songs, 'Just As I Am'."

I knew that song from listening to Susie and Debbie sing it all the time. Thank God, Miss Patt let me go and I got to go back to my seat and join the other kids singing the song until it was finally over. Miss Patt handed out red licorice and Life Savers. I took the licorice, which was my favorite, but it didn't taste so good. I think it was a little stale. It sure was some of the hardest candy I ever had to work for.

Me and Corin went home and told our mom that we had been to a prayer meeting. Mom was peeling potatoes the fast way she always does, but as soon as she heard where we were she stopped, and stared at us like we just said we'd been playing on the freeway.

"Yeah, and guess what? Marci accepted Jesus today."

What a big mouth my sister has. At first Mom didn't say a word, then suddenly, *both* her eyes puffed up so big they looked like blue and brown sunny-side-up eggs popping out of her face.

"So what does 'accepting Jesus' mean exactly?" she asked me.

I scrunched up my lips and looked away. "It's nothing, Mom. The lady just asked us who would accept Jesus, and all I had to do was say I would. Nothing else."

Mom seemed ready to strangle me. "From now on, I don't want you two going to prayer meetings or any other Okie-holy-roller-hootenanny."

Corin and I started giggling.

"It's bad enough that we have to live next door to them and put up with all their mierda."

We were still laughing.

"I mean it. I don't want you two going back to any prayer meeting. Qué prayer meeting! The only kind of prayer meeting you're allowed to go to from now on are the prayer meetings at our own church!"

"We don't have any," said Corin. "And if we did, we wouldn't go because they'd be boring."

"Corin, I don't want to have to repeat myself. I said"—

"Don't have a heart attack, Mom," I interrupted. "We only went there because we heard there was free candy."

"Which wasn't any good," Corin continued. "So you don't have to worry, even though *Marsha* is going to serve Jesus the rest of her life." Corin started laughing again.

I gave my sister another dirty look. "I went up there because I felt sorry for the lady."

"Well, I don't care why you two went there. I don't want you going back. And I especially don't want you going up to some Okie gabacha to accept Jesus." She pointed the potato peeler at us to show she meant business.

"Don't worry," I said. "We're not going back."

"You better not." She turned back to her potatoes.

We went to our bedroom.

"That was stupid." Corin said as she sat on her bed.

"Even though I felt sorry for that lady, I ain't going back."

"Me neither."

As I held the stale piece of licorice in my hands, I asked Corin, "Think you'd go back though, if the candy was good?"

She tilted her head to think about it for a second. "Yeah!"

*

Just one day after I accepted Jesus, my dad hit me again. We were at my cousin Max's house, whose brother, Jerry, was visiting from Colorado. Max had a wife named Sandy who nobody liked. Dad said it was because she had a "superior personality." He seemed to think it was because she was white. I asked him if she thought she was so superior, how come she married a Mexican? He shook his head and said, "things happen sometimes that we don't understand."

We went over to their house that night, and it looked like they'd just finished eating. Plates were still on the table, and most of the food was gone from the serving bowls. I went out to play with Corin, Jimmy and Rena. Jimmy and Rena were Max's kids. We were playing Superman, then we sat around and told jokes like: Knock knock. Who's there? Madam. Madam, who? Ma damn foot is caught in the door, will you open it up?

I went inside the house and looked around to see if Mom and Dad were getting ready to leave. They weren't, so I sat down to listen to them. This turned out to be boring because they were talking about some union thing and about how some guy wasn't "representing them worth a damn." I got up and walked over to the dining room to see what my cousins had eaten for supper. There were peas, some kind of rice, and a piece of fried chicken. On a plate were a few slices of cucumber.

I was hungry, not only because I'd been running around, but because we ate beans for supper and I didn't eat a lot since I didn't like the way my mom fixed them. "Frijoles guisados," she called them, which means she fries oil with flour, and then adds some bean juice and onions. This makes the beans thicker, but makes them taste awful. Mom fixes them this way because the king of the castle likes them like that. Since the king says, "I pay the bills," I have to eat them the way he likes them. Corin hates them too. Mom makes us eat one big spoonful each. After that, we get to leave the table.

When I saw the cucumbers on the plate there were two good reasons I thought I could eat them: 1) my cousins were done eating, and 2) I was hungry. Plus, everyone was so busy talking about the union that I didn't think anyone would notice. Boy, was I wrong. My dad's cat eyes caught me the second I put one in my mouth.

"Marci, who gave you permission to eat their food?" He asked as if I'd just murdered their firstborn son.

I wanted to lie and say my cousins did, but the cucumber was stuck in my throat.

"Oh, Eddie, it's okay." Sandy interrupted us. "She can eat whatever's leftover. We're done and besides"—she looked me up and down, "She looks hungry."

Dad looked at Sandy, then turned to me.

"Put it down."

I still had a cucumber in my hand. I slowly put it back on the serving dish. Too bad, because I knew no one would eat it now. For some reason, I still couldn't talk.

"Hey man, let her eat it," said Max.

"Yeah, Eddie," Sandy continued. "She's welcome to eat anything we got there."

"Says you!" He made Sandy back off with a snap of his eyes. "Marci, get over here!"

I didn't know what he was going to do. I was scared he was going to slap me in front of everyone. I slowly walked over to him. Everyone was staring at me. He grabbed my wrist.

"I asked you if you had permission from Max or Sandy to eat off their table?"

I shook my head.

"Where do you think you get the right to eat food off anyone's table without their permission?"

"I don't know," I said.

"You know goddamn well I didn't raise you to just walk up to someone's table and start eating."

I stared at my dad's hair. It was oily and black. I could smell the Brylcream mixed with his sweat.

"Marci, you know this means I have to punish you."

My eyes turned sharply to meet his. His voice sounded like God in the Moses movie when he was about to give out the Ten Commandments.

"Why?" I asked.

"Because what you did wasn't right. When we get home, I'm gonna have to spank you." He tried to make everything sound fair, like he was a judge giving out a sentence on *Perry Mason*.

"But, I only ate a slice of cucumber!"

"Chingao, Eddie! You're not going to hit her for that!?" Max set his beer down and looked like he couldn't believe what my father was saying.

Even my cousin, Jerry, spoke up. "Hey, come on, Ed, it's okay. Let her alone, man."

"Goddammit, Jerry, when you have a kid I'll make sure I won't tell you how the hell to raise it if you shut the hell up about how I raise mine!" he yelled, then turned back to me.

"When we get home, you're gonna get a spanking. That'll be to teach you a lesson." He held my hand like we were shaking hands on it.

If my dad had a pair of horns, he could have been the Devil's twin. I pulled my hand out of his.

"Now, vete. Go outside and play."

Outside, I told Corin what he was going to do.

"He's gonna hit you for eating a piece of cucumber?" Corin couldn't believe it.

"Yeah."

The other kids called Corin back to the kickball game they were playing. Corin turned to line up for her turn to kick. "Don't worry about it, Marci," she yelled out to me. "He won't do it. Come on, come play with us."

I started playing, but my heart wasn't in it. There's nothing like the feeling of doom hanging over your head. Finally, Dad and Mom left my cousin's house and called out to us to get in the car. Max, Sandy, and Jerry all stared at me like I was about to get fed to the alligators. Now I know what Jesus must have felt like when he knew he was getting crucified. Dad looked like he was in a good mood, so I started hoping he forgot or changed his mind.

When we got home he spoke a little to Mom about my cousin, Jerry, and how he couldn't figure out how Max could stay with Sandy. He said she was a bitch, and that if Max was smart he'd leave her sorry ass. Then he called me over to him. I walked into the living room still thinking he might've changed his mind. Instead, he told me to go to his bedroom and get a belt. My chest felt heavy, like it had fallen into my stomach.

"You're still going to hit me?" I asked, not believing he would do it. "Why don't you just forget about it? I won't do it again. I promise."

"No, and I already told you why." He had the TV on and wasn't even looking at me. "Now get it!"

I picked a belt that wasn't too fat or too skinny. I knew firsthand why one or the other hurt more. I wanted to run out of the room and sneak out the back door, but I knew he'd come find me, and then I'd really get it. It felt weird picking out my own belt. It's not like I ever got a choice before. All the other times he'd just walk toward me, undo the buckle, and slide the belt out of his pants. That slap of leather sliding against belt loops always scared me. It seemed weird getting a spanking without hearing it first.

I took the belt and slowly walked into the living room. I handed it over to him. He told me to bend over his knees. I'd been spanked in lots of different ways, but never over his knees. I felt stupid doing this, like I was in a movie. I almost wanted a spanking the regular way. I laid across his knees and he told me he was sorry, but this was so that I'd learn a lesson.

"Eddie, come on, hombre! Do you have to hit her?" Up until now, Mom had been sitting quietly. "It's not that big of deal. Let her go. She was just hungry."

"Goddamn it, Delia! If I want your opinion, I'll ask for it." With that, he hit me five times across the butt. I have to say it wasn't as hard as he's hit me before, but it was hard enough to make me cry. He let me up, then pointed his finger at me. "Damn you Marci, don't you *ever* embarrass me like that again."

"I didn't do nothing to you," I said, trying not to cry. "I was just hungry." I ran to the bedroom and put my head under a pillow.

I hated God for giving me the kind of dad I had, and I hated Mom for making us live with him. I wanted Dad to go away and find another wife, or jump off a bridge, eat a dead rat, or crash in a car. I didn't care. I just wanted him gone. Right now I wanted him dead.

✳

"Bless me Father, for I have sinned. This is my first confession ever." I was kneeling in front of a mirror practicing my first confession. "Pretty much I've been good." I stopped to think what sins I could tell the priest. "I said some cuss words, hit my sister, and talked back to my mom. I also missed Mass on Sunday two, no—three times." That's what I'd tell him. I was trying to think of a few more sins I could use as a back up. I could say I stole some candy. But I didn't think he needed to hear that. He might think I was sinning too much.

"A priest is the closest thing to God," said Sister 'Lizabeth. "Priests are holy men. When we tell our sins to them, we are essentially speaking to God."

I don't know who's telling these things to the nuns, because it was really hard for me to think that God was as boring as old Father O'Neal.

It was February when we started training for our first Holy Communion. Having to do first communion with a bunch of seven-year-olds was not fun. But then the Mother Superior brought in a new girl named Gloria. Sister 'Lizabeth said Gloria was in the class because she didn't receive communion yet and she was eleven, too! When Gloria came to class she had on pink pedal pushers and white tennis shoes. She walked into the class on the first day with her head up like she knew somebody in the back of the room. She sat down, opened her book and stared straight ahead. I sat near the front so I heard Mother Superior whispering to Sister 'Lizabeth in the corner about Gloria and me.

"This is the second one we've had this year. It's such a surprise, you know. It's not like the Mexicans to keep their children out of catechism, especially since it's free. Something must be going on at home." She talked like she was an FBI expert on Mexicans. Then she saw I was listening and motioned to Sister 'Lizabeth to walk out of the classroom with her.

I looked over at Gloria, stared at her till she saw me, then waved. She smiled and waved back. I decided right then we'd have to be friends.

✷

I hated stupid Holy Communion. Didn't need it and didn't want it. I even hated catechism and told my mom so. Here's what she said back: "Malcriada! Reponosa! Over my dead body! Especially after you've been listening to all those Okie holy-rollers trying to convert you. You damn right are gonna receive your Holy Communion. No me diga nada about it anymore."

So she made me stay in catechism and go through the training with the seven-year-olds. Corin was doing it, too, except in the other catechism class next door. Sister 'Lizabeth never did Holy Communion training before, so we had to get a special lady to come teach us. Her name was Miss Beauchamp and Sister 'Lizabeth was supposed to sit and watch. Miss Beauchamp didn't let us talk, chew gum, or speak out of turn. She looked at our hands at the start of every class and sent us to the bathroom to wash them even if they were just a little browner than our real color. Once, during the first week, she caught Claudine and Juanita sending notes to each other. She got mad, yelled at them, and made them stick out their hands. Then she hit them with a ruler so hard they cried.

When Miss Beauchamp talked, her voice was high and raspy, like a high note on an organ. On top of that, she talked like she was French, even though everyone knew she wasn't. She said she was born in Eau Claire, France. But I found out later from Sister 'Lizabeth that she was really born in Eau Claire, Wisconsin. Her husband was the great-great-grandson of a French explorer. She sure liked being French, though, because we had to say her name in a Frenchified way. She said it should sound like "zee wind sweeshing through zee trees, Boo-shaum." Every time she talked it sounded like Pepe le Pew. I told Gloria and we laughed so hard Miss Beauchamp came over and asked us to share our joke.

"It's nothing, Miss Boo-chaump, it's just that"—I started laughing even though I didn't want to. "It's about this cartoon I saw and I was just telling her." I nodded my head toward Gloria, trying hard to keep from really letting go. Gloria was laughing, too, which didn't help.

"Well, gihls, would you like zu go speak to zee Mother Zuper-ior about zis great cartoon?"

"No, I don't think so, Miss Boo-chaump." I said. Seeing that old tree sloth was one of the last things I wanted to do.

"Mah neme iss Boo-shaum," she corrected me in her Pepe le Pew accent. I was trying so hard not to laugh that water leaked out from the corners of my eyes. Gloria had to stare into her catechism book to keep from laughing again.

"Young ladees, I fail to see ze humor in zis exchange. Eef there are any firther outbursts from you both I weel immediately zend you to zee Mother Zuper-ior."

"Okay," I squeaked. This was going to be a hard class. Miss Beauchamp dressed funny, too. She was a big lady who looked as old as Mother Superior, except her hair was red and tied in a bun. Gloria said it was a French twist, and we started laughing again.

"That weel be enough," she yelled, looking at us over the top of her glasses. She always wore dresses with pearls, and lots of times I'd see her grab those pearls and hold them in her hand. Once, when she was bent over I saw a picture of Saint Peter pinned to the top part of her bra. I wasn't looking on purpose, I just saw it. Her chiches were big, and they were pretty like pink papier-maché Easter eggs. But it made me sick to think about them because they were hers. I didn't want to see them again, even if I didn't look on purpose. I loved chiches so much, but Miss Beauchamp could sure make you think twice about wanting them.

And that dumb ruler she used to whack us always seemed to be close by, like she was waiting for a reason to hit us. Mother Superior said I could join my grade in catechism once I went through Holy Communion. I guess she thought Miss Beauchamp would whip me into shape. Stupid Mother Superior. She didn't know how much I was used to mean people. Miss Beauchamp was a cupcake compared to my dad. Yeah, she was mean, but not mean enough to scare me. What was she going to do? Whip her pearls off and choke me with 'em? Plus, if she touched me with that ruler I'd tell my dad and he'd do something about it. I know he would. He wouldn't like anyone else hitting me.

But the thing about Holy Communion was that I was scared of doing it. First, we had to learn about the body and blood of Christ. Miss Beauchamp made it sound like it was the most normal thing in the world to eat Christ's body and drink his blood. I kept waiting for her to smile and say "jes keeding" but she didn't.

"Miss Boo-chaump!"

She pretended like she couldn't hear.

"Miz Boo-shaum!" I did my best to copy her French. Still nothing.

"Ma Cherie!" Pepe le Pew always said this to that dumb cat he wanted. This time the whole class started laughing, even Sister 'Lizabeth.

"Aauuhh." She put her hand up to her forehead like she wanted to faint. "Marhseeuh, in zis classroom we do not refer to zee teacher as one's cherie. Raising your hand ees zee proper way to get my attention."

I raised my hand.

"Yes, Marhseeuh?"

"Miss Boo-chaump, how come you keep talking about the body and blood of Christ? We're not really going to eat and drink it, are we?"

She looked at me like I had the brain of a pigeon. "Oh, no, no, no! If you read your catechism book, you would zee that the drinking of Jesus' blood and the eating of ees body ees zymbolic. Christ died for our sins. We eat hees blood and body because when we do, we become part of heem." She said it as if it was the most wonderful thing in the whole, wide universe.

I felt better, but not much.

"Who said we have to do this?" I asked. But I already knew the answer.

"God, of course."

I didn't trust her. I'd seen too many science fiction movies where people take over your minds. I couldn't believe Miss Beauchamp was trying to make a whole class think that eating a body and drinking some blood was holy. I wasn't ever going to make fun of Suzy, Beaver, and Debbie for being in a religion where they barked like dogs. The only thing that made it kind of okay was that the blood was really wine and the body was really a cracker.

But only the priests got to drink wine. When I asked why she said "that's the way it ees." Mass was always so boring they were probably glad, too. Some might be wishing for more, like Father O'Neal. He liked to pour lots of wine in. I could tell because I counted while he filled his goblet. Father Castro, who was new to our church, poured one drop in, and always made a face after he drank it. Maybe the wine was bad, like the white port Auntie Arlene drinks. They ought to give him Welch's grape juice. No one would know.

Miss Beachamp said the next part of our first Holy Communion lesson was to learn "The Act of Contrition."

"You have to say zees prayer," she said, "right before you

go to confession, wheech ees what you have to do before you receive zee Holy Communion."

I practiced that prayer so that I could say it so fast it was all one word.

Next, we got to eat unblessed wafers for practice. They tasted exactly like store-bought tortillas. What was scaring me the most though, was going to confession. I practiced the confession I was going to tell the priest. It wasn't totally fake because parts of it were actually real. I wanted it to sound like I wasn't making any of it up. It would be bad if the priest said I was lying during confession. But the truth was I didn't want him knowing the truth. I never talk to anyone about my feelings, much less my sins. I didn't even feel good talking to a priest about my little white lie sins. How was I supposed to trust some man I didn't know with my real sins, especially if he was going to say they *were* real sins, which I guess some of them were.

So I practiced my fake confession, the stuff he would think any eleven-year old girl would say: stealing, hitting, cussing, and missing Mass. I wasn't really sinning for not telling the priest everything. I talked to Baby Jesus, Mary and God, so they already knew what I'd been doing. They'd probably think it's okay not to say everything to some man I didn't know. Plus, my mom and dad sin all the time and they don't tell their sins to a priest.

So on Saturday morning I woke up, did my chores, then told Mom I was going to church.

"O'ye, Marcía. You're going to your first confession today, qué no?" Mom asked me this while pouring warm water into the bowl of flour for the tortillas. I stood next to the stove watching her form the masa into little balls for rolling into tortillas.

"Yeah."

"Hijo, you don't know how glad I am for this day. I didn't think you'd ever do your first Holy Communion; especially since you didn't go when you were smaller. Your father, ay!

Sometimes I think él quiere pelear con todo el mundo. Tell me, how many people do you know get into fights with their monsignors?"

"I don't know, five?"

She looked at me like I should know better. I watched the dance of her hands as she rolled out the first tortilla. It made a sound like a newborn baby getting its butt slapped. She finished rolling it and put it on the comal.

"It doesn't matter, though. I'm just happy you're finally going."

"So that's why I didn't go when I was seven?"

"Yah...We couldn't get you in until the monsignor went to another church. Man, am I glad he left." She flipped the tortilla over with the pink fingernails of her right hand, then looked at me. "You scared?"

"No," I lied.

"Make sure le dices todo al priest."

"I will." The crusty smell of the cooking tortilla filled up my head.

"I mean it, Marci, everything." She looked at me like she knew all the sins I ever committed since I was practically in her stomach.

"Don't worry." I told her as I grabbed the tortilla, spread butter on it and shoved it in my mouth. "See you later."

"And come straight home!"

I ran out the door before she could say anything else and rode my bike to church. I parked it, and walked inside. There was Miss Beauchamp with the class all around her. Everyone, even Gloria, looked sad.

"Well, hello Marhseeuh. Glad you could finally join us," Miss Beauchamp whispered so loud the whole class turned to stare at me. Gloria saw me and waved. Miss Beauchamp had the pearls on again, a blue dress and white high heels. She looked like she could be on *The Bob Hope Christmas Special*.

I pretended not to pay any attention and sat in the pew to

wait my turn. I checked each kid as they came out of the confessional. Their faces were the color of paste and their eyes were dark and hollow like the zombies from *Night of the Living Dead*. They walked with their heads bent and their hands together, up to the front row of the church. When they got to the front pew they knelt down, looked up at Jesus on the cross, and prayed.

My turn was next. I was sitting outside the confessional, shaking inside, but didn't let anyone see. I knew how to keep my feelings to myself. You had to, you know, in my house. My hands could give away my cover, though. They were wet and slid right off the top of the pew when I grabbed it. I tried one last time to practice the confession I was going to say, but all I could think about was the priest catching me in a lie.

I heard whispers inside the confessional. I listened hard to see if I could tell who it was. Someone was saying something about stealing and hitting. Then I heard the priest talking back. Jeez, it was Father Chacón. I could tell by the way he talked. I was sad it was him because he was the smartest priest in the church. My hands were still wet and now I was burping the tortilla. My legs started shaking which made the pew squeak, so I made myself stop. Remember when I talked about being scared of different things and that nothing was equal to how scared I was of my dad? Well, I just found a new kind of scariness: talking to a priest.

The door opened and Manny di Giacomo came out and walked hunched over and holy-like to the front pew. Miss Beauchamp mouthed "your turn," like I didn't know. She sat straight up in the pew as if she was going to hear my confession herself. I got up and walked over to the confessional. Then I opened and closed the door, nice and easy, just like I was going to the bathroom. I didn't want Miss Beauchamp to know how scared I really was.

It smelled like BO and Pledge inside. I knelt down on a little wooden platform. The bones in my knees hurt the second they touched it. I looked around to see if I could see anything, but it was too dark. I heard Father Chacón telling whoever it was on the other side to say five Hail Marys and ten Our Fathers. God! That kid must have robbed a bank! He gave the blessing, shut the little window and opened mine.

I saw the shadow of the priest's face. I couldn't say anything even though I knew I was supposed to. My tongue felt weak, like when I went to the dentist to get a filling. And there was a giant heartbeat in my head. I started breathing fast, like Bonita, the MacCormacks' dog, when she had her puppies.

"Hello, is anyone there?" the priest asked.

"Yes," I could barely get *that* word out.

"Would you like me to hear your confession?"

"I guess so." I didn't, but I couldn't say that.

"Well, go ahead."

"Okay." I breathed a big huge breath, then I tried to talk but the words still wouldn't come. More time passed. Father Chacón sat there waiting.

"Do you want to come back another time?" he asked.

"No." I can just see me walking out, telling stupid Miss Beauchamp, then having to come back in. "No, I'll do it." I remembered my practice confession and tried to pretend I was home in front of the mirror. I took another breath.

"Bless me Father, for I have sinned, this is my first confession ever."

"Tell me. What are your sins?" He let out a big breath, too. He must get tired sitting in that little room.

"Well, I hit my sister..."

"Sí?...How many times?"

"I don't know." I was too nervous to count. "Let's see." I tried to remember what I'd practiced. "I think ten, maybe twenty."

"Ten or twenty? Which is it?"

"I don't know, I guess, probably twenty."

"That's a lot, no?"

"No, not really. You ought to see how many times she

hits me. Let's see..." I was still trying to remember my fake confession. "I stole some peanuts from my grandma's bar, but that was a long time ago when I was little, so I don't know if it counts...Um, I also talked back to my mom, and missed Mass on Sunday."

"A lot?"

"What, talking back or missing Mass?"

"Both, I guess."

"Uh, talking back, just once and missing Mass one, maybe two times. I always try to go to Mass even though I usually go by myself."

"You go to Mass alone?" he asked with surprise in his voice.

"Yeah."

"Where's the rest of your family?"

"Home. Around. I don't know. They're busy. Mass takes up a lot of time, you know." Miss Beauchamp didn't tell us the priest was gonna be a damn detective.

"Bueno, I'm glad that church is important to you."

"I guess so." I thought of Baby Jesus. Please make him stop, I prayed.

"So, do you have any more sins you want to tell me?"

"I think that's about it."

"You sure?"

I couldn't remember if I told him I cussed.

"Did I say I cussed?"

"No."

"Well, I did."

"Was the cussing with bad thoughts and words, or was it just bad words?"

Boy, was he nosy. I was getting so scared I was beginning to lose track of everything. I needed to get the heck out of there.

"Bad thoughts, I mean bad words. Well, they go together sometimes." I didn't know if I was making sense.

"Okay, wait. Are they bad thoughts, bad words, or bad things?"

"Bad words. Yeah, that's it."

"Bueno, bad words, then...What kind of bad words?"

God, did he have to know everything?

"You know, like shutup and damn, though I got punished enough for saying them since my mom washed my mouth out with soap. And those words aren't even as bad as some of the words I hear my dad say."

"And what about your bad thoughts?"

Didn't he listen?

"Well they weren't that bad, just the normal bad thoughts that go with bad words."

"Yes, but I need to know what your bad thoughts were."

This priest wouldn't quit.

"I told you already," I said.

"I don't think so."

By then I was so scared I could hardly breathe. I had to get out of there. And it was so bad now that I decided to tell him the truth.

"Well, like wanting my dad to go away, wishing I didn't have Miss Boo-chaump for a catechism teacher, liking girls, and wanting to squeeze chiches. How's that?"

I thought I heard him laughing behind the screen.

"Bueno, bueno, that's plenty. Okay." He stopped talking for a second, I guess to think or something. "You know, you must try not to hit your sister, and not say bad words, or think bad thoughts. God put us on this earth to love and serve him. This means we have to live our lives with as much faith and purity as we can. Life isn't easy, even if you don't like your dad or Miss Beauchamp. But we have to do our best to be the best, even among great hardship. We must try to forgive those who hurt us. Remember, Jesus forgave all those people when they nailed him to the cross. And as for liking girls and wanting to squeeze chiches. I don't see a problem with this, except it seems you're still a little young to be squeezing chiches. I don't think this is a sin either, unless the girl doesn't want them squeezed. In that case, it is. But, you might think about waiting till you're a little older before you start."

I couldn't believe what I was hearing. He said it was okay to squeeze chiches. I was happy. But then, wait a minute, I forgot we were in the confessional. He can't tell who I am. He thinks I'm a boy! Ha! Ha! The heartbeat in my head stopped and I was smiling so big I'm sure my teeth would have glowed if he could have seen me better.

"This is the word of the Lord. For your penance you must do ten Our Fathers and ten Hail Marys, with an extra prayer to Jesus so that he can help you along the way. Okay?"

"Okay," I almost yelled out. I was so happy I wanted to tell him that I spoke to Jesus all the time, but then I remembered it was our secret.

"I hereby absolve you from all your sins in the name of the Father, Son, and Holy Spirit. Amen."

"Amen." He shut his little speaker door.

I got up slowly because my knees were stiff. I walked out of the confessional blinking because even in the church the lights were brighter than inside that dark little hut. I was still smiling but marched with my head down just like the other kids. I snuck a look at Miss Beauchamp who stared at me with barb-wire eyes. She was probably wondering why I was smiling. Nobody comes out of a confessional booth smiling, even if you are happy. I looked down at the floor and tried to look holy. I don't know if it worked because it felt like her eyes were two laser beams burning on my back.

Kneeling in front of the altar I started my prayers. I finished with the Our Fathers and was halfway done with the Hail Marys when Gloria came and knelt next to me. She clasped her hands and pretended to pray.

"Sure were in there a long time," she whispered.

"Yeah, it's that Father Chacón. He asked a ton of questions. I wonder if his dad was a cop."

"I don't know."

"What'd he make *you* do? I whispered.

"Ten and ten."

"Wow, I guess we have to do more because we're older, huh?"

Just then Miss Beauchamp came up to us.

"Are you ladees praying or playing?" She bent over and I saw her chiches again. Aaahh. I turned my head away fast, toward Jesus on the altar.

"Praying, Miss Boo-chaump."

"That better be what I see you doing," she said as she walked away.

"I hate her," Gloria whispered.

"Me, too."

After I was done with my prayers I told Gloria I was going home.

"See you tomorrow," I said and walked out the church. Even though I didn't like catechism and Miss Beauchamp, or having Father Chacón know my whole life story, I didn't care. I told the truth to that priest and didn't have to lie. He acted like everything I said was normal. It didn't even seem like my sins were that bad. I don't know what he would have done if he knew I was a girl. But I didn't care because the worst was over. Now, I could do Holy Communion, eat Christ's cracker body, and even drink his white port blood. Communion was nothing. Communion I could handle.

✳

Father Chacón was in charge of the spaghetti feed to raise money for Biafra. Uncle Tommy and Auntie Arlene were part of the spaghetti feed organizing committee and gave us a discount so we could go. They go to church every Sunday—seven a.m. I asked Uncle Tommy once why he went to church so early.

"Is it because you're used to getting up at five every day for work?"

He works as a cook at Harpoon Willie's, a restaurant in San Francisco, and has to get up early to start his shift.

"Nope, I go to the Mass at seven so I have the whole day free."

I told him he was crazy. Dad thought so, too, since he called Uncle Tommy and Auntie Arlene "holy rollers."

"What's a holy roller?" I asked.

"Someone who really likes going to church."

My mom rolled her eyes, then shook her head.

"What's wrong with going to church?"

"Nothing's wrong, it's just that"—he stopped and glanced at my mom. "Well, I just think your Uncle Tommy spends too much time in that church. That's all."

I wasn't getting it.

"But Auntie Arlene goes a lot. Is it because her daddy is a cop that makes her a holy roller?"

"Nooo. Your Auntie Arlene is one tough chick, y también, she *is* a holy roller, but I think your Uncle is a little more holier than her since he's always talking about that goddamn church, or is camped out over there kissing someone's ass."

"How much is too much?" I asked. "I go to catechism twice a week and church on Sundays. Does that make me a holy roller, too?"

Dad started laughing. So did Mom.

"No, you ain't a holy roller. A holy roller is someone who spends a lot of time with—priests."

This time, Mom gave Dad a dirty look.

"Well, I guess you don't have to worry about me, Dad," I said.

"Oh no? Why's that?" he asked as he picked me up and sat me on his lap.

"Because I don't say anything to priests. And they don't talk to me."

"That's good, mija. Then we got nothing to worry about," he chuckled.

My dad didn't want to go to the spaghetti feed, but since

we had the discount, he said we could go. Dad didn't like spaghetti, and hated going to church for any extra reasons, especially if he had to be polite to people he didn't like, like Father Chacón. Father Chacón was the priest I saw the most since he usually gave the nine o'clock Mass. Even though my dad never saw him more than a couple times a year, he didn't like him. I don't know why. I liked him because he was ten times better than Father O'Neal, who was getting so old he walked into Mass the other day with his little priest robe inside out.

Father Chacón was a good talker. During Mass he said something everyone seemed to like; everyone, that is, except my dad. After Mass was over Father Chacón shook people's hands at the front of the church. Dad kept his hands in his pockets but Mom shook his hand because she thought he was a nice man. Dad said he was a phony ("jotito" we heard him say under his breath). "He does that bullshit to win the popularity contest with the pinche monsignor." Boy, did Mom cut her eyes at him. I sure wanted to know what jotito meant.

We got in the car and waited for Mom to finish talking to the priest. Dad wouldn't even look at her.

"What the hell she doing?" he'd ask.

"Talking to Father Cabrón, I mean Father Chacón," said Corin. She looked at me and grinned.

I knew Dad wanted to scold her for saying cabrón, but he laughed softly to himself instead.

The spaghetti feed was Saturday night. I was excited. We got to the church and I saw my Uncle Tommy in a nice jacket and shirt and my Auntie Arlene in a dress.

"Qué pinche holy rollers," said my dad who was wearing jeans and a tee shirt. I had to say, Uncle Tommy looked good. It was a warm night and his muscles looked big underneath his shirt. He was swimming at the outdoor pool every day, so the hairs on his arms were all golden on top of his coppery colored skin. His face was smooth and handsome like Fernando Lamas, and his hair was thick, dark, and wavy. His teeth were so white they could be used on a toothpaste commercial. I knew he wanted to look like the guy who played Hercules. All he had to do was grow a beard and you could almost see him in the movie where Hercules knocked down a Roman city. And he'd have a beard, too, except he was a cook and they didn't like hair on men's faces. Plus, Auntie Arlene hated beards.

Auntie Arlene looked pretty, too. Her hair was blonde and her brown eyes reminded you of Bambi. She was tall with the world's longest legs. She wore a pretty blue dress with a white sweater over it.

We walked into the church building which was actually part school, cafeteria, offices, playground, and church. We paid our money, and went to the cafeteria at the back. Lots of tables were set up with red checkered plastic cloths on them. I peeked into the kitchen and saw Father Chacón with an apron on and his shirt sleeves rolled up. Everyone else in the kitchen was a lady. I didn't see any Sisters around. Father Chacón acted like he was the boss. He told all the ladies what to do. The pots of boiling water were so big they looked like bathtubs. The spaghetti sauce smelled good, and so did the garlic bread. I saw little bits of garlic on top of the bread before it went into the oven. Father Chacón was sweating so much his hair was wet.

Uncle Tommy and Auntie Arlene were sitting at the same table as us. Auntie Arlene quietly pulled a bottle of white port out of her bag and asked Mom and Dad if they wanted any. Dad smiled and nodded yes. Uncle Tommy went to buy two glasses of red wine for him and my mom.

He came back holding the glasses with his face kind of mad. "It's a fundraiser, you know," he said to my dad and Auntie Arlene.

"Yeah, but I only have a limited fundraising budget," she said laughing. Everyone except Uncle Tommy laughed. I could tell there was going to be lots of drinking tonight.

After a while we got to eat. I had thirds, but Dad and

Auntie Arlene hardly ate anything. Auntie Arlene's wine was almost gone and everyone was laughing loud. Corin went off to play with some other kids, and Uncle Tommy went to see if he could help in the kitchen. I was bored so I told my mom I was going out to play, too.

"Okay, but don't go too far," she said.

I looked in the kitchen and saw the ladies cleaning things up. They looked hot and tired. I felt sorry for them, especially the ones washing the big tubs that had the spaghetti sauce. I walked outside and saw a couple people smoking cigarettes, but no one I knew, so I came back in. I was hoping Gloria would come, but she didn't. After we received Holy Communion, I never saw her again.

David Quintana, a boy from catechism class, ran past me and pinched my arm, so I took off after him. I followed him back through the dining room, the kitchen, and into the church which had really big doors that were hard to open. He was faster than me so he had already dashed through the back doors of the church and into the parking lot when I gave up. I slowed down and walked through the church, then heard someone talking. Everything was dark so it was hard to see, but I could hear people talking from someplace inside.

I was a little scared, mostly because it was dark and I knew I wasn't supposed to be there. Plus, I didn't know what I would find. I started walking toward them. They were on the right side of the pews. I listened hard. It was coming from the confessional; it sounded like people were laughing inside. I didn't know whether to run or hide because it sure didn't sound like someone was getting their confession heard. I thought whoever was in there probably didn't want to know I was in the church, so I decided to lay down in a pew and wait for them to walk out. I picked a pew just two or three rows up from the confessional and laid down flat. I knew that unless they sat next to me, I'd be totally invisible.

I pretended I was in a Hardy Boy story, so it was less scary. My mission was to find out who was in that confessional without them knowing. I waited maybe five minutes, then heard someone laughing again. That's when I knew for sure it wasn't a confession.

I heard the knob turn and I peeked up just a little bit over the top of the pew. My breath was coming out hard, so I covered my mouth with my hand to make it quieter. The door opened slowly and a man walked out tucking in his shirt. Since the church was dark, it was hard to see, but it looked like Uncle Tommy. It was! I almost screamed out his name, I was so shocked to see him. He didn't see me as he walked quickly toward the church door that led into the cafeteria. He opened the door and slipped out.

I turned back toward the confessional. After about a minute, I saw a priest come out of the very same door as my Uncle Tommy. It looked like—it was—Father Chacón! Híjole! Father Chacón and Uncle Tommy were in the same confessional! Why in the heck were they in there? If Father Chacón was hearing my Uncle's confession, he'd be in the middle part, where the priest sits. And, he'd probably be doing it at some other time, not during a spaghetti feed. Father Chacón walked past me toward the front of the church. He knelt at the altar. I guess he was praying. After what seemed like forever, he got up, then went down the aisle and out a different door. That's when I slipped carefully out of the church and into the parking lot. It was pitch dark. I walked around the parking lot so I could stop breathing so hard, then went inside the building. Mom looked worried, and Uncle Tommy was back at the table with Auntie Arlene.

"Where were you?" Mom asked.

"Hanging out," I said, trying to sound normal.

"Well, stay right here. We're going soon."

I went over to where Corin was playing and waited for my parents. I couldn't stop thinking about what I just saw. What were they doing inside that confessional? I wanted to know bad, but I was too scared to ask. Maybe Father Chacón was giving my uncle a special confession. But he still would have sat in the part where the priest sits. I looked over at Uncle Tommy. His cheeks were red, but other than that, he seemed the same.

Finally, everybody was getting up to go. Father Chacón came over to tell us he'd been counting the money and that we raised $129 for the children of Biafra. While he talked, I saw him and Uncle Tommy look at each other for one or two seconds. Dad and Auntie Arlene were too drunk to see it and Mom was busy helping Corin find her jacket.

Father Chacón stood at the front of the building thanking everyone, smiling, and saying good-bye. He waved to me and said he was looking forward to seeing me in church next Sunday. I had a frog in my throat, so I just nodded okay, and dashed out the door.

✳

I couldn't stop thinking about wanting a birdy, not even for a day. I wanted to be with Raquel and I needed a birdy to do it. I figured with all the extra suffering I was going through, like going to catechism and putting up with my dad, that God would change me into a boy. I told God he needed to change me because he had to do what was right.

I don't know if I fell asleep thinking about it, but the next thing you know, I woke up, lifted my pajamas, and looked down like I do every morning. Low and behold, laying against my leg in all its tomato-worm-like squishiness was a birdy! I pulled my legs up to my stomach in shock. It finally happened! I couldn't believe my wish of a thousand nights had finally come true! I brought my legs down away from my chest and lay there not touching it or doing anything. I looked over at Corin, who was still sleeping. She wouldn't be for long, though, since it was almost seven and the alarm, which was my mother, would soon come in.

I thought maybe it was dream; a trick of sleepy eyes. I made my hand go toward the place where my cuca used to be but I couldn't touch it. Not yet. I lifted my pj's once more. It was still there, turned a little to the left. I didn't see any huevos hanging below, but I was too afraid right then to check if they were there. I started getting scared. I was wide awake now and wanted to scream out to my mom, but I didn't know what I would say. No one in the world knew I wanted to be a boy. Maybe I should have told someone, because now I really needed somebody to talk to. How was I going to tell everyone? And what would you say if you were a girl and you woke up one day and suddenly had a birdy? It's not like you can say "guess what I grew last night?" over the supper table.

I didn't move. But after a few minutes, I decided it was okay to touch it. I slowly reached down. My fingers inched closer and closer till the very tip of my finger slid over the skin. It felt good! Like a Vienna sausage fresh out of the can. Each time my finger touched it, it moved a little, like a teeny lizard getting petted.

I started getting excited. It finally happened! I got braver using the tips of my fingers to stroke it. It was soft and smooth like velvet. I thought I could look now to see if I had huevos. I never really thought about them much. I just knew they were part of a set. If you had a birdy, then you had to have huevos. I didn't know what they were for. And I didn't think I'd need them for anything. In fact, they looked like they could get in the way of lots of things like running, pooping, or riding a bike. But if I was going to be a boy, I guess I'd have to get used to them. I slowly reached down below my birdy. I wasn't sure what I'd find. Slowly, carefully, I moved my hand lower and lower. Just a little more and I'd be there.

Smack! Mom woke me up by slapping my hand hard through the blanket.

"Marrana! Keep your hands out of there," she hissed.

"I wasn't doing nothing!" I whispered back, mad as hell it was only a dream.

✳

The way I look at it, if Jesus could have gone to heaven without a holiday, we would have all been better off. Easter was a special day to lots of people including my mom who went to church and my dad who didn't like to. The only part of Easter I liked was the day before. That's when we got to dye eggs. We'd even get to use a whole dozen. Mom would boil them, and we'd sit at the table with our Easter-egg kit and clear crayons drawing flowers, or writing words like Happy Easter, and Eat Me. This time, my dad was in the kitchen while we were dying eggs and I wrote down every cuss word he said. I can't remember who he was mad at, but when I pulled the egg out of the dye it was covered with chinga, joda, pinche, asshole, and cabrón. I showed it to Corin and she cracked up. We hid the egg from Mom by saying we broke it and put it in our room on a shelf that was so high nobody saw it except us.

When Easter came we got new clothes so we could dress up for church. This meant going to J.C. Penny's to find our dresses, with my dad pulling out his charge card to pay. I got a hat, gloves, anklet socks, and black patent leather shoes. Mom made me buy them. I don't know what she was thinking. I told her I wanted to wear pants and a Nehru jacket, but she told me she'd die first. I knew it was bad when Corin laughed at me, but I didn't see how bad I really looked until we got the pictures back from that day. Depending on who you knew better, I either looked like Randy in a dress, or a young Miss Beauchamp.

We went to the twelve o'clock Mass, then came home. Dad made us take pictures even though we were dying to hunt for eggs. Mom said she'd hide them just as soon as she got out of her heels. We wanted to change, too, but Dad said no.

"This day is special. Christ went to live with His father

in heaven. He died for our sins, you know. Just like the priest said, Jesus didn't have to die for us. He did it so that me and you and everybody who tries to do good in este pinche world can go to heaven. This day is special, so you two stay in your clothes." He said this while he took off his tie.

Then he went into the kitchen and got a beer. He took his shoes and socks off and sat there barefoot at the kitchen table drinking it.

Me and Corin got our eggs and Easter baskets, then waited for Mom to come and hide them. Mom bought us all kinds of candy eggs: sugar, chocolate and marshmallow. Corin's favorite were the Peeps. She liked to bite their heads off and make them walk around. I picked up my favorite dyed egg and showed it to Corin who started laughing. It was a giant eyeball with lots of veins running through it. I told her it was God's eye watching her. I put it up to mine which made her laugh more.

"Hey, knock off that racket over there," Dad said, taking a drink and looking at us over his beer.

"Okay, you kids stay here till I tell you to come out. I'm gonna hide the eggs." Mom finally came into the room. She was still in her dress, but had on tennis shoes. "Don't peek. Remember, God's watching."

"Hurry up, Mom," Corin yelled.

"Hey! What'd I tell you? Cállate and sit still until she tells you she's ready," Dad yelled at Corin as he scratched the hairs on top of his foot.

Me and Corin whispered.

"Bet I can find more eggs than you," she said.

"Bet."

In a few minutes we heard Mom say "Ready!" and we ran outside and stood in line until she said go.

"I see one," Corin yelled walking over to the egg.

"'Spédate, Corin. Not until I say so."

We got ready like we were about to run a race.

"On your mark, get set, go!"

We took off looking for those eggs like starved dogs. I found two right away, but Corin already had four. I ran through the yard and found three more but Corin had the last two, beating me by one.

Finished, we went back inside. Dad was on his second beer. The first can was bent in half, lying on the table. He had a funny smile on his face as he watched Mom pass out the eggs and the candy. Then she brought out a big surprise, two chocolate eggs the size of little footballs from Uncle Tommy.

"Éstos son para both of you. You each get one," she said, cutting us a little piece. "But you can only eat a little bit at a time. Son muy ricos."

"When did he bring these?" I asked happily, shoving chocolate in my mouth.

"Anoche, after you guys were asleep."

"Yeah it was late because he probably had a special Mass with that little jotito he likes," my dad added, burping while he talked. Mom gave him a dirty look.

"Dad, what does jotito mean?" I asked.

"It's—"

"Nothing," said Mom, cutting him off. "It's a dirty word. Your daddy shouldn't say it and I don't want to hear you say it, either."

"But what does it mean?"

"Never mind. It's just a bad word."

My dad was trying not to laugh.

"Y tú," she said looking at my dad, "it wasn't after he went to church. He had to work late." Her eyes told him to shut up, but he wasn't looking at her. He bent over to pick the lint from between his toes. I looked the other way.

Corin was so happy with her chocolate egg and Peeps she didn't seem to be paying attention to what our mom and dad were talking about. She bit the head off two of the marshmallow chicks and made them walk around.

"Pawk, pawk, pawk, pawk, pawk, where's my head?" she

said, making one headless chick talk to the other, "'I don't know, where's mine?'"

Dad made that same funny smile again. He rubbed his feet together, unbuttoned his shirt, then stretched back in his chair, lifting up his arms which showed his hairy armpits.

"Corin, let's go eat our eggs in the living room," I said, grabbing our baskets.

"Uh-uh. No you're not. You have to stay right here at the table," said Mom. "I'm not gonna have you two make a mess on the couch." Mom sat down at the table to drink a cup of coffee.

"All right," I said trying to look away from Dad.

I started peeling one of the real eggs. Corin peeled one, too. She took off the white part and left it on the table and started eating the cooked yolk. Dad stopped smiling.

"Corin, how come you're not eating the white part?" he asked.

"Because," she grunted, her mouth filled with yolk.

"Because why?" he said, looking at her hard.

"Because I don't like it. I only eat the yellow." She was still playing with her candy and didn't pay him any mind.

"She doesn't like the white part, so I eat it," I said, reaching for it. But his hand stopped me.

"Just a minute. O'ye, Corin. Mira, in this house nothing gets wasted. Everything costs me money and it's money I have to bust my ass for. You peel an egg, you eat it. The whole thing. Not just the parts you like."

"But, Dad, I hate the white part. Marci eats it for me anyway." Corin said, still eating the yolk.

"Yeah, I like it, so nothing gets wasted," I added, trying again to grab the egg.

"Dammit, Marci, I said no!" He slapped my hand and the white part went flying across the kitchen floor. "Corin, go over there and pick up that egg. Bring it here so I can see you eat it," he said pointing to the table.

"Eddie, déjalo. It's dirty now. She'll eat the white part on the next egg." Mom spoke softly.

"A qué cabrón! If *I* say she has to eat it, then she's going to eat it! I don't care if she used it to wipe her ass! She's going to eat it!"

"Marrano, Eddie! Do you have to talk that way? It's Easter Sunday, you know."

"Shut up, Delia!" he said, looking hard at her. He turned back to Corin. "I'm not going to tell you again. Pick up that egg. Unless you know what's good for you, you better eat every last bit of it." Corin didn't move. "Now!" he said slamming his hand on the table.

Corin jumped when he slammed his hand and went to pick up the egg. She brought it over to the table, set it down, and looked at it. Her eyes were already watery.

"But Dad, I don't want to eat it," she cried still chewing the yolk. "Mom always lets me give it to Marci."

I didn't think now was a good time to tell her I didn't want it either.

"Corin," he said, pointing at her, "I'm counting to three. If you know what's good for you, you better pick it up and start eating." I could tell he meant it.

"One."

Corin shook her head.

I watched Mom carefully to see if she was gonna to do anything. But she seemed scared and kept looking at her hands and the Easter baskets.

"Two." He was already undoing his belt.

"Dad, I can't eat this. It makes me throw up."

"Dad, it's dirty. At least give her a clean one," I said. Silently hoping that Corin would pick it up and shove it in her mouth.

"Three."

SLAM! The belt came across her mouth so fast I don't think any of us saw it coming. I screamed and backed away.

"Sit down, Marci! And you too, Delia. I'll teach both of

you to tell me what to do. Don't forget *I'm* the one in charge," he said pointing to himself. With that, he hit Corin again. The Easter baskets went flying across the table, spilling candy all over the floor.

"Eat it!" he yelled.

"Eddie, stop! Stop it!"

"Eat it, goddammit!" He picked up the egg and tried to cram it into Corin's mouth.

"Dad, knock it off!" I yelled reaching over the table and grabbing his arm. He shook his hand free and backhanded me across the face, knocking me to the floor.

Corin's mouth was stuffed with the egg yolk she'd been eating, and the dirty egg white was now smeared all over her face.

"Eddie! Déjalo!" Mom yelled. Dad raised his hand up to hit her, too, but something stopped him. He turned back to my sister who was lying on the floor crying, a glob of yellow flashing each time she opened her mouth.

"Sonavabiche, you pinche kids ruin every goddamn holiday we have!" He stood over Corin, still holding the belt and breathing hard. "I'm not telling you again. Get up and sit at the table, and I want to see you eat every bit of that egg."

"Okay. Okay, Daddy." But she couldn't. She was still crying and choking on the yolk. Mom didn't move. She just sat there looking at us, squeezing her hands into fists; the black dots in her eyes darting back and forth.

I got up, grabbed our baskets, picked up the candy and eggs, and put them back in. I left them on the floor and started to walk away.

"Marci. Get back here! I didn't say you could go. You only go when *I* say you can."

I wanted to tell him to go to hell and shove the eggs up his ass, but I knew what would happen if I did.

He looked down, saw Corin crying on the floor, and something inside him must have snapped. "Señor," he said staring at the ceiling, "why...is...life...so...hard?"

"Oh brother," I thought.

He bent over to pick up Corin but she pulled her hands away.

"Don't!" she cried, pulling her arms back. "Leave me alone!"

"Mira, 'jita. I'm sorry I hit you. It's just that you and Marci sometimes drive me so crazy I lose my mind. I don't know what I'm thinking or doing. I'm sorry, mija. I'm sorry. Come here. Come over here. Let me see what I did." He talked soft now.

Slowly, Corin picked herself up, and stood there kind of wobbly. Her eyes were red from crying and there were pieces of egg on her face.

"Corin. Come here, mija. I'm sorry. Come here and let me have a look at you." He knelt down and opened his arms.

I knew she'd go over to him. We were always more afraid of what would happen if we didn't.

He grabbed her hand, looked at her face, and softly brushed off the egg. Then he hugged her. She pulled away from him but his eyes kept searching for something. There was a bruise across the top of her head, and her nose was bleeding. When her eyes looked at him, they reminded me of my cousin Danny's good eye, like they weren't really seeing.

"You know your daddy loves you, don't you?"

No answer.

"Don't you?" he talked sweet like an angel.

Still no answer.

"You know I do. It's just that you can't waste food around here. When your daddy was little we never had enough to eat. We were starving, all of us, your grandma and my brothers. Sometimes all we had were a few beans. Your grandma didn't waste a thing. Not a single thing! We couldn't...Understand?...Huh? Now do you see why I get so upset when you waste food?...Huh? Talk to me."

"I guess so, but I still don't like the white part."

"Mira, you don't know how hard it is to put food on the

table. I work my goddamn ass off day in and day out putting up with all kinds of bullshit just to be here for you guys, give you a little house to live in, and food to eat. All I'm trying to do is to get you and Marci to appreciate what I have to go through everyday. Not for me, but for you. You guys!" he said pointing to us. "I could go away and live an easier life. Have fun. But I don't. I don't. And you know why? Because of *you*. You! Not me. *You*! You think I do this for myself?"

No answer.

"Do you?"

"I don't know." She was looking at the floor now.

"You know goddamn well I don't do this for me. My life would be a *hell* of a lot easier if I didn't have you two, or your mother," he said glancing at her like it was her fault. "I live for you guys. That's all I do." He pointed his finger at Corin when he said "you." Then he let out a big breath. Come here." He picked her up and sat down in a chair with her on his lap.

I wanted to tell him that I wouldn't care if he took the easy way out.

He pressed her close to his chest.

"I spanked you because you have to get it through your head you can't waste food. I love you. I love all of you," he said, looking at us. "Hug your daddy." He was talking soft again.

She didn't move so he grabbed each of her arms and put them around his neck.

"Come on. Give your daddy a hug."

Nothing moved.

"Come on, 'jita, hug me. Come on."

Finally, she moved her arms a little bit.

"That's right. Hug your daddy. There's no one in the world who loves you like your daddy. No one! Got that?"

Corin nodded.

"And don't you forget it, either. Now tell your daddy you love him."

"Come on," he said looking at her. "Tell me you love me." He looked her in the eye. "Come on."

His face seemed different now, like he was someone else, someone we didn't know. His eyes were green and sparkly. He almost looked nice. He brought his nose up to Corin's neck.

"Come on. You know you love me. Tell your daddy you love him."

Corin turned her face toward the wall. "I love you, daddy."

"That's right, mijita. That's my good girl."

✳

I woke up to a pink sky. I don't know why it was that color, but when I went outside to water my corn, which was now as tall as me with stalks as fat as my wrist, I looked at the sky and wondered how it could be so pink. Maybe it had something to do with the fact that we lived close to Union Oil, or maybe it was because everybody was burning trash that day. I always thought the real reason was because Grandma Flor and Tío Alfonso drove up to the house that morning in their Cadillac convertible. I couldn't believe my eyes. There she was, sitting with Tío Alfonso right next to her. Grandma Flor owned the car but always made Tío drive it. She said she was a princesa and that was just the way it was.

Grandma Flor had a red scarf over her head. Her hair sticking out the sides was purple black like an eggplant. She had on cat's-eye sunglasses and red lipstick to match the scarf. She was the only person I knew who had a million lipsticks to go with anything she wore. She was smoking a cigarette and slowly getting out of the car. Grandma Flor was not little. She was taller than my dad and had no fat on her. Her skin was brown and wrinkled, and the muscles on her arms and legs were hard.

Tío Alfonso was moving kind of slow—from driving, I guess. His skin was as dark as a cooked frijole, and he had thick, black curly hair. He said he was from Gallup, but Dad said he was really from Louisiana and that he wasn't Indian like he said he was, but Colored, trying to pass. I didn't believe my dad because he didn't like Tío Alfonso, so he could have made anything up. Tío Fonso, which is what me and Corin called him, made Dad mad because he thought Tío was just a no-good freeloader who lived off my grandma.

Grandma makes her money from The Coronado, so she isn't rich, but she used to have these old shacks she rented out. When the city wanted to build a new courthouse right where they were, they had to, as Grandma put it, "pay the price." That's how she got the Cadillac and that's how she met Tío Fonso: he sold it to her. Mom likes Tío, even though she say's he's a little young for Grandma.

I was happy to see Grandma Flor. She lives in Gallup and as far as I know always lived there. I think about her a lot and wish I could see her more than I get to. She's smart, and good at bingo, too. I call her the seeing eye dog of bingo players. She's so good she can look at ten bingo cards, keep her eyes on mine and Corin's, and still talk to her friends. She smokes without stopping from the second she gets up till she turns off the light at night. When she talks, the cigarette hangs out the corner of her mouth. I don't even know how she sees with the smoke from the cigarette climbing like a snake into her eyes.

Grandma plays bingo, but she's no kitten. She stabbed Grandpa Chon once. His real name is Encarnación. We saw him maybe two or three times, but he never remembered who we were. He liked to drink, and my mom said she guessed Grandma got sick of it because they got into a fight where Grandpa was hitting her when she pulled a knife off the kitchen counter and stabbed him in the stomach. Twice. The police came and took Grandma to jail but let her go when she told them what Grandpa did. Everybody in Gallup knows

Grandma because of her bar. Grandpa Chon lived. Some said it was because of his name. Other people said it was because he was too mean to die. But he sure didn't come around anymore after that. When he took off with Coco Collins, a gabacha who used to come in to buy a six-pack of beer every Friday, Grandma said good riddance.

I ran up to Grandma to hug her. She raised the arm with the cigarette high over my head so it wouldn't burn me, gave me a kiss on the lips, and hugged me tight.

"Mira, look at you, look how big you are!" she yelled loud enough for practically the whole neighborhood to hear.

"Hi, Grandma!" I yelled back. "Hi, Tío."

Tío Fonso came around and shook my hand.

"Hello, good morning," he said, like I was a princesa, too. He's always nice to me and never talks very much. Mostly he smokes, drinks beer, and watches all-star wrestling.

"Qué estás haciendo? What are you doing? Where is your mama y tú daddy?" Grandma asked fast and loud.

"Dad is in the back doing something, I don't know what. Mom's inside."

Corin must of heard them drive up because she ran out of the house straight into Grandma's arms.

"Grandma Flor! Hi, Grandma!"

"Mira, y tú también. You're both getting so big."

She hugged and kissed Corin, then held her out so she could look at her close. I saw her eyes go all over her, then stop at the scars and bruises on her legs. She looked over at mine.

"Por qué están so flacas? How come you guys are so skinny, eh?" she asked, then smiled real big. "Did you say hello a tú Tío?"

"Hi, Tío Fonso," Corin said softly, then slowly reached up to shake the hand he held out to her.

"Hello, Corin. How are you?"

Tío Fonso looked tired, like he wanted a beer.

"Come in everybody," I said, like I was the boss of my house. "Did you drive all the way from Gallup?" I asked, but they didn't answer because Mom walked out with my dad right behind her. Tío Fonso walked around the car and opened the trunk to take out the suitcases. I went to help, but Dad beat me to it. They shook hands.

"Quehúbole! Cómo estás?" my dad said to Tío Alfonso, shaking his hand hard, then each of them grabbed a suitcase.

"Hi, mija," Grandma said as she hugged my mom. "Cómo 'stás?"

"Fine, fine."

"Well, I'll be goddamn! Talk about a surprise," said my dad.

"Hello, Eddie," Grandma said hardly looking at him.

She stood smoking with her hand on her hip and talked to us like she was giving a speech. "Pues, estamos a un drive en mi carro, so I said, 'The hell with it, Fonsito, let's go to California and visit my 'jitas.' So here we are." She reached down and hugged me and Corin.

I thought it was weird that she never told us she was coming, but I didn't say anything.

"Entre, entre. Come on in then," Dad said back to my grandma. "You guys must be muy cansado."

They walked into the house and sat on the couch.

"Sí, poquito, pero I'm just happy to see Marcía and Corin. Come over here and give me another hug."

We went over to her and hugged her again.

"Delia, get me a beer and get them something to drink. Flora, qué quieres?" he asked Grandma.

"Café, nada más."

"Y tú, Alfonso, café or cerveza?"

"Café, gracias."

Mom got up to get them their drinks and I followed her into the kitchen.

"How come Grandma's here?" I whispered.

92

"No sé," she said.

"She never comes without telling us," I said as I opened the fridge.

"Just get your dad a beer."

I got the beer and the canned milk. Mom came behind me with two cups of coffee. I could tell my dad was trying to do all the talking, but Grandma wouldn't let him. She talked fast, and when he tried to talk, she wouldn't even wait for him to finish his sentence. Tío Fonso was already in front of the TV watching *Roller Derby*, and Dad and Grandma had moved into the dining room. I wanted to watch *Roller Derby*, too, because I liked Big Anis Jensen, who played for the Bay Area Bombers, but I wanted to hear what Grandma was saying.

Grandma sipped her coffee with a really loud slurp. She untied her scarf and her pressed-down hair puffed up like a thick black sponge. She lit another cigarette. Lucky Strike was her brand.

"Well, I no gonna beat around the bush," she said as she took a deep puff off her Lucky. "I come here to take Delia and the girls with me to Gallup for a vacation." She blew out a bunch of smoke into my dad's face when she said this. "A long one."

"A qué cabrón." Dad's face wrinkled up into a frown. "Now just hold on there a minute. Who says you can come over here and do what you want with my wife and kids?"

"No te digo nada, except this is my daughter and my grandchildren and I gonna take them to my place for a little while." Grandma said this with the cigarette hanging from the corner of her mouth.

I don't think they saw me and Corin watching and listening. I looked over at Corin. Her eyes were round and scared.

"Delia, did you have something to do with your mom coming out here?" Dad practically yelled it in her ear.

She sniffed loud, but wouldn't look him in the eye.

"I thought so." He said it like it made him sick.

"La Delia no me dijo nada. She just say she was tired. The girls are on vacation, so I told her come out and visit me and Fonsito." When Grandma finished talking, she sucked in the cigarette for a long time, then let out the smoke with a hard puff of air. I thought Dad's head was going to explode.

"I want to go with Grandma," Corin piped in.

"Me, too," I said.

"You kids stay out of this. This is none of your damn business. Me and your grandma's talking here. Better yet, go into the living room and watch TV with your tío." Dad tried to flick us out of the room like flies. We didn't move.

"I said go!" he yelled, and scared us away with those eyes that could melt steel. We knew that look and got up to leave.

"Déjalos. Let them stay." Grandma said it soft but strong. We sat back down. Then, as if nothing happened, Dad seemed to forget we were there.

"Mira, Flora, this is *my* family. You can't just come here out of the blue in your fancy car, pick them up and drive away. These are my wife and kids. They ain't yours. They're mine!" His voice was loud and he was pounding the table with his pointer finger.

I looked over at Mom. She had one leg that kept bouncing up and down and held her hands together like she was praying. Her hands were pressed together so hard that her fingernails had turned white.

Tío Fonso quietly walked into the kitchen and got himself a beer. He didn't go back to the TV though, he just stood in the doorway, watching.

Grandma Flor put out her cigarette, then pulled another from her silver case and snapped it shut. She shoved the cigarette in her mouth and lit it with her lighter so fast you almost thought it lit itself. She took another long puff, and looked at my dad like she'd like to kill him.

"Mira, let me tell you something." She pointed her finger at my dad who looked like a bomb was ticking away inside him. "Your wife and kids are not your slaves. You married my daughter and you helped bring these kids to this earth, but I got news for you. You sure as hell don't own them."

That's all it took. He tried to choke her, but before his hands got a good grip on her neck, Grandma pulled a switchblade from her pocket and laid the tip under his ribs.

"Ay, Dios!" my mom gasped.

"Sit down, cabrón! And take your goddamn hands off my neck!" Grandma's arm muscles were hard, and the tip of the knife was dented into Dad's stomach. She looked like she was itching to use it, too. Slowly he let go of Grandma's neck. His hands didn't know what to do so they stayed in the same place, only now they were just in front of him. He looked down, saw what they were doing, then dropped them to his sides.

"Eddie, why don't you sit down like the lady asked you to?" Tío Fonso had quietly walked up behind him and spoke right in his ear. My dad looked like something was broken. His eyes, still hot, flitted all over the room; first to Grandma, then Mom, then me and Corin, and finally back to Tío Fonso. He carefully, quietly sat down.

Grandma laid the knife on the table, but kept her hand on top of it. With the other she smoked her cigarette. She didn't take her eyes off my dad. Except for the puffs from Grandma's cigarette, the room was totally quiet.

Finally, he looked away.

"Chingáo, man. I guess you wear the goddamn balls in this family, qué no?" he said like he was kind of laughing.

"Mira, I don't wear the balls, but I got enough of them to stand up to you. Leave these kids alone and treat your wife for once like she ain't your dog."

"Nobody!! Nobody!"—he pounded the side of his hand into the table like he was karate-chopping it—"tells Eddie

Cruz what to do! Not my wife, not my kids, and especially, not you." With that, he pushed himself away from the table.

"Eddie"—

My mom tried to grab him by the arm, but he shook it off and walked out of the house, slamming the door behind him. We heard the car start, then tear out as he drove away.

Mom ran into the living room and looked out the window like she wanted him back. I first thought this was going to be the luckiest day of my life until she turned around and I saw how much she was crying. Something told me right then that we weren't going anywhere. Mom wasn't going to leave my dad no matter what he did to her, or us. And, as if she read my mind, Grandma whispered to Tío, "She ain't never gonna leave him."

I went to find Corin and saw that she had sunk down into a corner, crying. Something about seeing her and my mom cry made me feel like I weighed a thousand pounds. Like I was sinking into the tar of the La Brea Pits. I knew then that even though I wanted to leave, I couldn't. Not by myself. I couldn't leave Corin and I knew she wouldn't leave without Mom. When I looked at Grandma, I felt what I needed to do. When I looked at Corin, I felt the same thing—but opposite.

Grandma put out her cigarette.

"Bueno. You girls want to go with your Tío Fonso and me, or are you staying here with your mama?" She asked the question matter-of-fact, like how I wanted my eggs cooked.

I thought about it for another second, then looked over at Corin.

"I can't go without my mom, Grandma," Corin said, crying harder.

"Y tú?" Grandma looked over at me.

I slowly shook my head.

"Bueno. Vamos, Fonsito." She started gathering up her things. She took the switchblade, folded it up, and put it back in her pocket.

"No quieres lonche?" Mom walked into the kitchen, her

eyes watery, and started getting things out of the fridge. I could tell she was trying to act like nothing happened.

"No, gracias, mija. It's better if we go."

Grandma and Tío walked to the living room. They picked up their suitcases and walked out the door. While Tío loaded the suitcases back into the car, Grandma hugged all three of us.

"You be good," she said to Corin and bent down to hug her. "And start eating a little more. You look too flaca."

Corin smiled.

"Y tú también." She hugged me hard and gave me a kiss on the lips. "You and Corin are gonna fly away with the wind." She stopped to puff on her cigarette. "Mira, toma. I almost forgot. I bring some presents for you two." She looked inside her big purse and brought out a present for me and one for Corin.

"Thanks, Grandma," said Corin. "Can we open it now?"

"No, no. Wait till I go."

Both of them were in long skinny boxes.

Grandma pinched my cheek and looked over at Mom. She turned back toward me. "You help your mama," she said, her eyes diving deep into mine.

"I will," I said, and started crying. Then she hugged me hard.

When she finished with me she turned to Mom and put her arm around her. "I no gonna tell you to leave him. He's your husband. But I want you to know that you and the kids can come and stay with me anytime. I mean it, Delia, anytime. Entiendes?" Then she stopped, stared at Mom, and put both hands on her shoulders. "Delia, if there's anything I wish I'd done, was not leaving tú papa sooner." She patted Mom softly on the cheek, then got in the car. She took her scarf out of her purse, tied it over her hair, and lit another cigarette.

Tío Fonso came over and shook our hands. "Cuídate," was all he said.

Grandma stared straight ahead as Tío started the car and gave it some gas.

"Bye, Grandma!" yelled Corin, her eyes filling up with water.

"Bye, Grandma," I yelled, too.

"Bye-bye mijitas," Grandma said, turning around to take one last look at us as Tío Fonso put the car in gear and drove away.

"Bye, Mom!" my mom yelled louder than anything I'd ever heard come out of her.

Grandma had already turned back around. She was almost out of sight when she lifted her hand up and waved like she was in a parade. She was still waving as the car sped around the corner.

Secretly, I opened my present. I lifted the lid off the box and there, against black cardboard, was a flicker of turquoise and silver. My very own knife.

✳

After Grandma Flor left, nothing was the same anymore, at least not for a while. Dad didn't come back, and even though I was dumb to think it, I wanted Mom to be happy about it. Instead, she cried every day and hardly ate—and I found a pack of Winstons on top of the fridge. Sometimes, she talked to us, saying she wished he'd come home. Mostly, it was Tía Leti she spoke to, who came to the house each night to check on her. I don't think Tía likes Dad very much, but she didn't even say mean things about him on account of my mom having such a hard time.

After Dad was gone about a week, Mom said she had to go out and get a job because he didn't call or nothing, and Mom didn't know where he was, or if he was ever coming back. Since she had to learn to drive, Tía Leti's son, Gordo, came over to teach her. Gordo was a nice guy, and not really fat, though everyone says he was as big as a walrus when he was little. His job was at Union Oil, but his hobby was working on cars. He told Mom he had a Ford Falcon he could loan her till she was on her feet. It had a clutch, but for some reason—either Gordo was a good teacher or Mom really needed the car—she learned how to drive it in two lessons. After practicing a little more, Gordo took her down to the DMV and she got her license. Finally, we felt like we'd been set free.

The next step was to get a job. Tía Leti drove Mom around town where she helped her put in applications at different places. Tía worked in a laundry where they washed and ironed clothes starting early in the morning. She said she'd try to get my mom a job there, but Mom said she wanted to work someplace else if she could. She told me Tía worked too goddamn hard for not enough pay and she sure didn't want to do that. Tía got off work so tired she could hardly stand up. But she'd still go over to Flavio's Flaky Pastries everyday for coffee with her friends before she went home to start supper.

Mom never finished high school, but she could read and write. She got a job right away at a factory where they made plastic bowls, but said it was too hot inside and she was always burning her hands. So she quit. Then she got a job as a substitute at Woolworth's. It didn't pay a lot, and they made her do every job in the store. They called her in for work when they needed help, which turned out to be almost every day. That meant one day she'd learn how to use the cash register, or the next day or two she'd be making hamburgers and grilled cheese sandwiches at the lunch counter. Other days she filed papers, answered phones, or stocked shelves. She said she liked it because she never knew what she was going to do when she left in the morning.

Mom got up early to get ready for work. Next, she got me and Corin up. After breakfast she drove us to school where we stayed at the playground till school started at 8:30. Mom started work at 8:00. So she dropped us off at ten till, and we had the whole playground to ourselves until the other kids started coming. We didn't mind being at school early. I taught Corin tricks on the monkey bars, or we read together.

When school was over, and unless we had a Girl Scout meeting (Corin had joined, too), we went over to the bakery and met Tía Leti. Then we walked over to her house to wait for Mom to pick us up.

Mom got to know everyone at Woolworth's, and they'd sometimes give her presents to give to us: nail polish and coloring books for Corin, and rubber balls and paint-by-number sets for me. The cook was nice to her, so lots of times we got to eat leftovers from the lunch counter for supper. This meant Mondays—meatloaf, Tuesdays—liver, Wednesdays—hot-dogs with macaroni and cheese, Thursdays—fried chicken, and Fridays—fish sticks. My favorite days were Thursdays and Fridays. When there weren't any leftovers, we ate grilled-cheese sandwiches, spaghetti, cold cereal, or weenies wrapped in bacon. This made us happy because we didn't have to eat beans so much anymore.

I don't know how long Dad was gone. It seemed like forever, but I think it was only a couple of months when I heard from Tía Leti, who heard from her husband, Tío Agapo, that Dad was living in another town in an apartment, and that he sometimes had a lady driving around in his car with him. Tío Agapo said it was some gabacha named Wanda. I couldn't believe it. It seemed weird to think of my dad with another lady. I wondered if she had big nalgas too. Tía Leti told only me and made me promise not to tell anyone, not Corin and especially not Mom. I told Corin first chance I got, only because I thought she should know.

I couldn't get over how quiet our house was with my dad gone. There wasn't any yelling going on and Mom didn't talk very much, at least not to us, so I read, watered my garden, or played outside. Corin read or played with the MacCormacks next door. This made the house so quiet I sometimes couldn't believe we were the same people. At night, we got to watch whatever we wanted on TV: *Gilligan's Island, Dobie Gillis* and *Green Acres*—all the shows Dad hated. Randy Torres even came over to watch TV, which was fun because he could talk like Mrs. Douglas on *Green Acres*. He could even do Ginger and MaryAnne from *Gilligan's Island*. Mom laughed at Randy when he did this. After a while she stopped crying and started laughing a lot more. I can't remember how long it'd been since I'd heard her laugh.

More people started coming over the house to visit and lots of times they brought little presents, like a dozen fresh tortillas, avocados from their trees, or eggs from someone's backyard. Uncle Tommy came by more and always let me squeeze his muscles. Even my cousin Danny stopped by once in a while, but he didn't stay long. He wobbled sometimes when he walked and his good eye was fuzzy, like it had clouds in it. I could tell Mom was worried about him when she saw him. "Este Danny, pobrecito," I heard her tell Tía Leti once. "It should be us who goes over to check on *him*."

The last time Danny came over I walked outside with him to his car which was a really cool '56 Ford. That's when he told me it was my dad who was sending him over to look in on us. I asked him why Dad couldn't come himself, and he said "I don't know, man. Your dad just told me to stop by from time to time."

"When you see him what do you tell him?" I asked.

"I tell 'em you and Corin are still doin' good in school and that your mama's working. Y'know, things like that."

"Do you just tell him or his girlfriend, too?"

Danny started laughing. "Girlfriend? Who told you your dad's got a girlfriend? He ain't got no girlfriend."

"Does too, and I know it because someone I know saw him with this girl named Wanda."

"Wanda? Wanda? No way on her, man. She's just hangin'"

with your dad. Your dad don't like her, at least not the same as your mama."

"For sure?"

"Yeah. Your dad still asks about your mom and everything."

"Probably wants to know if she's got a boyfriend." He seemed a little surprised by what I said.

"Well—well, that's just part of it." He got in his car. "I gotta go."

I was sad about my cousin. It looked like he was on some kind of drugs. Mom said lots of the guys who come back from Vietnam are on drugs. I wanted Danny to be the same as before he left. It made me mad that he was different now. I told Mom I was going to ask him what happened over there but she said "over my dead body."

But about my dad being gone, probably the best thing that happened to me and Corin was that we didn't get whippings anymore. Our legs and arms didn't have scabs and bruises on them, and I didn't get scared everyday at five o'clock. Since I like to count things, I used to keep track of how many times my dad hit me and Corin and it came out to two, sometimes three times a week. That's a lot of whippings not to have. The time I use to spend being mad, I read. And instead of worrying, I learned to fix things, like the cord on the iron or the leak in the toilet. I checked out books from the library on woodcraft and started to build things with Dad's tools. I built two more garden boxes and planted snapdragons, daisies and geraniums for Mom, cucumbers for Corin, and spinach for me. My corn was growing so fast it was taller than me. Our house wasn't the same anymore. It was different, but in a better way. Except for Mom being gone all day, I liked how everything was. I didn't know it, but I guess I must of spent a lot of time being mad or afraid. It was nice being something else.

✳

School was out and that meant no catechism and no teachers. Since Mom couldn't afford a baby-sitter, she said we had a choice of being watched by Auntie Arlene, who didn't have to work, or we could go to Summer Recreation, which was at a park a few blocks away. We went to Summer Recreation to see if we liked it and boy, did we. It was a place where these teenagers played with us all day. We came home, said "heck yeah," and Mom gave us the key to the house. The only problem was, it opened at ten. So Mom called Randy's mom who said we could come over and play with Randy, and she'd watch us for free. Mrs. Torres was sleepy in the morning and stayed in bed smoking cigarettes, which meant we got to watch whatever we wanted on TV and hardly saw her at all. Then, at 9:30, the three of us left for Recreation.

I loved Recreation. We stayed there the whole day until it closed at 4:30. We got to do lots of things like play softball, ride the swings, and act in plays. We were constantly making key chains and pot-holders. I was so good at making pot-holders that I made enough to send all my tías, Grandma Flor, and even cousins I hardly knew.

I liked some of the girls who worked there, too. They were nice and a lot were pretty. I especially liked one named Pippa, who was part Black and part Filipino. I wanted her to like me back as her girlfriend. But to her I was just a kid, plus a girl. It was the same old problem.

On top of everything, I finally figured out that as much as I loved Raquel, me and her would probably never get married. It's not that I didn't want to marry her. I did, more than ever. It's just that I didn't see her very much anymore. I didn't know where she was or what she was doing, except sometimes I'd see her get out of a car with an ugly guy in it. This guy was different than the other one I saw with the old Chevy. This one's face reminded me of a razor blade. His hair was long and black, and he was skinny like a mongoose. He usually wore white tee shirts that showed his muscles and he had a long pink scar on top of his arm. He always smoked and lots of times I saw him drink a beer, then flip the empty bottle into the back seat.

I found out his name was Ruben. He was creepy and I thought I was a heck of a lot cuter. I remembered Raquel told me about getting away as soon as she could. I hoped she wasn't taking off with that skinny razor blade face. He seemed awful. I wished Raquel would like me instead. The problem was, no matter how you looked at it, I was never gonna get her. She wanted a birdy. I had a cuca. She needed a car. I had a bike. She liked teenage guys. I was eleven. Raquel wanted to be free, and I wasn't leaving for a while. I had to face facts. It made me sad, and worse—I missed her. I still wanted her, but I already knew that I'd have to find another girl to love me. Who she was and where she'd be, I didn't know.

※

You know how every night before I go to sleep I pray to God to change me into a boy? And you know how I say a prayer, then look at my cuca every morning to see if it came true? And then there's my other wish for my dad to go away. I probably said those prayers for as long as I can remember. Well, one night when I was praying, I caught myself, and almost started laughing because my dad *was* gone! He really *did* go away! Finally, it looked like God was starting to listen. I guess people ask so many things from God that he can't always hear them and that's why Sister 'Lizabeth says we can't stop praying. "God's busy," she says. This is good news because it means he's finally paying attention to me. And it might mean he'll change me into a boy soon, too. I felt happy for a while, then started to worry again. Dad was gone, but I didn't know if he'd stay gone.

Then something happened that took me by surprise. I started to miss him. I couldn't help it. I'd remember how he was when he was happy and how fun he could be, laughing and play-wrestling with Corin and me. At his workbench in the shed I'd watched him hammer, saw, and make things. When he was making something he'd always answer my questions and he talked to me like a teacher. He never yelled or got mad. It was the only time I saw him that way. Then I remembered how he made my mom laugh. He'd dance with her, making up songs from his head. He had a way about him that was hard to forget.

Our house was better now, but I kept catching myself wanting him back. Maybe he'd be different. Maybe he'd be so sad to not have us or Mom that he wouldn't hit us anymore. It had to mean something that he sent Danny over from time to time.

I've wanted my dad to leave for as long as I can remember and now that he's gone, here I am wanting him back. I must be crazy.

One night before we went to bed I told Corin I missed him.

"You do?"

"Yeah, I know it sounds weird, but sometimes I wish he was back but, you know, only the nice part. Not the mean part."

"I don't," she answered. "I don't miss him. And I don't care if I ever see him again."

"You don't?"

"Nope," she said, her jaw set. "Even though Mom has to work, everything's better now."

She was quiet a long time. I was tired so I turned off the light. After a couple minutes she said, "Marci, you always think things are gonna get better. But they won't. You and Mom are both stupid because he's too mean."

"I know he's mean," I said, "and I hate him most of the

time, but I guess I've been thinking of his good parts, the parts I want him to be."

"He can't be just the good parts."

"Why not?"

"'Cause most of him isn't." Her voice sounded sleepy.

I sighed. "Yeah, I guess so. But if he does come back, something's gotta change."

"Uh-hmm."

"I don't know what."

"We'll think of something." With that, Corin turned over and fell asleep.

✳

Another month passed and Mom was working at Woolworth's as a steady instead of a sub. They made her a checker so she spent the whole day ringing up people's things. She missed going from place to place like before, but said working as a steady paid better and would give us Kaiser in six months.

After me and Corin talked, I didn't miss my dad as much. I guess what she said made me remember how he really was most of the time. Maybe I was sad because I wanted him to be different. But I knew he really wasn't gonna change. Three and a half months have gone and he hasn't called or nothing. I figured if he cared about us, he'd at least come back and say he was sorry. Even if he wouldn't change, he'd at least lie. Pendeja. I don't know what I was thinking. Now I was glad. Glad he wasn't coming around and glad we were free of him. Glad to see Mom laugh, Corin singing Beatles songs, and me not worrying about what the night would bring.

I looked at my legs. All they had left were scars. Uncle Tommy said me and Corin looked like we gained a couple pounds. I knew it was because we ate food we liked. And Danny didn't come over as much as he first did, but each time he did, he looked worse. You almost couldn't talk to him because he'd take a long time just to say one word.

Except for worrying about Danny, I was finally happy because my other wish of a thousand nights had finally come true; that is, until the day Dad decided to come back.

❊

"Where the hell is your goddamn mother and why isn't there any food on the table?" he asked, pulling out a chair and sitting down hard with pants so dirty they looked like he'd wiped the street with them.

I was learning to cook so I was making meatloaf when he walked in. I had an onion in my left hand, and a knife in my right. Seeing him, I gripped the knife a little tighter. It'd been almost five months. His hair was long and greasy and I could smell him from where he was sitting. He had grown a little pointed beard which made him look like the Devil.

"You don't live here anymore. So I don't have to tell you nothing." I answered back.

"I'll be goddamn! I'm your father and as long as I live I'll *always* be that!" He slammed his hand on the kitchen table. "Don't give me any lip, Marci. Just because I been gone don't mean I can't kick your little ass. Now answer me. Where the hell is your mother?"

Just then, Corin walked into the kitchen, saw our dad and screamed. He looked at her, gave her a mean look and turned back to me.

I hung on to the knife, gripping it hard. I wish I had the guts to use it on him just like Grandma Flor.

"You ain't been in this house for five months. You didn't call or nothing to see how we were, and you didn't give us any money. If you want to know where Mom is, why don't you call her at work? And, if you want food, why don't you go ask that girlfriend of yours to come over and cook it!" I was shocked I could talk to him this way. It was as if holding the knife gave me super powers. I was breathing fast because I was mad. I stood facing him, my right hand holding the knife, waiting to see what he was going to do. Corin stood with her back pressed against the wall.

He looked at me, then back at Corin. He started laughing. First so soft I could hardly hear him, then his laugh grew louder and he looked up toward the ceiling like God was the only one who understood how awful his life was.

"Hijo, Marci, what a big little man you are now." He walked over to me and stuck his pointer finger under my chin. "Qué hombre! I didn't know I had me un hombrecito. Here I was thinking you was my little girl. And goddamn if my dick didn't squirt out a boy."

I slapped his finger away.

"Oh, and a macho también."

"I ain't afraid of you." I held onto the knife even though I still didn't know if I could use it.

"I'll tell you one thing," he said, speaking so close I had to hold my breath. "If you ever decide to use it, you sure as hell better kill me, because if you don't—you might live to regret it." He grabbed the knife out of my hand and threw it into the wall about three feet from where Corin was standing. It scared her so bad she fell to the floor like a popped balloon. He looked at her, started laughing again, and walked out the door.

"Get out! Get out!" I yelled.

Corin got up from the floor and yelled, too. "And don't come back!"

"Mom doesn't want you, either," I almost spit the words at him.

He stopped, turned around and came back. His face was the color of blood. "You should never say things like that to your father." He looked at both of us, turned, and was gone.

"We can't tell Mom," I said, letting out a big breath of air.

"Why not?"

"'Cause she doesn't need to know he came over. It'll just

make her sad." I walked over to where the knife was sticking in the wall and pulled it out.

"Marci, if we tell her what he did, it'll make her mad, not sad." Corin said matter-of-factly.

"But Mom's happy now. I don't want to spoil everything. It won't be good for her to know he came over."

"I hate him." Corin pounded the table as hard as she could.

"Me, too."

"Okay. We don't have to say anything. But I'm afraid, because we don't know what he'll do to us, or Mom, if he comes back."

"Yeah, but if he tries anything, I'll do everything I can to keep him from hurting us."

"You're strong, but not that strong. You saw how he grabbed that knife out of your hand."

"I know," I said worried. "But if he does come back, I hope Mom won't take him."

"Me, too."

When Mom got home, she was so tired she didn't even care that supper was late. I made macaroni and cheese instead, and fried the hamburger into patties. Me and Corin tried to act like we always did. Mom went to bed right after supper. She didn't even ask us about our homework.

The next day, me and Corin stopped off at the library and came home late in the afternoon. When we got there Mom was sitting on the couch crying. Next to her were some roses in a fancy vase.

"Who sent you those?" I asked, already knowing the answer.

She looked at me, her eyes red from crying. "Your daddy."

I knelt down next to her. "Mom, please don't listen to him. Whatever he told you, don't believe it."

"Yeah, Mom, Dad lies really bad."

"What did he say?" I asked.

"Nada, he just left me a card."

"Well, what did it say?" I didn't want to beat around the bush.

"He wants me to go back with him," she said, holding the card. It was written in Spanish: "Quisera tú en mi vida," she read out loud, then started crying, hard. I never saw her cry like that before.

Even though I couldn't remember the last time I touched my mom, me and Corin both sat down next to her and put our arms around her.

"Mom, what're you going to do?" Corin asked.

"No sé. I wish I knew. I guess all this time I kept thinking he would come back and cuando no se regresó, I just figured he wasn't going to. Now he says he wants me back and I don't know what to do."

"Mom, don't. Don't take him back." Corin grabbed Mom's hand and looked into her eyes. "He's mean to us. Please don't go back with him." Corin took her hand and put it up to her face. Mom looked at Corin, but her eyes didn't see.

"Mom, listen to her. If Dad cared about you, he would have given you money for rent or tried to see you. He didn't even phone or nothing." This time Mom switched her eyes over to me, but I could tell she still wasn't listening.

"Probably his girlfriend, Wanda, broke up with him and that's why he wants you back," Corin added.

Mom's eyes flickered like she just woke up from a nap.

"Qué dice? Your daddy has a girlfriend? How come you know this and I don't?"

"We didn't tell you," I said. "We found out a few months ago from Tío Agapo."

"Him? He's just a mustedo. I don't believe your daddy had a girlfriend."

"He did, Mom," I persisted. "We know it, because Danny

knew who she was and Tío Agapo saw them together in Dad's car and she was sitting real close."

"Cabrón! How come you guys didn't tell me sooner?" Mom took the card he gave her and threw it across the room.

"We knew you were sad about Dad going away so we didn't want to make you sadder," said Corin.

"Well, you should have told me. Cabrón, pinche, jodído. If I saw his chicken-shit, skinny little ass right now, I'd kick it all the way down to that goddamn—who?"

"Wanda," I said.

"Wanda's house and back."

I smiled inside.

"Next time he comes around you *should* kick it, Mom," Corin said.

"He ain't coming around, and if he does, I'll tell him to go to hell! And to kiss my ass on his way there!" Mom's eyes looked like they meant business; even the blue one. I don't think I ever heard her say so many cuss words either.

"Can we tell him to go to hell, too?" Corin asked.

Mom smiled and said, "No, I think you better leave the name calling to me. Now go on. Watch TV or something. I have to make some phone calls."

We went to the living room and turned on the TV. As I listened to Mom talking to Tía Leti over the noise of the TV, I was happy because Mom was mad. I knew Dad would be back. He wouldn't give up, not yet. Mom was mad now, but who knows how long it'd last.

✳

I was right. Two days after he left the flowers, which Mom threw in the garbage can, he called. I could tell it was him even though she never said his name. I watched her face for a sign that would tell me what she was going to do. She looked like she was listening to somebody trying to sell her encyclopedias. She saw me listening and shooed me out of the kitchen. I pretended to leave but stayed in the dining room next to the kitchen. I heard her say a lot of "uh-huh's" and "hmmm's," but not once did she say "too bad, no way, or don't call me again," which is what I wanted her to say. She talked maybe five minutes before she hung up.

"Well," I said, walking into the kitchen. "What did he say? 'Come back to me, mujer. Te quiero tanto, mujer. Soy tu hombre, mujer. Mi corazón is empty without you'?"

"Nooo, well, sí, poquito like that." She rolled her eyes just a little bit.

Corin walked in and in two seconds knew right away what had happened. "Dad called, huh Mom? What'd he say, 'honey come back.'" She said in a mimicky voice. "Or, be mine again?'"

"Yeah, he probably just copied four or five Valentine heart candies. You know, 'I'm Yours, Kiss Me, and You're Cute.'" Mom tried not to laugh.

"So what did you tell him?" asked Corin.

"Yeah, did you ask him about Wanda?" I added.

"I didn't ask about la Wanda and we didn't talk long. I told him I didn't want to see him and that he needed to grow up. Then I told him I had to go and hung up."

"He'll call again," I said.

"Well, I'll just tell him the same thing."

"He never takes no for an answer," Corin continued.

"Well, this time he will. No soy la misma. I drive a car and have my own job. I support you guys and I don't have to listen to him tell me what to do anymore."

"I hope so, because he'll keep trying," I added.

"Don't worry. We don't need him. I'm not talking to him again. Okay? So, vete, I got work to do. Go play or something."

She started washing the morning dishes.

I went to our room and tried to read a book so I could think about something else, but nothing seemed to work.

After a while, I gave up, took the five cents Mom gave me the day before and went to the store to buy candy. Then I went to a field by the store and sat on a giant rock. I sat there thinking about what I would do if Dad came back to live with us, and nothing, not a single thing, entered my mind.

✻

Dad drove up to the house the next weekend in his Chevy Impala that was so shiny you could use the chrome for a mirror. This time he was clean. He had a haircut and smelled like Old Spice. He was carrying a rose. When he knocked on the door I opened it but didn't let him in.

"Aren't you going to let your father into the house?" he asked, acting polite like the Fuller Brush Man.

"No. We told you we didn't want you here, so go away," I said as I started to close the door.

"Quién es?" Mom hollered from the kitchen.

"The Fuller Brush Man," I said, trying not to laugh.

"It's me, Delia! Your husband. Can I come in?"

"Eddie?" I saw the way Mom rushed from the kitchen to the front door.

My dad bent down to kiss her on the cheek and handed her the rose. I couldn't stand to watch so I left the room and walked out to what was left of my garden. The corn was gone and there were just a few radishes and cucumbers left. I picked two cucumbers and the radishes for supper that night. Then I pulled weeds and sat there for so long it started to get dark. Corin was next door, so I went over to get her. I told her what happened. When we walked out of the MacCormacks' house, his car was gone. I looked over at Corin and felt so sad I could hardly talk.

"She's gonna take him back," I said.

"I know," Corin said looking at me. "I knew she would."

✳

It didn't take long.

He came over the house every night after work for two weeks. At first he stayed in the living room and watched TV. Me and Corin went to our room when he did that. Then, after a few days they went into the bedroom and shut the door. I heard my mom giggling and laughing a lot. When this happened we went over to the MacCormacks' or to Randy's or just turned the TV up loud. After a while he started staying the night. We got up after he left for work, so we didn't have to see him except at night, when he came home and we had to eat supper with him. He acted nice. The way he used to when he was happy and played or joked with us. We wanted him to be changed, but after what happened in the kitchen, we knew he was faking. As soon as he thought he had her back he'd be mean again. We didn't talk to him unless we had to. After two weeks, he brought the rest of his stuff over in an old suitcase and a couple of cardboard boxes. And that was it.

I know I'm supposed to love my dad. But those are God's wishes, because I don't. I don't even like him and maybe I hate him, even though I know it's probably a sin to hate. I could never figure out why God made it so hard for people to tell the truth. If I told the truth, it would be a sin. If I didn't tell the truth, it would be a lie, which was a sin. So either way I sinned. I hope God understood. I think he owed me that much since he wasn't doing anything else.

It didn't take long for Dad to hit us again. It was after me and Corin told him we disowned him. He always said he'd disown us if we did things he didn't like, like marrying Black, Chinese, or Filipino men. I said he was prejudiced and I would marry whoever I wanted. So I told him if he disowned me I'd disown him. He said he was the father and that meant only he could do the disowning. Since me and Corin didn't want him as our dad anymore, we decided we could disown him, too. So that's what we did.

We waited till Mom went to the grocery store and left us alone with him. We walked into the living room and woke him up where he'd been sleeping on the couch.

"We have to tell you something," I said after shaking him awake.

"Qué quieres? Why'd you wake me up? Didn't you see I was sleeping?" he said, rubbing his eyes.

"Yeah, but we have to say this to you now," said Corin.

"We decided," I continued, "to disown you."

"What?" his eyes went totally open, then he sat up. "You can't disown me. *I'm* the father and that means only *I* do the disowning!" He was already yelling.

"No, we're disowning you. We told you we didn't want you to come back to this house ever again and you did. You were mean to us and to Mom and you never cared what happened to us while you were gone. So we decided we don't want you for our dad anymore." I said it just like I practiced it, slowly and carefully.

His face was now the same color as the rust on the gutter and his eyes had turned dark green. All the bad signs.

"So from now on you're not our dad. And we're not calling you that anymore." Corin said it cold, like a cop.

"That's right, Eddie."

He slapped me across the face. It was hard enough to knock me to the floor, but I got right up even though my face was stinging.

"Don't you *ever* call me Eddie! I'm your goddamn father and you're allowed to call me father and nothing else! You hear me? You girls are shit! You're nothing without me! If you lose me, you lose everything. Everything!" He was shaking me by the shoulders.

I didn't care anymore. I'd been hit by him before and I wasn't backing down.

"It doesn't matter, 'cause you're still going to be Eddie

to us. And you can hit us all you want but it ain't gonna make us take you back," I answered and looked him right in the eye.

"Pinche, cabrona, I'll show you who's boss." He whipped off his belt, lifted it up to hit me, then stopped. He slowly put the belt down and faced me. In a heartbeat he slapped me across the face. I fell over. Then he used his elbow to smash the top of my back so that I fell hard on the floor. He kicked me in the back, right above my butt. It hurt so bad I couldn't move. After that he went after Corin, who ran to the kitchen. I heard her trying to get out the back door. He must've caught her because she screamed.

"Let go! Let go! Marci!"

I got up as fast as I could and ran to the kitchen. He was twisting her arm behind her back and pulling her hair at the same time. She kept screaming.

"Let her go!" I yelled, looking for something to hit him with.

"Shut up, you little bitch!" he said, turning to me. "This will teach you to think you can call the shots in this house." He let go of Corin's arm and wrapped his hands around her head, then he lifted her off the floor, and slammed the back of her head into the wall. She screamed and kicked her feet up which got him right in the huevos. He dropped her like a rock and fell down grabbing his balls. She crawled away from him while he was still on the floor. He turned to us, his eyes in pain. "Cabronas. I'm not gonna forget this."

"Neither will we," I said. We ran out of the house and walked across town to Uncle Tommy's. When we got there he was outside watering the lawn. It wasn't easy for us to walk because everything hurt, but we did it because it was too scary to stay home.

Uncle Tommy turned off the water and asked us what we were doing.

"We came over because our dad hit us," Corin said, starting to cry.

He knelt down next to Corin and hugged her.

"Yeah," I said. "He hit us so hard he scared us. He's back, you know."

"Yeah, Mom took him back even though we said we didn't want him."

"I know. I guess I was hoping he'd be different this time." He took his gloves off and put them in his back pocket, then came in closer to get a better look. "What did he do to you?"

I told him.

"Hijo," he said, then whistled. "He hit you so he wouldn't leave any marks."

"I don't know if he did or didn't," I said, "but it sure hurts."

"Well, go on in. I think we got some leftovers from supper we can give you. I'll be right in. I don't know if that goddamn brother of mine is ever going to amount to anything."

We went inside but we didn't want to eat. Corin had a knot on her head. When I went to the bathroom to pee, the water was red. We watched TV with Auntie Arlene, who was drinking wine. Uncle Tommy checked on us, then started doing the dishes. The phone rang and I knew it was Mom by how Uncle Tommy talked to her. He got off the phone and said our mom was coming to get us. He didn't say anything more. I saw Auntie Arlene look at him, but he looked away.

When Mom came we didn't want to go. She said we had to and that we would talk about it when we got home. Uncle Tommy gave us a big hug and said to come over anytime we needed to. I could tell it made Mom mad, but she didn't say anything. No one said a thing until we got in the car.

"Your daddy—"

"He's not our dad," I said angrily.

"Yes, he is. Now listen to me. Él dice que you two got in a fight and he had to stop it. Then he said tú, Corin, kicked him in his privates. So when we get home, you better apologize. He's very hurt."

"He's lying!" Corin cried out.

"Malcriada. Don't use that language to talk about your daddy. You keep this up, little girl and I'm going to spank you."

"So what? What's another spanking?"

"He *is* lying, Mom," I said, trying not to cry. "He got mad because we told him we didn't want him as our dad anymore. We told him we disowned him and he got so mad he hit us."

"Yeah, he hit us hard. Like when a guy hits another guy."

She kept driving and didn't say anything.

"Didn't you hear her? She said he kicked us and hit us with his fists."

She was quiet for a second, then said, "I don't believe you. Your daddy hit you before, but he wouldn't hit his girls como un hombre. It's not true."

"But it is," I pleaded.

She parked the car in front of the house, killed the motor and turned around to look at us. "I don't see nothing that shows me he hit you. God's going to punish you both for being mustedas. Come on. Let's go inside."

We were afraid to walk in the house. When we went inside we saw that Eddie wasn't home. I guess he was at the bar. I didn't ask.

✳

The next day was like all the other ones since Eddie moved back. School started, and Mom said we were big enough to stay by ourselves. So we came home, and started cooking supper after we finished our homework. Mom came home at 5:00 and Eddie at 5:30. When Eddie walked through the door me and Corin wouldn't say anything to him. In fact we didn't say nothing to no one unless asked.

"Did you do your homework?"

"Yes."

"Yeah."

"How was school today?"

"Fine."

"Okay."

You get the picture. Eddie ate his food fast, then left the table and went to lie down on the couch. The whole time he had a hurt puppy dog look on his face like something terrible had happened to him. Corin's head was sore, and she could hardly move her elbow. I was sore all over and only stopped peeing blood that morning. Eddie barely got his huevos touched and he acted like we'd cut them off. After he left the table, Mom told us to apologize again.

"No way. I'm not ever saying nothing to him and especially not sorry," I said.

"Me neither," said Corin.

"Your daddy"—

"We told you, he ain't our dad. His name is Eddie, so call him that," I said.

"Now that's enough! Mira! He's your daddy and that's final. And I want both of you to tell him you're sorry for what you did. If you don't I swear to God, I'll pinch you so hard you'll wish you had."

Corin stuck out her hand. So did I.

"Here. Get it over with. I'm not saying sorry to him. He got kicked in the huevos by accident, and it was only because he was holding Corin by the head and slamming her into the wall. Look at the bump on the back of her head if you don't believe us." I stared right at her. "So go ahead. Pinch us."

We kept our arms out. She gave us a dirty look, then poured a cup of coffee and took it to Eddie.

✳

After Eddie hit us, everything in the house went back to the way it was, except Eddie was always feeling sorry for himself and Mom was mad because we still wouldn't say we were sorry for kicking him in the huevos.

"Shoot, I wish you would have kicked him harder," I said to Corin as we made our beds one morning. "Maybe you could've smashed 'em."

"Yeah," she said. "I wish I would have kicked him in the head so I could've knocked him out, or at least poked him in the eye."

Right then I felt guilty. "I don't know. Maybe we shouldn't talk like this."

"Why not?"

"I don't know. I guess 'cause it's not right. We're not supposed to even think about doing bad things to our mom and dad, much less wish it."

"Says who?"

"Says Sister 'Lizabeth, God and everyone else," I said, spreading my arms out like the whole world agreed with me. "It's one of the Ten Commandments, you know, 'Thou shall not kill.'"

Corin thought about it for a second, then asked, "Okay, Miss Holy Roller, is there a commandment that says thou shall not beat up your kids?"

"No," I said, cracking up.

"See? They brainwashed you into believing only the dad side of things. Is there a commandment that says anything about us?"

"You mean about kids?"

She nodded.

I thought of all Ten Commandments. "One, sort of."

"And what's it say?"

"Honor thy father and thy mother."

"Like I said."

"Yeah." I still felt guilty.

"Marci, you go to church too much. Plus, I didn't say I'd kill him—at least not on purpose. I don't think I'd kill anything on purpose, except maybe a slug or a mosquito." She giggled after she said this.

"Okay, but if you put a slug on Eddie's face, killed the

slug with a frying pan, and accidentally killed Eddie, would that still be an accident?"

"Yeah! Except not the slug part."

We cracked up.

＊

That Sunday, I saw Sister 'Lizabeth on her way out of church and went over to talk to her. I guess I was thinking about a lot of things, so instead of just saying hi, I asked her a crazy question.

"Sister 'Lizabeth, if you lived in a house with a really awful and mean dad, what would you do?"

She looked at me like she was trying to figure out what I was really asking her.

"Marci, let's go over here and sit on the bench for a little bit." She pointed toward a bench outside the church. "Is there something you want to talk about?"

"No. I just wanted to know what you would do since you're holy and everything..."

"Well, I don't know about that. But in regard to your question I guess it would depend on a lot of things. If I lived with a mean dad, I guess I would pray a lot and ask God for help." For some reason her eyes were open really big.

I studied her closely. "That's it?"

She seemed a little mixed up. "Um, yeah, I think so. We all have to live in situations that aren't always good. You know this from what you've learned in catechism. There are many people who live with great suffering and pray to God so that He will help them." She stopped for a second and looked at me hard. "Now tell me, is there something you need to talk about?"

"No. Not really." I played with my shoelace. "So you say you have to pray, huh? Well, what if you pray, I mean a lot, and nothing gets better. What if this father hits you, then what would you do?"

"Marci, is your dad hitting you?" She took my hand. It seemed like she really cared. But as much as I wanted to tell her yes, I knew I couldn't. I still remembered our little talk with the Mother Superior.

"No. I'm just asking because I know someone who's getting hit a lot by her dad. I just wanted to know what I could do, I mean for her, you know, to help her." I didn't know if she believed me or not. It wasn't a total lie. I could've been talking about Corin.

"Marci, if you know someone who's being hurt, it's your duty to God and to your friend to tell somebody who can help, even if it's a relative. You know you can always tell me or a priest. If there's some way I can help this friend of yours, please tell me so I can." She moved her hand very softly to my arm. I started to feel funny inside.

"What would you do?" I asked.

"I, I, I'm not sure," she said. She seemed surprised. "But I'd do something."

I looked at her and thought maybe the only thing she could do was hug me. Maybe that's all I wanted. I really didn't know.

"Okay. Thanks Sister." I got up to leave. I turned and walked toward my bike. I turned around and saw her looking at me with her face knotted up. I waved good-bye, then rode away.

When I got home I played football outside by myself for a while, hoping I'd see Raquel, but I didn't see her. I don't remember when I last saw her. I knew I wasn't going to be her girlfriend, but it didn't stop me from wanting to see her and wishing she was with me instead of that pendejo boyfriend. After a while I sat down and looked at my cuca, then looked at the sky. God was supposed to be up there watching over me. He was supposed to be answering my prayers. But it sure didn't seem like God, Mary or Baby Jesus were doing anything, and that included listening, much less answering.

I didn't know what to do. I thought about everybody who prayed: the people at churches, all the priests and the nuns, and probably tons more that I didn't even know about. If so many people are praying, then God must be doing *something*, right? Otherwise, it seems that people would stop. I mean why keep asking for something if you never get it? If I'm supposed to have faith, like Sister 'Lizabeth says, then how do I keep having it? How does everyone else?

✳

Eddie was sneakier now. He acted nice to us when Mom was around, but the second she wasn't, he bossed us like we were his slaves; then he yelled at us, and called us 'stúpidas or ugly Indians. He still hit us in that new way where it hurt a lot but didn't show anything, so when we told Mom she wouldn't believe us. I couldn't understand why. We'd be crying, our faces red, and even Eddie would be breathing hard, but he would just say we got in an argument and that we weren't, as usual, doing what we were told. Then we'd try to tell Mom what really happened and she would say "Cállate, don't talk back," or "Are you calling your daddy a liar?" Even if we said yes she still wouldn't believe us. She'd say she was gonna hit us, too, if we kept calling him a liar.

We learned that no matter what we told our mom, especially if we said Eddie was lying, he'd come back and get us for it after she was gone. I was getting more and more afraid of him. I know Corin was, too. Each night after supper, we went into our room so we didn't have to see him. Sometimes our mom went to visit Tía Leti, or sometimes she had to work late, and we would have to cook supper and keep the food hot for her in the oven. That's when Eddie was the worst. He hated it when Mom wasn't there when he got home, and yelled at us for any reason. He didn't like how we cooked either. 'Course I cooked bad on purpose. I knew how to fry some kinds of meat and make spaghetti, even mashed potatoes. And I could cook things really good if I wanted. But if Mom called and said we had to make supper, I would always burn the meat, cook the green beans too long, or put garlic in everything, which Eddie hated. Corin said I was dumb to do it because it made him meaner. I didn't care. I did it because I hated cooking for him. Just because I had to cook didn't mean it had to taste good.

One night he got really mad because Mom had to work late and we had to cook again. There was a pound of hamburger on the sink that was thawed from the morning and Mom said to make spaghetti or whatever I wanted. I tried to think what Eddie hated more, hamburger patties or spaghetti. I picked spaghetti.

When he got home and saw spaghetti and no Mom, he threw the biggest fit I've ever seen.

"How many times do I have to eat that goddamn shit?!" He took his lunch-box and threw it on the counter. It slid across and slammed into the wall. Corin was setting the table and looked over at me.

"Chinga, chinga, chinga, I put up with este pinche mierda all goddamn day, then I got to come home to this kind of crap. I hate this shit! Every time your mom has to work I gotta eat dog shit for supper." He walked over to where I was stirring the spaghetti sauce on the stove, put his hands on his hips and yelled in my face. "Why do you cook this crap, huh?"

I didn't say anything.

"You hear me? Answer me when I ask you a question!"

I kept stirring the sauce and didn't look at him even though he was standing close enough for me to feel his breath on my hair.

"Mom told me to make spaghetti," I looked up at him, "and you don't have to eat it."

That did it. It was as if a dam broke. He slapped me across the face, knocking me down. "You damn little bitch! If it's the last thing I do, I'm gonna teach you respect." He started kicking me. In the stomach, in the back, everywhere it seemed. I covered my head but he had his work boots on and the toes of the boots were so hard it felt like ten feet were kicking me.

"Eddie, leave her alone!! Leave her alone!" I heard Corin yelling at him. But he kept kicking me, and it didn't seem like he would ever stop.

"From now on, if you don't learn some respect for your father, I'll just have to knock the shit out of you until you do!"

"Leave her alone!" I heard Corin yell again, and through the slits of my arms, I saw her trying to hit Eddie. He turned, and without saying anything, backhanded her so that she was thrown across the room where she fell against the wall. I couldn't tell if she was okay or not. She wasn't moving.

He finally stopped kicking me. Everything hurt bad. I couldn't get up and even if I could, I didn't want to. Then I saw him grab the pot of spaghetti sauce.

"This is what I think of the fucking mierda you cooked," he said. He held the pot over my head and started to tip it. I screamed. He laughed, like it was the best joke in the world, then moved it away from my head and poured it all across the kitchen floor. I felt the hot splatter from the sauce hit my arms and legs. He dropped the pot on the floor and kicked it as hard as he could toward Corin, where it landed against her legs. Corin moved them out of the way as much as she could which told me she was okay.

He stood there breathing hard with his hands knotted in fists.

"I'm gonna say it just one more time. If you two don't start showing some respect toward me, I'll kick your little asses every day until you do. Now, clean up this shit. Both of you!" We didn't move. There was spaghetti sauce everywhere. "Now!"

Corin slowly stood up and picked the pan up off the floor. I sat up part way, but couldn't move very much.

"Oh, and another thing," He turned back toward us and pointed his finger as he spoke, "I don't ever want to eat this spaghetti crap again. You hear me?! If you have to cook, you'd better cook me some goddamn beans and chile. And learn to make tortillas, too. I ain't eating none of this shit you cook anymore. It's about time you started learning things that's gonna do you some good, and that's learning how to cook food a man will eat. I wouldn't give this shit to a fucking dog. Don't fix this crap again, Marci. You hear me?"

I didn't answer him.

"Answer me!!"

"Okay," I said. Then he walked out of the house.

We heard his car start and the tires screech as he took off.

"We have to tell Uncle Tommy." Corin sat back down against the wall. Her left eye was purple and it looked like it was swollen shut.

"I know, but we can't walk to his house. It hurts to move." I tried to sit up and had to lie back down. I looked at my legs and arms and saw bruises everywhere. My hand had swelled up and felt broken. My eye was bleeding by my eyebrow.

Finally I crawled over to the phone. I already knew Uncle Tommy's phone number by heart. I heard the phone ring three times, then started to get scared. On the fourth ring he picked it up.

"Hello?"

"Uncle Tommy. It's Marci."

"Hi Marci. What's going on?"

"Well, our dad hit us again. This time, really hard. I can hardly walk and Corin is messed up, too. Can you come over and get us?"

"Where's your mom?" he asked.

"At work. Eddie left, but I'm not sure when he's coming back. We're too scared to stay here. Come and get us, okay?"

"All right," he said. "I'll be right there."

I hung up the phone and looked at Corin. "He's coming."

"Do you think we should clean this up?" Corin asked, looking at the mess on the floor.

I looked at the kitchen. The noodles had been boiling the whole time and the pot was over by the wall with a big dent in it. There was sauce over most of the kitchen floor. The brown tile with the red all over it made it look like the floor was part of us.

"Nah. Leave it. That way Mom will know what happened."

In a few minutes Uncle Tommy came over. He looked at both of us and the mess.

"Híjole!" He walked over to Corin and looked at her eye. "Jeez, what'd he do to you?" He saw me leaning against the stove and looked at my bruises, my hand, and the cut over my eyebrow.

"Hell," he breathed out. "This time I think my brother's really lost his mind. Let me clean some of this mess up first. Sit tight for a second."

He turned off the noodles, got the dish rag and wiped up the sauce as best he could.

"All right, let's go."

He got our sweaters and Corin's doll, then slowly led us out of the house. It hurt to walk. We got in his car and drove to his place without saying a thing.

Auntie Arlene's eyes got big when she saw us. Both her and Uncle Tommy helped clean us up.

"You think we need to get them to a doctor?" she asked.

Uncle Tommy grunted, but didn't say anything.

"Tom, I think these kids need a doctor."

Uncle Tommy was checking Corin's eye. Then he looked at my hand.

"Let's hold off a bit, at least till we talk to Delia."

We stayed at Uncle Tommy's for about an hour. We watched TV, and drank the Cokes Auntie Arlene gave us. Then the phone rang and we guessed it was our mom seeing where we were. We heard Uncle Tommy telling Mom he "didn't think it was safe for us," then he spoke in a whisper so we couldn't hear anymore. When he came back to the living room Auntie Arlene asked him what my mom said.

"She's coming over to get you guys," he said, looking at both of us, then at Auntie Arlene.

"Tom, the same thing happened not too long ago and look at them. They're in worse shape now than ever. I don't think it's a good idea for them to go home."

"I know, I know," he said, his voice trailing off. "I don't know what to do. Delia says they're her kids and they should be with her. How can I tell her no?"

"Uncle Tommy, you have to help us," Corin said.

"Yeah," I added. "Eddie is really mad and Mom doesn't believe anything we say. She thinks we're the bad ones and that Eddie is perfect."

Corin walked up to Uncle Tommy and looked at him with her one good eye. "Please don't make us go back there." She grabbed his hands.

Uncle Tommy sat down and put Corin on his lap. He softly brushed her hair and started to cry. Auntie Arlene looked at him, but didn't say anything. Corin sat there like a doll, staring straight ahead.

"Honey," Auntie Arlene finally turned to me, "you can call the police." I could tell she'd been drinking because her words sounded fuzzy. She got up and wrote down the number for the police on a piece of paper and gave it to me. I put it in my pocket. "Tom, you want to call the cops? They might be able to help the kids."

He shook his head. "No, they'll just put them in a home with some stranger and I don't want that to happen."

"We could come live with you," Corin said.

They glanced at each other, but I could tell they didn't seem very sure of it.

"It'd be better than what they have right now, don't you think?" Auntie Arlene continued as if Corin hadn't said a thing.

"I don't know, Arlene. I don't know what's good for these kids anymore."

Then we heard a knock followed by the door opening. It was Mom and Eddie.

"Hey, kid brother. Quehúbole, Arlene," Eddie said it loud, like he was the boss of their house. His cheeks were red and I could smell beer the second he walked in.

I saw Mom look at Corin's eye, which was now swollen shut and turning an even deeper purple. She saw the Band-Aid over my eyebrow and my fat red hand. She seemed a little scared.

Uncle Tommy put Corin down and turned toward my dad.

"They ain't going with you, Eddie." He stood facing my dad, making sure we were both behind him.

"Uh, I think you're a bit mistaken, there, kid brother. These here are my kids, and if I say they're going with me, then that's exactly where they're going." He jabbed his finger into Uncle Tommy's chest while he talked.

Uncle Tommy slapped Eddie's hand away.

"I said they're not going. You keep beating the shit out of them, and it's not safe for them to be around you. So they're staying here till you cool off."

Mom came from behind my dad and told us to get our sweaters.

"Now hold on there, little brother, I think me and you are having a bit of a communication problem here. First of all, I don't beat my kids. Son muy chingasos and they get into lots of fights, but that's with each other. I didn't hit them before, and I didn't hit them tonight. That stuff that happened to them was from them fighting together."

"He's lying!" I yelled out. "He hit us and is trying to make it seem like it was me and Corin."

"You better shut up, little girl, before you learn what's good for you."

"I already did, Eddie. So tell me something new," I said standing behind Uncle Tommy.

"Don't lie to me, Eddie. I know damn well you did this." He stretched his arm out toward me and Corin.

Eddie turned back toward Uncle Tommy. "I don't think you heard me, so I'm gonna say it again. These here are my kids and that means only I call the shots on 'em. Nobody has any say-so on these kids except their mother and me. So you'd better think twice before you say anything else. In fact, you'd best keep your mouth shut before you find out what's good for you, too."

Uncle Tommy's eyes were hard. "I ain't afraid of you. You got a big mouth and you ain't nothing but a little man who blows it off too much. You talk a good-daddy line but the way I look at it, if you were such a good daddy you wouldn't have these kids constantly running to my house to get away from you."

Eddie smiled just a little. He looked over at Auntie Arlene who was sitting on the couch.

"Anybody want some wine?" she asked. No one answered. "Well, I do." She got up and wobbled to the kitchen where I heard the cabinet open.

Corin was sitting next to me. She held her doll tight to her chest. Mom came over and sat next to us.

"Mira, you two don't live here. You live at our house. Now go get your sweaters so we can go."

"We're not going," I said, like I was my own boss, even though having Uncle Tommy there was the only reason I could be that way.

Eddie's fingers curled in and out as he looked at me.

"What did I just say to you back home? Now go get your sweaters like your mom asked you before I show you what's good for you."

"I already told you we're not going." I wasn't backing down.

"Then that's it," Uncle Tommy said. "The kids are staying here."

Eddie glanced at Auntie Arlene who came back to the

couch with a glass full of wine. He turned toward Uncle Tommy.

"The hell they are! These kids are going home with me and that's final." He made a move to grab Corin.

Uncle Tommy blocked Eddie with his chest. "No, they're not. They ain't going anywhere." Uncle Tommy's hands were balled up into fists. His chest was big and puffed up like Popeye's after he ate spinach. Uncle Tommy was bigger than Eddie and Eddie knew it.

"Well, well, well," Eddie sneered. "So my queer little brother thinks he can kick his big brother's ass, huh?" He folded his arms up like it would be nothing to beat him up. "Now I sure as hell know that no queer can kick nobody's ass. Just because you got a few extra muscles don't mean shit. Because a queer with muscles—is still a queer." He looked over at Auntie Arlene but spoke to Mom. "Ain't that right, Delia?"

"Who you calling queer?!" Uncle Tommy was really mad and pushed his chest against Eddie's.

Auntie Arlene gripped the couch—her eyes were wide like a scared rabbit.

"Eddie, cállate!" It was Mom talking. "Stop being so hateful. Why don't you get the girls' sweaters so we can go."

Eddie didn't even look at her.

"Well, it seems to me, that if the queer shoe fits, then the queer," he paused to look around the room, "should wear it." He started laughing.

Uncle Tommy slammed his fist into Eddie's face. I saw my dad knocked down in one punch. Mom went over to help him, but he threw his arm out to push her away.

"Get away," he said as he pulled himself up. "I can take care of myself." He got up slowly, and turned to face his brother.

Auntie Arlene had a funny face now, like she was eating something awful. I didn't know what queer meant, but I could tell it was bad.

"Hijo, Tommy. Guess that was a sore spot, no?" Eddie asked as he rubbed his chin. He started laughing again. "Tell you what," he poked his finger into Uncle Tommy's arm. "I'm going to let you keep them for the night. No problem. Delia will come by to get them in the morning. If it's that important for you to knock the shit out of your brother over the girls spending the night, well then, go ahead. Take 'em." He flung his hands like he was throwing us away, then moved toward the door. "Let's go, Delia."

My mom picked up her purse.

Eddie opened the door, stopped, and turned around. "Yeah, it must be pretty damn important for you to hit your brother over his kids sleeping over. Unless," he looked at my Uncle, then at my Aunt, "it's something else." He walked out the door laughing.

"I'll be by in the morning," Mom said, looking at me and Corin, as she followed Eddie out. "Be ready by a quarter to eight."

She shut the door and was gone. Uncle Tommy was still breathing hard. Auntie Arlene got up and walked over to him.

"Nice guy." She reached out and softly touched his face. "I'm going to bed. G'night kids."

"Good night," we said together.

"Uncle Tommy, what's queer mean?" Corin asked.

"Quiet, Corin," I corrected her. "It's not a nice word. Don't worry," I said, looking at Uncle Tommy. "Eddie's mean. You just can't listen to him or he'll get you."

Uncle Tommy cocked his head a little to the side and looked at me. "Oh, I know all about your dad." Then, suddenly, his face smoothed out and he pretended like nothing happened. "Okay, kids. Let's put you guys to bed."

My hand was killing me. Corin said her eye was hurting, too. Uncle Tommy gave us some ice packs and a half aspirin each. He laid us down on each end of the couch. I guess the aspirin worked because I slept pretty good. At eight the next day, Mom came. Uncle Tommy walked us out to the car and told Mom to take us to a doctor. Then he said if we ever needed him, to come over, or call, and he'd be there to get us.

"They won't need to do that anymore," Mom said to Uncle Tommy.

"Why's that?" he asked.

"I had a talk with Eddie last night, y pienso que the girls won't need to be coming over here again." She opened the car door and we each got in. Uncle Tommy looked at us through the window.

"Oh yeah? Eddie say he was going to stop hitting them?" He leaned on the open window. "Look, Delia, both you and I know Eddie's got his charm, but he can be a real son-of-a-bitch. And a man who hits his kids isn't really going to change. At least not in my book."

"Mira, Eddie's not as bad as you say. Es muy cariñoso. He's good to these kids most of the time. He just needs to watch his temper. Y, last night, he said he lost his temper. But we talked, and he said he won't hit 'em again."

"It's a lie!" I cried out from the back seat.

"Come on, Delia, you know he *has* said that before." Uncle Tommy looked over at Corin with her closed up purple eye. "How much more are you going to let these kids get beat up? Is he gonna have to kill one of them to make you listen?"

Mom started the car. She looked hard at Uncle Tommy and pointed her finger as she talked. "He said he's going to stop and I believe him!" She put the car in gear, gunned the motor and sped away. I looked out the back window. Uncle Tommy was standing there with his hands in his pockets. He stood there until we drove out of sight.

✳

I think I figured something out. I mean about this word, queer. As far as I know, it means being different. I don't know how it means something bad. But I know if Eddie is calling Uncle

Tommy queer, then it probably is. I could tell by how Eddie said it. Plus, Eddie wouldn't have said it unless he wanted to make Uncle Tommy mad, which he did. I've never seen Uncle Tommy so mad. It felt good to see him knock Eddie down with one punch. That's what I'd like to do someday, but you already know that and I'm getting off the track. I decided to look up queer in the dictionary. I didn't have one, but the library did. This is what it said:

"**Queer**: adj [origin unknown] **1 a**: differing in some odd way from what is usual or normal **b:** (1) eccentric, unconventional (2) mildly insane: touched **c**: obsessed, hipped **d:** *slang*: sexually deviate: homosexual **2 a:** *slang*: worthless, counterfeit [~ money] **b**: questionable, suspicious **3**: not quite well : Queasy; **syn** see strange — queer-ish / *adj* — queer-ly *adv* — queer-ness *n*."

I sat in the library a long time. Why did Eddie call Uncle Tommy queer? It could be for lots of reasons, but none of the ones in the definition seemed like they fit Uncle Tommy. The number one thing Miss Buck says to pay attention to in the dictionary is the first definition. Then after that, you can go to the second or third if the word has one.

I started thinking about all the things Uncle Tommy does. He lifts weights, but lots of men lift weights and there's nothing queer about that. He goes swimming, but tons of people swim, and it's just exercise like my mom used to do to Jack LaLane before she started working. He drinks wine, but look how much wine Auntie Arlene drinks, and Eddie didn't call her a queer. He goes to church, but practically everyone I know goes to church except my mom and dad. Eddie says Uncle Tommy's a holy roller; someone who goes to church a lot. Does going to church make you queer? The nuns go to church every day, and they for sure seem queer, especially that Mother Superior. The priests go to church, and they seem different, but they sort of *are* the church, so I don't know if that counts.

Maybe the queer word and church go together, but I'm not sure how. There was the time I saw Uncle Tommy in the same confessional booth with Father Chacón. That seemed kind of queer. Why were they in there and what were they doing? If they were just talking, they could have found a corner or sat in a pew. It seemed weird, plus, it didn't look like Father Chacón was hearing a confession, either. And why did he pray at the altar when he walked out? I need to think like a scientist. Better yet: a detective.

I took a piece of paper and wrote the word queer. Then I wrote down all the things I've been thinking about, plus a little more.

Queer:
the church
too much of the church = holy roller
holy roller = queer?
queer nuns = Mother Superior
queer priests = Father Chacón
queer people = Miss Beauchamp
Uncle Tommy called a holy roller
Uncle Tommy called a queer
Father Chacón acting queer
Uncle Tommy and Father Chacón in the same
    confessional booth = queer.
Uncle Tommy hitting Eddie hard when he called him a
    queer
Queer = something bad.
Too much church makes you queer, or
You're already queer and that's why you go to church.
The church is queer.
If the church is queer, then God must be queer.

Hmm. It seemed that Uncle Tommy did something bad or too much with the church and that's why he's queer. So what could he've done? The only thing I could figure out is that Uncle Tommy shouldn't have been in the same confessional booth with Father Chacón. If Father Chacón is queer because he's a priest, then he might of done something to make Uncle Tommy queer.

Or, could it be that Uncle Tommy likes Father Chacón?

I went back to two words in the definition that I didn't know: "eccentric" and "homosexual." I looked both of these up.

The first word, eccentric, means "not having the same center or deviating from some established pattern or from conventional or accepted usage or conduct." I didn't totally understand this, but it sounded a lot like the first definition. The second word, homosexual, means "of, relating to, or exhibiting sexual desire toward a member of one's own sex."

That could be it! I walked back to my study table and pulled out my list again. If Uncle Tommy and Father Chacón liked each other, then that could be why Eddie called Uncle Tommy a queer. But, I don't know. Father Chacón is a priest, and priests aren't supposed to get married or have girlfriends. They're supposed to be like God, so this means they have to be holy and they can't kiss anyone. Uncle Tommy is a macho and he's married to Auntie Arlene, so it doesn't seem like he would like Father Chacón. The more I thought about it, the more mixed up I got. Auntie Arlene and Uncle Tommy don't have kids and they've been married a long time, *and* they're Catholic. Auntie Arlene drinks lots and lots of wine. I don't know why, or if it has anything to do with this queer stuff, but it just seems like it could be evidence or something. And remember when I was in confession with Father Chacón and told him I liked girls and he didn't even care? And remember I thought it was because he thought I was a boy? Well, maybe he knew I wasn't. If he knew I was a girl and I said I liked girls, then can you see why he didn't care?

So if being in the church makes you a homosexual queer, or a man loving a man, or lady loving a lady makes you a homosexual queer, then this must be what I am. I'm a girl. I like Raquel. That makes me a girl liking a girl, which is a homosexual queer. And since I like God, Baby Jesus, and Mary, and they're the church, then I must be a double homosexual queer. I looked over at Miss Buck who was whispering something to a lady. She saw me looking at her and smiled. But then what happens if I want to be a boy. Does that make me a triple?

✳

If your dad throws spaghetti against the wall, two things can happen: 1) it can stain the walls, which it did, and 2) you don't eat it again. Nothing else changes when you throw food against walls, at least not in our house. If you thought it might, then you'd be thinking like me, and not like my mom. I think she's got something deep inside that keeps her wanting to stay with Eddie, some kind of claw that keeps hold of her. He can tell lies and she'll believe him. He can do anything and she'll forgive him. I love Mom, more than anything. But after what Eddie did to us the last time, I don't know if she loves us the same way she loves him.

Me and Corin stayed home from school a whole week to let my hand get better and her eye go down. We stayed with Mrs. Torres who said she didn't mind, especially after she saw Corin's eye. She asked Mom what happened, and if she took us to the doctor. Mom said we fell off the gate in the back yard and that, yes, she did.

"Why did you lie?" I asked her later.

"Qué dices? What are you talking about?" She was cleaning the bathroom sink, something she did every morning before she left for work. Eddie left around seven so I asked her without him being around.

"I said, why did you tell Mrs. Torres we fell off the gate and that you took us to the doctor?"

She kept wiping the rag around the sink. I stood next to her, my eyes following her hands. She didn't answer.

"You know, Mrs. Torres always says, 'I may be stupid, but I wasn't born yesterday.'" I tried to catch Mom's brown eye. "I know she knows what Eddie did to us."

Mom stopped.

"Y qué? Did you tell her? Did you? Did you tell her so she can talk about it to todas las vecinas? Huh? Did you?" She threw the rag down hard into the sink.

I turned to walk out of the bathroom.

"Marci, you better answer me."

"And if I don't? What are you going to do, hit me, too?"

"Dígame!" She put both hands on her hips. "Did you tell her?"

I don't ever remember seeing her so mad.

"No, I didn't tell her, so you can keep telling everyone your lies." I started to walk out the door, then faced her. "It's not like people don't know. But, if she asks, I'm gonna tell."

Mrs. Torres never did. She watched TV all morning. At twelve she fixed us peanut butter and jelly sandwiches. Then she watched more TV. Around two o'clock she started cooking and cleaning. At three o'clock cartoons came on and she let us watch those.

It seemed that everyone wanted to believe my mom. No one said anything when she said we fell off the gate, even Tía Leti and she knows about Eddie's temper. So me and Corin decided to write Grandma Flor a letter. We wrote the letter while Randy's mom watched her soap operas. This is what it said:

September 19, 1967
Dear Grandma Flor,

Hi. How are you? Fine, we hope. Me and Corin are writing you because we want you to know what's been going on at our house. Our dad, who we now call Eddie because we disowned him, is still really mean. Eddie is living with us again because our mom took him back, even though he never gave us any money while he was gone and had a girlfriend named Wanda, too. While Eddie was gone, Mom learned how to drive and got a job at Woolworth's. We didn't think she would take him back, but she did. Why? Who knows.

Eddie is mean. He hits us a lot, and then he lies to Mom about it. The other day he threw a pot of spaghetti against the wall that I was cooking for supper, and then hit us so hard I got a broken hand and Corin got a black eye that swelled up till it closed. Eddie keeps lying to Mom, saying it's me and Corin that's fighting and not him who's hitting us. Nobody believes Eddie (except our mom), including Uncle Tommy who got in a fight with him and knocked him down with one punch!

We want to know if you can come and help us. If you can't come here to help us, please tell us what to do. Okay?

Thank you grandma. We will be waiting for your answer.

Love,
Marci and Corin

P.S.
Don't tell Mom we sent you this letter.

We found a stamp in Mom's bills box and Grandma's address on the back of one of her birthday card envelopes that we always saved. We mailed it on Tuesday and got a letter back right away. This is what it said:

September 26, 1967
Mijitas,

I feel bad for you. I have to be here for Tio Fonso porque he is sick. He had un heart attack—not to bad. He is fillin mejor. I think he gonna be fine. I am sending you money to take the bus to come hear and stay with me. Your mama is too crazy over your daddy and she no gonna leave him. So come hear and be with your gramma Flor and your

Tio. Tell your Tia Leti or Uncle Tommy to show you how to
catch the bus. I give you my phone number so you can call
me when you get hear. I will come and get you.
555-525-7764

Love,
Gramma Flor

PS
Mijitas, go stay with your uncle if your daddy gets
mean again. I don't want you sticking around putting up
with his shit.

In the envelope were two twenty dollar bills. We took
Grandma Flor's letter and the money and hid them both
between Corin's mattresses, way in the back where Mom
wouldn't find them.

"What are we gonna do?" Corin asked. We were sitting
on the bed talking low, just in case Eddie or Mom came home
early from work.

"I don't know, I don't want to go to Grandma Flor's unless
we have to."

"Eddie ain't gonna change."

"I know, but I wish Mom would see what he's really like,
so she can come with us."

"She won't."

"I know." I let out a big breath of air, then went over to
my drawer and took out the knife that Grandma had given
me. It was four inches long and about an inch wide. It was a
pretty knife, silver and black with a piece of turquoise in the
middle. "Corin," I said flipping open the knife. "Let's *make*
Eddie change. Let's show him that we're not gonna take
anymore shit from him."

"Like how?" she asked.

"I don't know, but we can think of something." I looked
at her and she looked at the knife. Then I smiled real big.

✳

We *did* want to kill Eddie, if that's what you were thinking. God says not to kill, but it sure is hard to obey him with a father like Eddie. I wonder if God gave Moses those Ten Commandments for people who were in tough places like me and Corin, or were they just regular rules that he had to write to keep everybody in line? Who knows? Even though Sister 'Lizabeth seems to think she knows what God is thinking, I don't think she really does. I think she makes up most of what she says about God, just to keep me believing in him. Either that or she thinks I'm really dumb.

Probably the easiest thing we could have done about Eddie was move to Gallup and live with Grandma Flor. But leaving your house and your friends, your aunts, uncles, and cousins, is hard to do. Mostly, I think it was Grandma Flor's last words that made me and Corin want to do something about Eddie, even though we were scared to death. Grandma's tough. You have to be that way if you raise a bunch of kids by yourself and run your own bar. Mom told me Grandma has a loaded shotgun behind the bar. She's fired it, too. Grandma says some men and even some ladies are mean as yard dogs when they're drunk. She doesn't mind if they hurt themselves, but she sure don't like it if they start hurting other people or messing up her bar. Nope. Out comes the gun, and she tells them to get the hell out till they can act civilized.

Our grandma isn't scared of anyone. But me and Corin are just kids and we don't have Grandma here to help us. All we have is ourselves. So this is what we did.

We needed some help. We told Randy what happened and asked him to help us. Randy's a sissy, but he's big and strong. We went over his house after my hand got better and talked to him on the lawn outside where no one could hear us.

"You want me to help you tie up your dad?" He asked it like he couldn't believe it.

"Yeah. That's all though. You don't have to do nothing else. You'll wear a mask so Eddie won't know who you are just in case he wakes up." I said it like it was as normal as buying a pack of M&Ms.

"I don't know, Marci. Your dad's way meaner than mine. I could get hurt or in big trouble."

"Randy," I took my finger and poked it in the grass, "don't be a chicken. You gonna be a chicken all your life?"

"Yeah—" Corin said with a laugh before he could reply.

He looked at her, then said, "Probably."

"No you're not. This is your chance to stop being a chicken. All you have to do is get us some of that rope and duck tape your dad has in the garage and get your butt over to our house when we give you the signal. Our mom won't be home, so all you do is tell your mom you're coming over to watch TV."

"Come on, Randy," Corin added. "If we mess up, then we have to pay the price and you know what that is."

He looked like we were forcing him to jump off the Empire State Building.

"Randy," I said, "our dad won't hit you. He knows your dad would come over and kick his butt."

"Yeah, Randy. Your dad is lots bigger than ours."

"Mean, too," Randy admitted. His eyes were far away, thinking. "Okay. I'll do it. I'll get the rope and the duck tape, and help you tie him up. But that's all. I'm not doing anything else."

"That's okay. That's all we want you to do," I said.

"And you can't tell anyone, not even the MacCormacks," he added.

"Don't worry. We don't want them or anyone to know."

We all shook hands and made our plan.

We decided to do it when things were exactly right. That meant that Mom had to be gone for a long time and Eddie had to be drunk. What was good was that the two usually went together. Two weeks passed, and Eddie started drinking one day when he got home from work. Well, he always drank a beer after he got home from work. But this time he started drinking a lot. Mom was working till nine that night, and Eddie was mad about it, so he kept drinking. He brought a six-pack home with him, and I made a good supper of beans and chile. That way he'd at least be happy about the food. I didn't want him to have any reason to hit us. I made the beans guisados, just the way he likes them, and I even tried to make tortillas, but they came out looking like a map of California. It made Eddie happy anyway.

"Mira," he said, as he shoveled beans and chile into his mouth with the tortilla. "This is the kind of comida you should always be cooking for your old man. Don't give me none of that damn spaghetti shit you're always making. When you cook for your father, and I *am* your father," he said, pointing to himself, "cook me some goddamn beans and chile. That's what I want. You hear me?" He turned to make sure I was listening. His words were slithering all together, so I knew he was drunk.

I nodded. Corin took one of my tortillas and heated it up on the comal. Then she spread butter on it, brought it to the table, and started eating it. Eddie watched her.

"Hey!" he yelled at Corin. She kept eating her tortilla and didn't even look at him. "Corin, goddammit, I'm talking to you."

"What?"

"Hey, those maps of Califas taste pretty good, don't they?" He started laughing.

"Uh-hmm. Yep, they're crooked, but good."

"Our little hombre, Marcito here, can cook pretty good, huh? Huh?"

Corin looked at me.

"Oh, poor Marci," he said when he saw he was making me mad. "What's the matta, chiquito?" He talked like I was a little baby. "You don't like it that I called you hombrecito? Well hell, that's what you are. I'm not gonna lie to you. Right? Right? Your daddy never lies." He started laughing again.

"My name's Marcía. Call me that or Marci," I said, my voice hard.

"Este, mira, Marci. Your mother and I made a big mistake when we named you. We should have called you Mauricio. No? Mauricio. Pero, how did we know you'd be a boy when we saw your little bizcocho? We just went with what we saw." He took a long drink from his beer and slammed down the empty can on the table. "We didn't know no better."

I cut my eyes at him, but said nothing.

"Corin, get me another beer." Corin got up from the table, went to the refrigerator and got him a beer. He grabbed it, opened the can and took another long drink.

"Ahhhh," he said, then burped. "But hey, I'm happy. I thought I just had me two daughters. Instead, I got me a daughter," he looked over at Corin, "and a son." He gave me a big fake smile. I gave him another dirty look.

"But I'll tell you one thing," he said pointing at me, "you're gonna have to figure out sooner or later that you ain't never gonna be man enough to take on your father. Not as long as I'm still standing. Hell no! Your daddy here's the one with the balls." He pointed to his birdy. "And he ain't scared of nothing. Nothing! You hear me? And I'm gonna tell you something else, he's got this big peter here to back up these huevos, too. You, girl," he pointed at me, "ain't got shit down there except a little piece of tail. And that, little hombre," he got up from his chair, "is all you'll ever have." He staggered over to the fridge and grabbed another beer. He took his half-drunk can and the new can and walked out of the kitchen.

"I'll show you how tough I am. You watch," I said. But I don't think he heard me. He walked into the living room and turned on the TV. Then he sat on the couch and finished off the can. He opened the second and started drinking it. After a while he got up, turned off the TV, and went into the bedroom. I started cleaning up the dishes. Fifteen minutes later I peeked in while pretending to go to the bathroom and saw that he'd fallen asleep.

"He's asleep," I said.

"Think we should do it?" Corin opened the fridge and looked for more beer. "He drank every one of 'em."

"Just a second. Let's go check again." We went back to the bedroom. Eddie was snoring as loud as a dump truck.

"I think we should," I said.

"Think so?"

"Yeah. Yeah, I do."

"Okay," she said. "Let's go then."

"I'll get Randy." Corin started toward the door.

It was 6:45. "No, wait! Not till seven. That's when they're done eating supper."

"All right."

We cleared and washed the dishes, and put away the food. At seven Corin ran over to Randy's house.

In about ten minutes Randy and Corin showed up at the back door with rope and duct tape.

"I got the stuff, Marci," Randy said breathing hard. His eyes were big and wide. His cheeks were red and his panza heaved in and out, as he tried to catch his breath. He held a bunch of rope in one hand and Corin had the role of duct tape in the other.

"Okay, Randy," I said, patting him on the back. "You did good."

We must've been out of our minds. Maybe we were, because that night something else inside of me was doing the thinking.

When I saw the rope and tape, I didn't know if I could go through with it. But when I remembered what Eddie did to us, and how he said I could never stand up to him because he's got big balls—even though Grandma Flor sure stood up to him and she's just a grandma—well, something about it all made me think I could.

Corin didn't waste time. She got more rope we found in the shed. I got the scissors and cut some duct tape about as long as my hand. I stuck the tape on my arm. We had our knives in our pockets and checked to make sure Randy was still ready to help us. He seemed scared, but he didn't look like he was going to chicken out on us. We told Randy to put the scarf he got from his mom over his mouth to hide his face. I thought it was going to be a scarf like what Tonto wears on the *Lone Ranger*, but his mom only had something silky, like what you get at Montgomery Ward's. It was red with black and gold knots all over it. When he put it over his mouth, he looked more like a harem lady, than a robber guy.

I went to the living room and closed the drapes, even though it was still light out. Eddie's loud snore came from the bedroom. I peeked in on him again and saw his hands were over his chest. I gave the signal and we got our stuff and tiptoed into the bedroom. I motioned to Randy to kneel by Eddie's feet. Corin was on one side of the bed and I was on the other. I knelt down without making a sound, holding one end of the rope. Randy had another piece of rope. I looked up at the ceiling, hoped that God was watching, and gave the signal.

Taking one of Eddie's arms, I slowly wrapped the rope around his wrist. Then I took his other arm and, leaving just a couple of inches between his hands, I wrapped the rope around his other wrist. I was really scared he was going to wake up, but maybe God *was* watching, because Eddie kept snoring. I gave Corin one end of the rope, I took the other and we tied each end to the front of the bed. Randy did the same thing with Eddie's feet. Randy was so nervous he was sweating all over his mom's scarf. He did good though. He moved carefully, lifting up each of Eddie's feet and tying the rope around them.

I finished tying my end of the rope to the bed's leg and checked on Randy. So far, Eddie stayed asleep and everything looked good. I couldn't believe he didn't wake up, but after drinking a whole six-pack, it didn't seem like he was gonna be waking up for a while. After Eddie was tied up, I motioned for Randy to leave. He stood up and snuck out of the bedroom. In the hallway he turned toward us and pulled off his mask. I gave him a thumbs-up, which I learned from watching *The Avengers*. Randy gave me a thumbs-up and walked down the hallway and out the door.

Next, I peeled the duct tape off my arm and slowly lowered it over Eddie's snoring mouth. I knew he'd wake up as soon as his mouth was blocked so Corin went over to the other side of the bed and took her knife out. My knife was already on the floor by my feet. I checked the time on the bedroom clock. It was 7:25. I slapped the tape over Eddie's mouth. He woke up like he'd just had a heart attack.

His eyes got big and he tried to talk. All that came out of him, though, were words we couldn't understand. We had a pretty good idea what they were, though. He tried to pull his arms free but couldn't because we made the ropes tight. Then he tried to move his legs, and when he saw that he couldn't move those either, he got madder. We could see it in his eyes. Nobody's eyes get as green and hard as his. Poor Eddie. We knew right then that he wanted to hit us bad. But what was he going to do? He kept struggling, trying to loosen the ropes, but it didn't do him any good, because this was a bed made a long time ago by one of my tíos. It was heavy and hard to move, which was why cousin Inez left it in the room when she moved out. Our knots were tight, too, which was about the only good thing we learned from Girl Scouts.

"No use struggling, Eddie," I said, checking all the knots and making sure they stayed tight.

"Yeah. It ain't going to do you any good to try to get loose. We got you tied up good," Corin added.

"Mmmmfffhh, mmmmmfffh mmmm!"

"What's he saying?" I asked Corin.

She raised her shoulders like she didn't know.

"He's trying to say something, I think." I looked at Corin.

"I guess so," she said. "Too bad we can't understand him."

"Yeah, too bad." I went up close to him. "Hey, Eddie, want me to loosen the tape so you can talk?" I said it nice-like.

He nodded his head fast, but his eyes looked like they wanted to kill me first.

"Think we should?" I said to Corin. Eddie looked over at her.

"Nuh-uh. Not yet. I don't want to hear him. Let's go get ice cream first. Mom bought some last night."

"Okay!"

We both got up, took our knives with us, and walked out of the room. I was breathing fast. Corin's eyes were big like she couldn't believe she was doing this. We walked over to the fridge and sure enough, there was the "three-kinds" of ice cream in the freezer. Neapolitan. What a weird name for ice cream. We were never allowed to have treats unless we asked. So it was fun to walk up to the refrigerator, grab the ice cream, and get our bowls like *we* were the bosses of ourselves. After spooning up a big pile of ice cream, we walked back to the bedroom, sat on the floor, and started eating in front of Eddie.

"Maybe he wants some," I said.

"I don't know. He only likes the strawberry and vanilla part, and I got mostly chocolate. What kind did you get?" Corin took a big spoon of it and shoved it in her mouth.

"Pretty much chocolate."

"Well, give him some. He might like it."

"I don't think Eddie likes chocolate very much," I said, knowing for sure Eddie hated chocolate.

"Yeah, he does. Give him some."

I took my knife and laid it next to the bed. Then I slowly lifted the tape off Eddie's mouth, but only part way.

"There, I think that's enough room to swallow something, don't you?"

Corin looked at the tape.

"Mmm-hmm," she said as she shoved in another spoonful.

"Eeef yooouu keeds doon't entie me, ahhmm goein tooo keek yurr leetle esses."

"Corin, I don't know about you, but I don't think I like the way Eddie's talking to us."

"Uh-uh. Me neither."

"We're putting the tape back on. Sorry, Eddie. No ice cream for you. Maybe if you're nice to us, we'll give you some. That is, if there's any left." I laughed. This was fun.

"I don't know, Marci. Do you think we should give him any, since it doesn't look like he's gonna be nice?"

"Mine's almost gone, so probably not."

Corin giggled.

"Mmmfffhh, mmmmfffh mmmm!" Eddie's eyes were hot little sparks. I was kinda scared because if he got loose, I knew he'd probably kill us. But right now, he couldn't kill a fly.

The sound of spoons scraping the bottoms of bowls was all the noise we could hear for the next few minutes. We finished our ice cream and set the bowls down. Eddie started pulling hard against the ropes. Corin looked scared, but seemed to feel better after I checked all the knots again. They were still holding tight, but to make sure, I tightened them.

"Let's wrap some tape around his hands and feet to really hold him," I said. "Corin, could you get me the tape and scissors?"

She brought them over to me. "Okay, hold the scissors ready. I'm gonna wrap tape around each arm and then tape 'em to the bed. Eddie's eyes got even bigger, and he tried as hard as he could to pull the ropes loose. Finally he stopped and lay still, breathing hard. "Looks like he'll be quiet for a minute."

I wrapped tape around his left wrist a few times, then brought it to the side of the bed. I wrapped it again, but brought it the opposite way so that his arm was held in a big V. I did this to his other arm, and then each leg. We were careful to tape him above his work boots.

"I never knew duck tape was so strong, did you?" I asked Corin.

"Uh-uh."

Eddie was sweating a lot. We looked at the clock. It was 8:05. I looked over at Corin and nodded to her. We sat down on each side of him, close enough to smell him.

"Eddie, we did this because we have to have a little talk with you," I said.

"Yeah, and we wanted you to hear us instead of hit us."

"We couldn't think of another way to do it, so sorry about all this." I raised my arms up, like I couldn't help it.

"Some of the things we wanted to say we've been wanting to tell you for a long time, but you never listened. And every time we told Mom, she believed you, not us."

"We just wanted to talk to you for a while, and if it looks like you're listening and will do what we say, then we'll let you go."

Eddie's eyes darted back and forth from Corin to me. He glanced at the clock to see what time it was.

"Corin, I don't think Eddie needs a clock right now."

"Here, I'll move it." She got the clock, unplugged it, and moved it to the floor, where she plugged it into another outlet so Eddie couldn't see it. "How's that?"

"Good." I turned back to Eddie.

"Eddie," I said, speaking close to his face which was now

looking up at the ceiling, "we have a few things we want you to do."

"We don't want very much, Daddy, I mean Eddie. Plus, we think it will be easy to do what we say."

"That's right. What we want are just three little things. Ready?"

Corin pulled a piece of paper from her pocket and gave it to me.

"You want to read it?" I asked.

"No, you read it."

"I unfolded the paper. Here's number one. You, Mr. Eddie Cruz, can never hit us again. Not with your hands, not with the belt, not with anything, no matter how much you want to, or how mad you get."

"Did you hear me?"

He nodded, then breathed hard through his nose.

"Number two. You, Eddie Cruz, can never call us names or say things to make us feel bad, or look stupid, even though that's what you might be thinking."

He didn't give any sign he heard me.

"Did you hear that one?"

He nodded.

"Number three. You, Eddie Cruz, can never be mean anymore to anybody. That includes us, Mom, Uncle Tommy, Father Chacón, and especially Grandma Flor. You have to always be nice to us and them, even if you don't want to."

Eddie wasn't moving.

"Got that?"

He didn't move.

"I said, did you get that?"

He finally nodded, still breathing hard.

"Hey, Marci. I don't think he liked the last one. Let's ask if he's gonna do what we say."

"Now, Eddie, I'm going to pull this tape off your mouth. But if you yell, I'm going to slap it back on. Hear me?"

He nodded again.

"One peep out of you and I won't take it off for the rest of the night. Got it?"

Nothing.

"Okay?"

He nodded.

I slowly pulled the tape off his mouth. He licked his lips, then started jabbering away.

"A qué joda! You little sons of bitches. I'm going to kick your asses to Kingdom Come the second I get free. So you better untie my ass right now before you know what's good for you."

"Marci, I told you he wouldn't listen to us."

"Cut me another piece of tape. That piece we had on him is getting slimy."

She cut another piece.

"Joditas! Let me go. I'm warning you!"

"What are you going to do Eddie? Huh? Huh? Where are those balls of yours now that you're always talking about? They aren't helping you very much right now, are they? Are they?"

"If it wasn't for these huevos, you wouldn't be here today." He jerked his head in the direction of his balls. "Now do as I say and cut me loose! You hear me?! You guys got a lot of nerve doing this to your father. I'll tell you one thing, God's gonna punish you for what you're doing to me."

"How?" Corin asked.

"He's gonna make your hands dry up."

"Dry up?" Corin looked at her hands.

"That's right, dry up. They're going to shrivel up and waste away because you've struck your father."

"We didn't hit you," she said. "We just tied you up."

"It's the same thing. You're hurting your father, and God's gonna punish you."

"When?" she asked.

"A qué cabrón! How the hell do I know when it's

supposed to happen? It's one of the Ten Commandments, pendeja, and you just broke it. God'll do it. You wait!"

Corin studied her hands carefully, then made them into tight fists. She opened and closed them a few more times.

"I don't know, looks like they're still working to me."

"Just watch."

"I think he's talking too much, don't you?" She looked at me, still flexing her hands.

"Sure is." I took the tape and put it over his mouth again, which was hard because he kept moving his head back and forth. Then he tried to bite me.

"Does God say anything about fathers biting daughters?" I asked.

"Jotito!"

"There." I finally got the tape on his mouth. "Damn, Corin, I should have asked him what that meant before I put the tape back on." I rubbed the tape hard across his mouth to make sure it stuck. "Oh well, next time."

I picked up my knife and motioned for Corin to do the same. I rested the blade against his face. Eddie's eyes looked scared now, like he was about to get branded.

"We're not going to hurt you, Eddie. But you have to do what we say."

"Yeah, we want you to do what we asked. It was just three things. But you know what, Corin?" I looked over at her. "I thought of another thing. We have to make him say he's never going to kill us."

"God, how'd we forget that?" She turned back to him. "Okay, Eddie. We forgot to say you can never kill us. I can't believe we forgot that one!" she said, looking back at me.

"I guess we weren't thinking all the way. So Eddie," I looked at him hard, "you can't ever kill us."

"Or Mom, either."

"Or Mom, either. Got that?"

He didn't move.

"Maybe we should show him we mean business, Corin."

We took our knives and slowly pulled the tips across each of his cheeks, cutting a thin line on both sides of his face. A small trickle of blood dripped from the cuts.

"Don't cut too deep yet, Corin."

"Mmmfffhh, mmmmfffh mmmm! mmmmfff! mm-mmm!"

"Eddie, do you think we like doing this? We're getting a little tired, too. We just want you to do what we're asking, and so far you aren't showing us you will." I sighed because I was getting tired.

"Like we said, we aren't asking much."

"Just do what we say. Eddie. You going to do what we asked?"

Eddie didn't move.

"Did you hear us?" I repeated.

He still didn't move.

I nodded at Corin. This time we took our knives and cut him across his throat. We made sure the cut was just light enough to bring some blood, but not too deep. We could do this because we'd practiced on one of his old leather belts to make sure we knew how to cut light or deep.

Eddie got all excited again. He kept making all kinds of noise under that tape.

"Shut up, Eddie. I'm tired of hearing you piss and moan." It was fun saying his own words back to him.

I looked over at Corin. She seemed really mad.

"Corin, think we're going to have to kill him?"

"I think so. He doesn't want to do what we say."

Eddie started nodding his head up and down really fast. His eyes switched back and forth from one of us to the other.

"He looks scared," I said. "Maybe he will."

"Just because he's scared doesn't mean he's not going to hurt us," she said.

"Yeah. You're right. Let's get it over with." Eddie's face was so red it looked like his eyes were going to explode.

"We should cut his balls off first, though," Corin said.

"Good idea."

We moved from Eddie's face over to his pants. Eddie's eyes followed us. His chest was going in and out fast, with the breath coming out of his nose like a little train engine. He kept trying to talk. As we held the knives up over his huevos, I took another look at him. His hair was wet from sweat; his face was a bloody mess. And the white bedspread held little pools of blood from the cuts on his throat. He watched us raise our knives right above his zipper, then his eyes rolled up toward the ceiling and he passed out.

"Marci! Hey Marci!"

"Huh?" I turned and saw it was my sister calling me. I was holding the knife Grandma Flor gave me.

"You were watching TV, and when I asked you a question a long time ago, all you did was stare at the TV."

I turned from her back to the TV and saw that *I Dream of Jeannie* was on.

"I did?"

"Yeah."

"What'd you ask?" I said.

"I said don't you wish we could be like that master guy on the show and have our own genies?"

I looked at the genie on TV, then down at the knife. I opened it up and quickly closed it.

"Yeah, I do." I said.

"Know what I'd wish for?"

"What?"

"It's a secret."

"I won't tell."

"I'd wish for a new father." She smiled when she said it.

"Yeah," I said. "I'd wish for that, and some other things, too."

"Like what?" she asked.

I got nervous for a second, because I couldn't tell her what else I wanted.

"Well, more wishes, I guess."

"Yeah, that's good."

I looked the knife, closed it, and put it back in my pocket.

❋

Sometimes I wonder if I'd be happier if I didn't think. I know things would be a lot easier. After I thought of all the stuff we could do to Eddie I couldn't get it out of my head. I know it was a daydream and nothing I could ever see us doing, unless Uncle Tommy helped—which I knew he wouldn't.

I dealt with Eddie now by going along with everything he said, just so he wouldn't get mad. But it's harder now because he's gotten tons meaner. Mom's dumb, too, because all she wants is for him to stay, so she pretends he isn't doing anything. She's almost as bad as him.

I tried to think of what Grandma Flor would do and the only thing I could come up with was a shotgun, which I didn't have and wouldn't know how to use even if I did. I could use Eddie's rifle since I'd seen him bring it out and load it tons of times, but it's long and I don't know if I could shoot it before he grabbed it from me. I tried to think of other things I could do. I went back to the library and sat at my favorite table just so I could think in peace. After a while, Miss Buck came over and asked me what I was doing.

"Thinking."

"About what, Marci, dear?"

"Stuff. Life, I guess." I had a piece of paper and pencil in front of me. The only thing written on the paper was the date.

"Well, if you have any questions, don't hesitate to ask. You know where you can find me." She looked at me like she wanted to know what the heck I was up to.

"Thanks, Miss Buck." I thought about it for second. "Miss Buck, if someone was mean to you, what would you do?"

"Well, that depends," she said clearing her throat. "I

suppose if there was a mean person who was hurting me I'd ask him to stop, and if that didn't work I'd have to come up with something else." She sat down in a chair next to me. "Is someone being mean to you?"

"No." I looked around the library, then stared at a row of books. "Well, sometimes." I started feeling hot and I think my breath was getting smelly, you know, like after you drink milk.

"Do you want to talk about it, Marci?" She folded her hands in front of her and stared at me through her cat's-eye glasses.

"No. There isn't anything really wrong. It's just once in a while this person is mean, and I can't figure out how to make him stop."

"Have you tried asking him?"

I smiled, which I guess told her the answer to that.

"Have you tried telling his mother?" she continued.

"She doesn't live here."

"Oh, I see. Hmmm." She rubbed her chin. "Is there anyone in your family that you can ask to help you?

"Yeah, but that didn't work either, at least not much. And don't ask me to pray," I said. "Because I tried that, too."

She looked a little scared. "Perhaps you should find a way to defend yourself against this person."

"Like how?"

"Well, you could learn karate or something. Maybe that would work. People always seem to be afraid of karate experts. I suppose there must be a reason for it. But I really think you should try to get somebody in your family to help you. I'll bet there's someone who can give you a hand with this."

"Yeah, maybe," I said. She got up to leave.

"All right, Marci, you just let me know if I can do anything for you, you hear? Don't hesitate to ask me for anything, dear."

"Thanks, Miss Buck."

I looked at my blank piece of paper. Then I got up and went over to the card catalog and looked up karate. I found a couple books on it. One of them teaches you how to do it so I checked it out. Diana Rigg used it all the time in *The Avengers*, and she beats up lots of men. I didn't know if I could learn karate from a book, and I didn't know if it could really help me, since TV and Eddie are two different things, but I didn't know what else to do.

I took the book home and read it, then started practicing some of the moves. I learned to hit and kick. I had to get a little ball and tie a string around it, then hang it up from somewhere so that the ball was my target. It was easy to hit, but I felt kind of stupid. Plus, I didn't want anyone to know what I was doing, so I couldn't yell HAH! which is what the book said to do. Next, I learned how to hit someone coming at you. I pretended somebody was after me and practiced the moves over and over. First, you hit them in the solar plexus. I never heard of this before, but a picture showed you where it was. After you hit them there, you knee them in the huevos. It seems like men's huevos was their Achilles heel. I don't know much about huevos because I've never even seen them, but the book said to kick men there if you can because "it will put a quick stop to your opponent." I remembered when Corin accidentally kicked Eddie in the huevos and boy, did he go down fast. In fact, that's how we got away from him that night. The huevos kick might be the way to get Eddie. On top of that, he's always talking about them like they're what make him special. I don't get it. If I change into a boy, I don't think I want huevos. Why would I want to go walking around with an Achilles heel right in the middle of my crotch? I'll have to remember to ask God not to include huevos when he changes me. *If* he changes me.

I kept reading. The book said if you couldn't hit them in the solar plexus and knee them in the huevos, then try kicking the attacker hard on the knee, and when they bent over, slam them with your fist on the back. They said a little person can do this to a big person but they didn't say anything about a kid doing it to their dad, so I didn't know if it would work. I practiced and practiced, but it's hard to do it when someone's not there. When Corin came in, I told her what I was doing, then showed her. She said I was stupid since Eddie was too big. I said maybe, but we had to try something. I thought it would be good to practice on someone bigger than us.

Randy was bigger but I don't think he liked it very much. We were over his house in the backyard.

"Randy, try to get me so I can practice my karate on you."

"Karate? What karate? Since when did you learn karate?"

"I'm learning it from a book." I grabbed his arm. "Now come on, let me practice. I won't hurt you."

Corin was standing on the side watching us.

"What do I have to do?"

"Come after me like you're gonna get me."

"Like I want to beat you up, or steal something from you?"

"Beat me up, dum-dum. What do I have to steal?"

Corin laughed and sat down on the grass to watch.

"You sure you won't hurt me?"

"No. Now come on, come after me."

"All right. Here I go."

He made a charge but all I did was push him away.

"Randy, do it harder! That was like pushing a balloon. Now come on, be tougher. Pretend like you're really beating me up."

Randy stood back and for a second, then he revved up like a car starting a race. He churned his legs up and down and his arms round and round, then came charging at me like a two hundred-pound bull. I was scared but did what the book said. I took my fist, slammed him in the solar plexus, kneed him in the huevos and chopped him on his back. Boy, did it work. Boy, did he cry.

"Whaaaaaa! Whaaaaaa!"

I knew his mom would come running so I tried to get

him to shut up. The second Corin saw him cry she made a dash to the side gate, and left me alone with Randy.

"Randy, quiet, quiet. Shhhhh. Shhhhh. I'm sorry. I'm sorry. I didn't think it would make you cry."

"You fuckin' hurt me, Marci. Ahhhhhh! You said you wasn't gonna hurt me. Ahhhhh! Mama!" Randy was sitting on the ground holding his stomach with one hand and his birdy with the other.

Out the back door came his mom.

"What's going on?" she said standing there with a white scarf around a head full of rollers.

"Hi, Miss Torres. I was practicing karate with Randy, and I accidentally hit him too hard. I said I was sorry and that I wouldn't do it again."

Randy was holding his birdy with one hand and rubbing his eye with the other. He was still crying, though not as much.

"Mama, she hit me hard in the stomach, then in the nuts, and then karate chopped me in the back!"

"Marci, you did all that?"

"Yeah, I guess so. But I didn't mean to hurt him, Miss Torres, honest."

"Looks like he's pretty hurt to me. I don't think it's a good idea to practice karate on Randy. He's not used to playing rough. Tell him you're sorry and then I think you'd better go on home."

"I did tell him I was sorry."

"Well, tell him again."

Randy had finally gotten up and stood next me, all six inches taller and fifty pounds bigger.

"I'm sorry I hurt you Randy."

"Is that okay, honey?

He nodded and stood there rubbing his eyes.

"Sorry, Randy. I won't do it again."

Randy walked over to where his mom was and leaned against her. She put her arm around him, then gave him a kiss. I went home through their side gate. Corin came running from behind the fence where she'd been hiding the whole time.

"Dang! What the heck did you do to him?"

"All I did was what the book said. I didn't think he'd go down so easy."

"Me, neither."

"I wanted to try it on him because he's big, but I forgot what a sissy he was."

"Randy's not good to practice on. It's like practicing on Baby Huey."

"Yeah."

We were almost at our house. Eddie's car was there, so we knew we couldn't talk about it anymore.

"I know who we could practice on." I was happy because it was the best way to solve the problem.

"Who?"

"Uncle Tommy! He's tough, plus he won't cry if I hit him like Randy did."

"Yeah. He'd be good. We can do it when Eddie's gone."

We walked into the house. I looked at my hands. They were little, but they sure made Randy cry. Even though he's a crybaby, I think that karate book had some things that really worked. After that, I practiced every day until we went over to Uncle Tommy's.

✳

Sometimes people do things you don't expect. Me and Corin were down in the basement watching Uncle Tommy lift weights and when we asked him if I could practice my karate on him, he said "no." Now don't you think a guy with muscles as big as his would let you try to beat him up, or practice your karate? You might think so, but not Uncle Tommy.

"I don't like violence," he said as he picked up two fifty-pound dumbbells.

"But Uncle Tommy, it's not violence, it's practice!" I walked over to him while he did the exercise to make your arm muscles bigger. "All you have to do is let me try a couple things to see if they work. You don't have to do anything except try to beat me up."

He stared straight ahead. Sweat was all over his face and his muscles bulged from the weights that weighed almost as much as Corin. I started to think twice about it. But I learned all this karate and I didn't want to give up.

"Marci," he said breathing hard as he set the weights down. "I know you said you're learning karate, but why do you want to practice on me? I'm too big for you. Why don't you practice on some of your friends?" He sat down to rest for the two minutes he gave himself between each lift.

"She did, Uncle Tommy," said Corin who went over to try to lift one of the barbells. She grunted, but couldn't budge it. "That's why we're here." She looked up at him. "Marci beat up our friend, Randy. And he's big. We need someone stronger, though, like you."

"Right," I added. "Someone with muscles."

"And tall."

"Well, I wouldn't say I was tall," Uncle Tommy chuckled.

"You're taller than us," I said.

"Way taller."

"And you got big muscles. Please, Uncle Tommy. Let us try it just once," I pleaded.

He looked at us. "You girls just want to practice on a man, don't you?"

We didn't say anything.

"Marci, how come you want to practice on someone my size? Most kids want to practice on other kids. Why do you want to do it with me?"

"I told you, Uncle Tommy, I did practice on another kid, and it was too easy. So I need to test it on a bigger person."

"Why?"

"I told you. To see if it really works."

He went back to the dumbbells and lifted them ten times on each side. He set them down with a loud thud and came back to his chair.

"Okay. Come on," he said still breathing hard. "Let's try it. Let's go outside on the grass so you won't get hurt."

So *I* won't get hurt?

"What do you want me to do?" he said, standing with his hands on his hips.

"All you have to do is come after me like you're going to get me," I said as I got into my fighting position.

Uncle Tommy sure looked like he didn't want to do this.

"Come on, Uncle Tommy, go after her!" Corin yelled. "Pretend you're getting her."

"Okay."

Next thing he did was walk straight for me with his arms out. I'd been practicing my kicks and the book said to use your legs if your arms were too short to reach the solar plexus, so I stood on the balls of my feet like the book said and got ready to kick him in his knees. As soon as he got into range, I raised my left foot up to kick him, but in one second all I saw was grass. I looked up. Uncle Tommy had caught my foot, which knocked me off balance, and down I went.

"One more time, Marci," Corin yelled from the side.

But I already knew it was no good. Uncle Tommy was bigger than Eddie, but I knew I wasn't strong enough to fight either of them. I tried to think of other moves I could try, but couldn't come up with anything. I laid in the grass thinking what else I could do for a few seconds.

"Marci, you all right?" Uncle Tommy asked.

"Yeah," I said as I picked myself up. Corin gave me a "back to the drawing board" look.

"Come here, both of you." He knelt down on one knee and put his arms around us. "I know why you guys want to practice on me."

"You do?" I asked.

"Sure. You want to fight your dad. That's why you needed

somebody bigger to practice on. The problem is that you two are dinky kids and little kids can't really beat up a grown-up, especially one like your dad."

"Well, that's why I've been learning karate."

"Yeah, karate is good to know, but it doesn't always work when it's kids against grown-ups."

"I guess so," I said. "But, Uncle Tommy, I don't know what else to do when he's hitting us. I guess we could call the cops, like Auntie Arlene says."

"I tell you what," his arms were still around us. "The next time your daddy comes after you, you run to the neighbors and call me and I'll come over and make him stop."

"You will?" Corin couldn't believe him.

"That's nice, Uncle Tommy, but I don't know if you can come over in time."

"I'll get there as fast as I can. You call me, and if your daddy's coming after you and I'm not there, then stay at the neighbors' and wait for me. I'll be right there, okay? I promise you. Okay?"

"Okay," I said, nodding.

I felt a little better. But not much.

✳

My cousin Danny died. The last time I saw him was at Thanksgiving, which I didn't talk about because it was like all our other Thanksgivings except it was at Uncle Tommy's and Auntie Arlene's. They invited us over, which made Mom happy because she didn't have to cook. Other people came, too: Tía Leti and Gordo, my cousin Berta with her dumb husband Lalo, and their little son, Lalo Jr., Father Chacón, Danny, and a few other people from Auntie Arlene's side of the family. Eddie said he wasn't going over to a house that had "a bunch of queers in it." Mom said fine, and we drove over in her car. She had to bring the pies so I spent the night before helping her make them. When we drove over to Uncle Tommy's, both me and Corin held a pie in our laps.

We had a pretty good time. Things were always better when Eddie wasn't there. Father Chacón was in black pants and a black shirt and had that little white thing around his neck. It always took me some time to get used to seeing a priest first, out of church, and second, not wearing robes. Father Chacón was a good cook so he was in the kitchen helping Uncle Tommy. Auntie Arlene "couldn't boil water if she tried," which is what Mom always said, so she was in the living room laughing a lot and drinking wine. I spent most of the time watching Uncle Tommy and Father Chacón, since I needed to figure out whether they were queer or not, and more important, if I cared.

Danny stayed in the living room. He was drinking Auntie Arlene's wine and talking loud, loud like he was at a baseball game or something. When he talked, though, his words sounded like a bunch of slugs stuck together sliming around in a way that didn't always make sense. He was talking to Lalo and Gordo. He kept saying Gordo only cared about himself and that if he really cared about other people he'd do something different with his life. This is a little of what he was saying:

"Hey, Gordo. Hey man. You ain't doing shit man, because if you were, you'd be doing, you'd be doing more. Because hey, if it was the thing to do, you'd do it and no mothafucka would stop you. You hear me? It'd be different, y'know. It'd be your thing, man. Your thing. You know? You hear what I'm sayin'? Huh?"

Gordo didn't say anything. He just looked at Danny and drank more wine. Lalo was trying to watch TV. Everybody else, including Mom and Tía Leti, were in the dining room around the table drinking, smoking, and eating guacamole. Pepito sat on Tía Leti's lap eating the chips she fed him. As usual, he snapped at Corin when she tried to pet him.

"Cuídate, Corin! You know Pepito no le gusta," said Tía, pulling him back from Corin's hands.

Corin grabbed a chip, dipped it in guacamole, and carefully held it out to the dog. Faster than you could say chip, he snapped it out of her hand.

Pepito licked his lips and Corin smiled, but I knew better. That little dog would just as soon bite Corin's finger off, chip or not. I turned back to the living room and heard my cousin Danny still jabbering away.

"I'll tell you what *you*, mothafucka, need to think about. You—need—to—start—thinking—about—love! You hear me? Love! Love is what really counts, man. Not money, not your goddamn cars, not women and shit. It's love, man. I'm telling you, because you ain't got shit if you don't have that. 'Cause *I* know. I've had lots of women and cars, money—well, not a lot of that—but until you have love, none of that shit means nothing. You hear me? Not a goddamn thing."

Well, that part made sense to me, but most of the time he sounded like he just opened up a cuss-word dictionary and pulled out a bunch of words that didn't go together and strung them in a long, loud, line of bad air. Even Eddie said Danny sounded like he was talking through his asshole most of the time. After a couple hours, he passed out, the glass of wine still in his hand. Gordo made sure he was out and took the wine from him so he wouldn't drop it.

I went into the kitchen to watch Uncle Tommy and Father Chacón again. Both of them had on big, white aprons. Uncle Tommy was wearing a white shirt with rolled up sleeves and, as usual, looked really handsome. On top of the stove cooling off was a giant turkey that he'd cooked with some kind of stuffing in it. He made mashed potatoes—well, he cooked them and told Father Chacón to mash them. Father Chacón ("Diego, Diego" he kept telling me) was sweating a little. He took the electric beater and added butter, salt, and heated-up milk to the potatoes and whipped them till they were super creamy. Whenever one of them got in the way, they used their hands to steer around each other so they wouldn't bump together. Uncle Tommy was making biscuits now and asked me to put some butter on a plate to go with them. After I did that, I sat down and watched them. I saw how they looked at one another when they talked, and I thought I could see something different than how regular men talk. I don't know exactly what it was, but the closest thing I can think of was how I might have looked when I talked to Raquel.

I don't know. I'm still not so sure what queer is. They don't seem queer like the dictionary says, they only seemed a little different. I wanted so bad to ask them if they were queer, but I knew I couldn't. I guess it's probably not that big of a deal, because if they really are, and they really do love each other, then I guess it's okay, except that Uncle Tommy is married and Father Chacón is a priest. So I wonder what they're doing about that? And where do *I* fit into all of this? I looked at them again. They seemed happy. I wish somebody could give me some answers around here.

"Where'd you guys learn to cook so good?" I asked.

"I learned in the Army," said Uncle Tommy, as he rolled out the biscuit dough. "I was a cook in Korea."

"Y, yo. I learned by watching mi mamá. She's a great cook," said Father Chacón.

"You don't usually see men cooking," I said.

"No, you don't," said Uncle Tommy. "And for sure, not in our family."

"But I'll tell you one thing, if you go to almost any good restaurant, it's usually the men who are the chefs," said Father Chacón as he scooped some butter and put it on top of the mashed potatoes.

See what I mean?

You never know what is, and what isn't. Like my cousin, Danny. You wouldn't of known he was going to die. There were lots of people in my family, here and in Gallup, who drank as much as Danny did. It's part of living, I guess. But at the same time, when he did die, I wasn't surprised because every time I saw him after he came home from the war, he was more messed up on drugs or wine or whatever. It made me sad, because he used to be so much fun. Now it was hard just being around him.

We found out Danny died the Sunday morning right after Thanksgiving. I was awake already and, as usual, looked down at my cuca to see if anything changed. I was still in bed thinking about what I wanted to do that day when I heard the phone ring. It was early in the morning, so I was a little scared it would be something bad.

Eddie answered the phone, and since he talks loud this is what I heard: "Hello.—Sí?—Cuándo?—Dónde?—That's terrible. Who found him?—He did? But it was too late, huh?—And, his mom and dad, how are they?—Ooohhh.— Yeah, he was looking pretty bad.—That's terrible, man.— Yeah.—Yeah.—Pobrecitos.—Yeah. Yeah. No kidding.— Pobrecito.—When will it be?—Tuesday?—Okay.—Okay.— All right.—All right.—Okay, thanks, Leti.—Thanks for calling.—Ba-bye."

After Eddie got off the phone, he told us Danny died from an overdose. His friends found him Saturday night passed out at a party but since everyone was used to seeing him passed out, no one paid any attention. He was messed up on heroin. Nobody knew it. We sure didn't. I thought he was just doing reds and smoking pot like some of my other cousins. Danny stopped breathing that night, but no one saw it. Everyone left him alone and thought he'd wake up and go home. This time, he didn't.

Corin started crying when Eddie told us about Danny. Eddie's eyes were watery from crying. I felt sad, but I didn't cry. Like I said, it's not like I was surprised. I think I was more mad than sad. I don't know why Danny had to go to Vietnam in the first place. We live close enough to Berkeley to hear about all the protests. It seemed if that many people were mad about the war, then something about it was wrong. I don't know very much, but what I do know is that a lot of my cousins kept getting sent there, and they never came back the same. Danny was the first. He got drafted and Tía Leti said his mom and dad were worried but proud. They had a big 8x14 picture of him in his fancy Army uniform on their living room wall. When he left I prayed for him to come back alive. But I should have asked for more. No one told me that lots of men came back crazy or on drugs. I wanted to tell all my tías and tíos not to let my cousins go to Vietnam. My tíos and tías think it's important to serve your country. I don't know why they think this, because a lot of people die. They could do what Mohammed Ali did. I'd tell them that, too. But I know they wouldn't listen. Kids aren't supposed to know anything.

Tuesday night was the rosary at the funeral home. They were burying him the next day. Tío Esteban and Auntie Lucy, who were Danny's mom and dad, wanted the funeral in Albuquerque, where they lived. But Danny lived in San Lorenzo so before he left for Vietnam, he made his parents promise to bury him out here on a hill looking over the bay because he said that's where he wants to be, looking out across the water. Tía Leti asked Auntie Lucy one time when they were out visiting before he left, "Pues, por qué? He not gonna be able to see it?" and Auntie Lucy lifted up her shoulders and said, "Porque, that's what he say he wants." Danny's mom and dad flew out from Albuquerque and Gordo picked them up at the airport.

At the rosary on Tuesday, everyone was there. Danny was in a coffin with a suit on, and his hands were crossed on top of his chest. They put makeup on him to smooth out the pits in his face and his eye patch looked new. His hair was shiny and combed, and except for his good eye being closed, he looked like he was going to a wedding.

Before I got there I kept telling myself that Danny was dead and that was the way it was. I thought I was ready to see him. I kept saying he was in a better place now. I pictured what to expect. I remembered my catechism: Danny was in the coffin, but his spirit was with God. Sister 'Lizabeth says dead people aren't even in the room anymore. I felt ready to see him. Nothing, though, helped me when I actually saw his body. He laid there, totally still. I stared at him and waited. I wanted him to sit up and say "psyche!" and start laughing. But nothing moved. Nothing, that is, except me. My chest grew hollow, and my eyes crunched up. Then I cried.

I thought about how Danny was alive just the other day, laughing and talking loud. Now he was dead, and wasn't ever coming back. Even though I knew he was dead, I couldn't believe it until I saw him in that coffin. Corin cried, too. Eddie, who wasn't crying until he got to the coffin, stood in front of Danny, then leaned into it and grabbed his hand. I wanted to pull Eddie's arm away and tell him he shouldn't do that, but I knew better. As soon as Eddie saw Danny, he started crying loud. He slumped over the coffin and yelled out sounds that I didn't think could come from a man, much less Eddie. Mom tried to pull him from the coffin, but he wouldn't budge. Finally, he let go of Danny's hand and told him good-bye. He stroked Danny's face and cried so much that his tears fell all over Danny. Eddie pushed himself away and shuffled back to the pew. He slowly sat down, shaking his head, still crying. Turning toward Mom, he whispered, "He was cold, Delia, so cold!"

There was organ music playing and I hated it. Tía Leti was crying, too. "Ayyy! Ayyy!," she yelled out. She kept crying about her hijo, even though he wasn't really. Danny had spent so much time at her house he felt like a son. Almost everybody was crying, except Mom. Sometimes I don't know if she is made of steel or straw because it sure takes a lot to make her cry. Auntie Lucy and Tío Esteban looked sad. Tío Esteban held Auntie Lucy's arm and led her past the coffin, where they stopped for a long time. Finally they each leaned over and kissed Danny and slowly walked back to the pew. I can't remember what else happened that night. Mostly, it was lots of people crying, everyone saying the rosary, then something about the funeral the next day. After that, we all got up and went home.

The next day at the funeral it was the same thing all over, except this time the coffin was moved inside the church and Father Chacón gave the Mass, which made Eddie mad. He kept saying "Danny would turn over in his grave if he knew that pinche queer was saying his last Mass for him." Mom told Eddie to be quiet, and Eddie gave her a look that could kill the devil. But I thought it was a good Mass. Father Chacón said nice things about Danny. He talked about the things Danny did and how he was before he went to Vietnam. He didn't say anything about how Danny was when he came back. Later on, Mom told me "It was because it's more polite to say nice things when people die. Besides," she added, "Everyone knows what he was like when he came back. So why talk about it?"

When Father Chacón finished the Mass, the coffin was closed and Danny was taken in a hearse to the cemetery. We had yellow stickers that said "funeral" on them that we put on the windshield. We followed the hearse in our cars. Danny got his wish, because Auntie Lucy picked a spot under a tree that was on top of a hill. If you squinted your eyes a little, you could see part of the bay. Auntie said she thought Danny would like the spot. I wasn't so sure because I couldn't see very much of the bay, but I didn't say anything. Tío Agapo spoke under his breath that he sure as hell hoped Danny liked it, since it cost an arm and a leg to bury him there. Tía Leti heard him and cut him a dirty look. Bet she gives him some of her hierbas in his supper tonight.

Father Chacón blessed the coffin. Then everyone walked past it to say good-bye one last time. Eddie, Tía Leti, and Auntie Lucy stopped at the coffin and started crying again. My mom and Tíos Agapo and Esteban had to pull them away. The coffin lid was closed so I didn't have to look at Danny, which was fine by me because I didn't know if I could stand looking at him again. Finally, it was over and we went to Tía Leti's house for the wake.

I don't know why, maybe it's because people are sad, but I hate getting together after a funeral almost more than the rosaries. Everyone is glad it's over with, which is why I guess they're eating and laughing. Mostly, though, everyone drinks. Eddie drank so much Mom had to drive us home. Even Uncle Tommy was drinking, something I hardly ever saw. Auntie Arlene was asleep on the couch with an empty wine glass on the table next to her, and Father Chacón was buzzing around like a humming bird trying to help Gordo and Tía Leti with the food.

Me and Corin ate some sandwiches and then went outside to hang out. The sky was pink again. I don't know why, but every time it turned that way, something always happened.

✳

That week I found out Raquel left during the night and married that razor-faced boyfriend of hers. I couldn't believe she married that guy. He was ugly and creepy. Miss Maestas, who lives across the street, found out what happened from Raquel's mom and told my mom, who told me. I was sad. I still thought I had a tiny chance with Raquel, even though I hadn't seen much of her since she's been with that dumb boyfriend.

Boy, was I mad. And I was double mad because Raquel left me for that scarhead and didn't even say good-bye. I tell you one thing, God, I hope you're paying attention now because I'm not talking about little baby wishes like wanting candy or a new bike for Christmas. This is almost the same as people starving in Biafra. Maybe you're busy, like Sister 'Lizabeth says, but start paying attention to me, will you?

That night someone knocked on the door. It was Carmella, Raquel's mom, holding a brown paper bag. Eddie answered the door and invited her in, but she wanted to stay outside. Her eyes were red, like she'd been crying. I was on the floor watching TV, but could see the door from where I was sitting.

"Hey, Carmella. Entre. Entre. Come on in," Eddie said, moving his hand toward the living room.

She shook her head.

"No thanks, Eddie. I gotta a lot of things to do, you know, with Raquel leaving and all."

"O'ye, I'm really sorry about her leaving like that. It must be hard on you."

She nodded again and sniffed loud. "It is. But hey, life goes on, y'know?"

"Tell me about it. Tell me about it," said Eddie with his Mr. Know-It-All way of talking.

Carmella bent over and started opening the bag. "Raquel left a note telling us good-bye and saying where she wanted some of her things to go that she couldn't take with her. She bought these tools herself, and said they were for Marci." She stopped for a second and looked at me. "Said she was moving to an apartment with no yard and wanted Marci to have them since she wouldn't be doing any gardening for a while."

Eddie took the bag from her, opened it up and looked inside.

"Well, that was nice of her, Carmella. I'm sure Marci will appreciate this, won't you, Marci?" he said turning to me. "Come over here and thank Mrs. Alvarado for these nice tools." He turned back to Carmella. "You sure you don't want to come in?"

"No, no. I gotta go."

I got up and took the bag from Eddie. Together in a little pile were all Raquel's tools. They were things I didn't have: the claw, two different size scoopers, and a weed digger. I looked at Carmella.

"Thanks, Miss Alvarado. I'll use them for sure. If you talk to Raquel, tell her thanks, too."

"You're welcome, honey. Be a good girl. I'll see you later, Eddie." She turned and walked away.

"What'd she give you?" asked Eddie.

"Her stuff for gardening. A claw for raking the dirt, two scoopers and a weed digger."

"Well, that was nice that she thought of you. Too bad she didn't think a little more before leaving her mother and father. Carmella looks bad, man. Bad. I feel for her, having her kid up and leave for that low-life S.O.B. I swear to God I'll kick your little asses to hell and back if you and Corin ever do that to me."

"Don't worry," I said.

I don't think he heard me because he went back to watching TV. I took my bag of tools and walked into the kitchen to look at them again. There was a small piece of yellow paper underneath everything when I took the tools out. It was a note from Raquel.

Dear Marci,

I'm leaving to marry Ruben and I want to give these to you because I know how much you like to garden. You're a good kid. Don't ever give up your dreams.

Love,
Raquel

PS
Grow some popcorn for me.

I folded up the note and put it in my pocket. I wanted to cry, but I was afraid Mom or Eddie would see me, so I held it in. I was happy Raquel remembered me. Really happy. That night, after I prayed for everybody, I said a prayer for her.

❋

What a day Tuesday was. The first part was just like any other day. Mom and Eddie went to work, and me and Corin went to school. At five thirty, though, Eddie didn't come home. Mom cooked beans and chile, and we all waited around till six for him to walk in the door so we could eat, but he still didn't come. At first Mom was worried.

"Dónde está tú daddy?" she said, checking her watch. "I wonder if he got in a wreck."

"Probably not," said Corin.

"I'll bet he's at the bar," I said. "He's done it before."

"No, he always tells me now when he's gonna have a drink after work." She looked out the window, as if his car was going to magically appear.

"He's probably at the bar, so can we eat now?" Corin asked.

"Yeah, Mom. Come on. I'm hungry."

"Bueno. Let's eat. I'm not gonna wait for him anymore. If he comes home late and complains about the food being dried up, I'll tell him it's his own damn fault."

So we ate supper and watched TV. Right in the middle of *The Beverly Hillbillies* I heard Eddie's car. I knew the sound of it, because he always did things to the motor to make it have more noise. Mom sat on the couch waiting for him to walk in. She looked mad. It's been a long time since I've seen her like this.

I heard Eddie talking. He wasn't alone. Corin peeked through the drapes.

"Ooohh, Eddie's with a lady, Mom."

"Qué?!" she asked, surprised.

I ran up to the drapes and peeked, too. It was pretty dark, but I could see him leaning against his car talking to some lady who was laughing a lot.

"He sure is. She's laughing and he's laughing." Eddie's

arms were crossed in front of him and he threw back his head and laughed some more. Mom couldn't keep herself away, so she poked her head through a crack.

"Cabrón!"

"Maybe it's a good joke," said Corin.

"Qué pinche joke." She closed the drapes hard. "That sonnavabitch." She went over to the couch sat on it and crossed her legs.

Eddie and the lady stayed outside laughing for a long time. Me and Corin looked at each other because we knew something bad was about to happen. *The Beverly Hillbillies* was still on and even though I tried to listen to Granny rant and rave about Jethro's cousin, Jethrine, I couldn't pay attention since there was a better show going on outside.

"O'ye! Did I raise you two in a barn? Get away from those damn drapes."

"Aw, Mom, let us see," Corin said, both hands still grabbing the curtains.

"Come on, Mom. You know you want us to tell you everything Eddie's doing," I said taking one last peek.

"I seen all I need to know."

"Nah-uh. No you didn't," said Corin.

I saw it, too. Eddie's arm was around the lady.

"Get over here, right now!"

"Okay, okay. But do you want us to tell you what we just saw?" I asked, pretty shocked myself.

"No, I've seen enough."

"I don't think so," Corin said giggling while she still peeked through a crack. "Now they're walking over here and his arm's around her."

We heard the keys in the door and in walked Eddie with a tall lady in a short black skirt and red high heels. She had poofy blonde hair ratted up so much it looked like giant motorcycle helmet. She smelled like cigarettes and Prince Machebelli. And when she walked in she smiled and looked around like she didn't care about anything. Eddie was smiling, too. Mom wouldn't even look at them.

"O'ye, Delia. I want you to meet a good friend a mine." He put his arm around the lady and stood there facing Mom. "This here is Wanda. Me and her go way back. We were in high school together. I stopped off at Tink's to have a beer and there she was. We started talking, catching up on ol' times. And after a few drinks I told Wanda I wanted her to meet my family." He turned to face her and moved his arm from her shoulder to her elbow, like he was giving her a tour of us. "Wanda, this is my wife, Delia, and my two kids, Marcía and Corin."

"Hi Delia. Hi kids."

Nobody said anything. Eddie looked at me and Corin.

"Did you two just hear the lady say hi to you?"

"Hi, Wanda," we both said.

Mom stared at Wanda, but didn't say anything.

"Well, Eddie," she said looking at her watch. "I think I'll head on out. It's getting late, and I know these kids've got to get their sleep."

"Sleep? Hell, who needs sleep? These kids get all the sleep they need. Stick around and have a drink before you go."

"I don't know, I feel like I'm imposing," she said, glancing over at Mom.

"Qué imposing. Shit, if I say you're welcome in my house, then godammit, that's what you are. Ain't that right, Delia?"

"Whatever you say," she said rolling one eye toward the ceiling.

"Marci, go get me three glasses and the whiskey. Sit down, Wanda. Make yourself at home."

Wanda and Eddie sat next to each other on the couch. Mom was on the lounge chair. Me and Corin were on the floor, watching the show.

I got up to get the whiskey.

"I don't want nothing," Mom said, yawning.

"Oh, come on, Delia. This here's a party. A reunion, hombre. Celebrate a little."

I set three shot glasses and the Canadian Club on the coffee table.

Eddie filled two glasses and was filling the third.

"I guess you must be deaf 'cause I said I didn't want any. You and your güisa can drink it." Mom studied her fingernails, then looked at Eddie like she wanted to kill him.

"You're gonna drink it because I said you're gonna drink it." Eddie filled the third glass, then slammed it down in front of her, spilling some of it on the table.

"Oh, Eddie, let her be. If she doesn't want it, don't force it on her." Wanda's hand slid out for the glass easy, like she's probably done it a thousand times before.

For once, Eddie didn't throw a fit about having someone do what he said. He either liked Wanda a lot, or was too drunk to care. I figured it was probably both.

"Delia, do you mind if I smoke?" Wanda asked, reaching into a small black purse for her cigarettes. She pulled out a pack of Winstons. It was the same kind Mom smoked.

"Do whatever you want. It's Eddie's house. Pienso que you should ask him." For some reason, Mom wasn't joining in the smoking.

Wanda looked over at Eddie.

"Smoke! Smoke! Light one up for me while you're at it."

We never saw our dad smoke before. Wanda gave Eddie a cigarette, lit his, then hers. He took a puff and blew the smoke out toward the ceiling. I wanted to laugh, but I didn't. Mom stared at Eddie, shocked, too, I guess. He held the cigarette in a funny way, between two fingers, kinda like a girl. He put it to his lips, sucked it, then blew out the smoke with a kind of "tuufftt," like he was spitting.

Wanda and Eddie finished their drinks. Eddie took Mom's drink, then poured another glass for Wanda.

"Let's toast this time," Wanda said.

"Okay, to what?"

"Let's toast to the future."

"Sí, cómo no? To the future."

"To the future."

They clinked glasses and started laughing. Boy, were they drunk. Boy, were they flirting, and right in front of Mom, too!

Now it was Mom who looked at her watch.

Eddie saw we still had the TV on. "Hey, turn off that goddamn TV! We got company here. Turn it off!"

"Aw come on, Eddie. *Gilligan's Island's* on now." Corin didn't want to miss her favorite show. Not me. The show in front of me was a lot better than dumb Gilligan. In fact, I couldn't think of anything better than what I was watching right then.

"Eddie? Your kids call you Eddie? How cute. Kind of radical, like the hippies. I didn't know you were so cool." Wanda squeezed Eddie's arm and giggled.

"I don't know if I'd call myself cool. These kids just like to make fun of their dad, that's all. I'm always the big joke in the family it seems," Eddie said, taking another tuufftt puff and looking at me and Corin.

"Como un payaso," said Mom.

"What'd she say?"

"Payaso. A clown. She said I was like a clown."

Eddie looked hard at Mom, like he wanted to slap her, but the cloud passed, and he went back to Wanda.

"Eddie, you remember Rick Tafoya?" Wanda lit another cigarette. "You played on some kind of team with him? Football, I think."

"You played football?" Corin asked, surprised as much as I was.

"Hell, yeah, I remember Rick Tafoya," Eddie answered, ignoring Corin. "Nice guy."

"Yeah, and remember he was so big the coach made him

a blocker or something? I used to know what he played. Let's see." She put a polished red fingernail up to her lips. "I can't remember. He was just one of those big guys that stand in front of the quarterback, y'know?"

"Yeah, yeah. Tackle, Wanda. He played tackle," Eddie said, spitting out some more smoke. "What about him?"

He probably wanted to know why she was talking about another guy instead of him.

"You know he was married right out of high school to that Norma Fuentes?"

"Yeah, I remember Norma."

"I found out she divorced him, just last year."

"Really? I thought they was gonna be together forever, the way they acted around each other." Eddie put out the cigarette, but waved when Wanda offered him another.

"Right, everyone did. Turns out ol' Norma met some guy in a night class she was taking and next thing you know, pfftt! That was it! Said she was in love with this guy and so long Rick."

"Ain't that a bitch? And Rick was a hell of a nice guy, too."

"Uh-huh." She glanced at her watch again. "Well, it's getting late, and I got to get going and let you all have a little peace." She stood up and smoothed down her skirt. "It's very nice meeting you, Delia. Eddie's told me so much about you." She held her hand out to shake Mom's, but Mom just waved. Wanda pretended not to notice and turned to us, instead. "Ba-bye kids. Now keep up the good work in school. Eddie tells me you two are really smart in school. Nothing like me. It was a cold day in June when I opened up a book."

Eddie laughed. "Yeah, I remember, too. I'd be going to class, like a good boy with my pants hitched up to my ears, and there you'd be, standing across the street smoking cigarettes and laughing your ass off. That's what I liked about you, Wanda. Always having a good time."

"Yeah," she laughed. "I'd cut class and smoke all the time. I guess I *was* a bad girl."

"Was?" Mom practically choked on the word.

"Yeah, Delia, but I think I'm slowing down a bit. Age does that to you, y'know. Having kids does it, too, though I wouldn't know since I didn't have any. Had me a hysterectomy at twenty-five. Can you believe it? Female problems. Doctors said if I didn't have one I'd be dead by thirty. So here I am, thirty-one, and still kicking." She held her arms out like she was a walking miracle.

"Well, Wanda," Eddie said, getting up to lead Wanda to the door. "It sure as hell's been great seeing you."

"Good seeing you, too, Eddie, and it was nice meeting your family."

Eddie walked her to the door and opened it. She turned one more time and said ba-bye to us. We raised our hands up and waved. Eddie shut the door.

"Ain't she a riot?"

"Ain't she?" Mom said.

"Ah, come on now, Delia! Don't go there. Don't go there. We were just having a drink and going over old times. There ain't nothing wrong with that."

Mom cut her eyes at him.

"You got nothing to be mad about. We was just catching up, that's all. Shit. If I wanted to mess with her I wouldn't have done it and brought her home to my family. Would I? Huh? Would I?"

"No sé. How am I supposed to know what you do and don't do with your girlfriends."

"We're friends, Delia, friends. Nada más." He looked over at me and Corin. "Tell your mom not to get jealous."

"Are you jealous, Mom?" Corin asked.

"Nope."

"She's not jealous, Eddie."

"Oh, ella está celosa, all right. Qué quieres, Delia, huh?

Qué quieres? For me to come home every damn day and eat my little beans and tortillas without ever having any fun? Can't have one pinche drink at Tink's without you throwing a fit. You didn't marry a goddamn pansy, for Christ's sake. You married a man! And if that means drinking a few beers with his buddies, or—"

"Or bringing home some drunken floozy," Mom interrupted.

"Hey! Now you better watch your mouth, little girl. She ain't no floozy. She might have had some hard times, but she ain't no floozy."

"How the hell do you know?" Mom asked.

"I know. I know these things. I sure as hell should know," Eddie said, mad.

"She looks like a floozy to me," I said.

"What's a floozy?" asked Corin.

"A qué cabrón. Now you see what you've started! You got the girls calling someone they don't even know a floozy."

Mom shrugged her shoulders.

Eddie undid his belt and pulled it out of his pants. I thought he was going to whip us for calling Wanda a floozy, but he was just getting ready for bed.

"Marci, come over here and help me take off these boots."

I went over and pulled one boot off. His foot was stinky and sweaty.

"Corin has to do the other one," I said.

"Corin. Get your skinny ass over here." Corin was slow about getting up. "Come on, girl. I can't wait all night."

She walked over to where Eddie was sitting, turned around, and straddled his leg holding the boot. He used his other foot to press against her butt, pulling off his boot. Corin practically fell to the ground when the boot came flying off.

"I wish to hell you kids would grow. Looks like you're going to be puny midgets all your lives."

"Give them a chance," Mom said. "Maybe they'll grow up to be big and tall, like their dad."

Eddie looked over at her. "I'm tired of your shit, Delia. I'm going to bed. You're making a big deal out of nothing!"

He picked up his boots and stumbled into the bedroom. Mom got a blanket and pillow from the closet and slept on the couch. Eddie must think we're stupid, living like ostriches with our heads in the sand. The only time I've ever seen Mom get mad enough to do something was when she thought Eddie was fooling around. She never does nothing about him hitting us or treating her like dogshit, but she sure gets mad if she knows some other girl's got her hands on him. I don't know what she thinks is so great about him. Whatever it is, it must be good, because she always takes him back.

* * *

Híjole, man. Mom sure put the ice to my dad the next day. She didn't even fix him his breakfast. Then she told him, "pack your own damn lunch, or better yet, get Wanda to come over and do it since you like her flabby ass so much." They almost got into a fight again, but I could tell Mom wasn't gonna talk to him. Eddie tried to make her pack him a lunch anyway, but she told him "come mierda." He left saying he'd make her pay for this, and she said, "try it." As soon as he was gone, me and Corin told Mom that Wanda was the same Wanda he was with that time when he went away.

"What, you think I'm stupid or something? I know it's the same pinche Wanda he was with before. I'll be damn if I stick around while he cats around town, expecting me to cook his food and clean his house. He can live like a pig and eat shit, for all I care!"

Mom was cussing and that always meant something was going to happen.

"O'ye, Marci, cuantos días till you get off for Thanksgiving?" she asked later that morning.

"I don't know, four, I think."

"Cuatro, eh? Then you and Corin can take it early. I want

you to go pack some underwear, socks, shirts, a pair of pants, a dress, a sweater, and your jacket."

"Where're we going?" I asked. "San Francisco?"

"No."

"Where then?"

"You'll see." She was smoking a cigarette, puffing away like it was her last day on earth.

"Mom. I want to know where we're going."

"No te preocupes. Help Corin pack. And put everything in your little Barbie Doll suitcases."

"Barbie doll suitcase? I can't use it anymore. It got wrecked, remember?"

"Then find something else."

The day I use that Barbie doll suitcase is the day they'll have to take me to the State Hospital. Eddie and Mom bought us Barbie doll suitcases one Christmas and I thought I'd die, even though I faked I liked it. My case was black vinyl with a big blond Barbie head on the front. Midge and Ken were in the back doing I don't know what. Mom and Eddie must have gone to the Mother Superior for ideas on getting me a present, because they sure didn't pay any attention to what I really wanted: a gun and holster, cowboy boots, and a hat. I think both of them thought if they got me a Barbie doll suitcase I'd act more like a girl. They even gave me a brown-haired Barbie doll to go with it. I hated her, except for her chiches. So after I stared at them a long time and even felt them a little (too hard), I gave her to Corin.

After Mom told me to go pack, I went to the kitchen, got some scissors and a big paper bag. Then I went to my room and cut a few holes in my suitcase just to make sure. I used the paper bag instead.

"Where do you think we're going?" asked Corin.

"I don't know. I asked Mom if we're going to San Francisco and she said no. But she wouldn't say anything else."

"Maybe we're going to Grandma Flor's!" Corin said, all excited.

"Yeah, maybe. I can't think of where else we would go except for San Francisco. I guess we'll just have to wait and see."

I helped Corin finish packing. She was putting in her Barbie doll.

"Corin, if you're going to take your Barbie, make sure you at least take the knife Grandma Flor gave you. We might need it more than that dumb doll. And bring a book, too."

"I love my Barbie," she said, hugging her then kissing her on the mouth.

When we finished packing, I picked up Corin's suitcase and my bag and brought them into the living room.

"We're ready, Mom," I called out.

"Ya mero," she yelled from the bedroom. "Get the keys from the dresser. Then I want you to get the bread and chorizo, and put 'em in that bag we got from Tía Leti. You know, the green one with the plastic handle. Y, put in otras cosas that look good to eat."

I went to the garage and got the bag. I took it into the kitchen, cleaned it out, and started putting in what she said, plus whatever else looked good. There were some Hostess Cupcakes that were for Eddie's lunch, some Oreos Mom gave me and Corin every once in a while, and some oranges. I took them all. I found little bags of chips. "Snack size." More stuff for Eddie, more stuff for us. Then I checked for the M&Ms that I knew Mom kept hidden inside the giant bowl way up on the top shelf. There was half a bag left, so I brought those, too. I hid them in my pocket, so I could have them whenever I wanted. Finally, I grabbed some napkins and threw those in.

"Marci, did you finish?" Mom yelled from the bedroom.

"Yup."

She walked into the kitchen and opened the bag. "There's nothing but junk here."

"I got what you said."

She didn't take anything out. Instead, she went back to the fridge and got some cheese. There was cooked ham I forgot. It was also for Eddie's lunch. It cost too much for *our* lunch, except for today.

"Okay. Vamos!"

We loaded the suitcases in the trunk, put the food bag in the back seat, and got in the car.

"Can't you tell us where we're going?" I asked.

"You'll see."

We drove down to the bus station. Mom was still driving the old Ford Falcon that used to belong to Gordo. She was supposed to give it back to him when she got on her feet, but instead Gordo sold it to her for $300. All of it was Mom's own money she saved from working at Woolworth's. I could tell she was proud of it, too. She washed it every week, and carefully shined the chrome. And even though Eddie didn't really want Mom driving, he gave in and spent a few hours changing the oil and spark plugs. We parked down the block from the bus station and got our suitcases out of the trunk. Then we walked to the station dragging our bags and the food.

"You two wait while I go get the tickets. Stay right here," she said, pointing to some seats. "Don't go anywhere and don't talk to anyone. 'Horita vengo."

She walked over to where a line of people were buying tickets from a lady behind a glass window. I looked around and saw people waiting, sleeping, or staring off in space. Lots of them were smoking cigarettes. There was a big sign that had all the places where the buses were going and the times they were leaving next to them. I saw Mom go up to the booth and buy the tickets from the lady behind the glass. She put the tickets in her pocket and walked over to us.

"Where we going, Mom?" Corin asked.

"I told you you'll know when we get there. Now sit still

and read your book or something. The bus we want comes in twenty minutes."

Ten minutes later Mom told us to grab our bags and follow her. She looked at her ticket and went to the bus that said Albuquerque on the front. We stood in line waiting for the man to put our bags into the bottom of the bus.

"So we're going to Albuquerque?" I asked.

"That's what the ticket says, doesn't it?" she snapped. "No, Marci, we're not going to Albuquerque."

"Can I see it?"

"No. Now give the man your bag and get on the bus. You and Corin get in the same seats. Get something close to the front. I don't want to be smelling that hediondo bathroom for the whole trip."

I gave the man our bags and we got on the bus. There was a lady wearing a jingly bracelet across from us who smiled when she saw Corin. She looked like she could be somebody's grandma.

"Are you two traveling alone?" she asked.

"No, our mom's coming. She's just loading the suitcases."

She nodded and looked around, kind of nervous.

"I just hate riding the bus. But I don't have a car." She stopped and looked outside the window for a second. "I'm visiting my son in Los Alamos. He works for the lab they have up there. Home of the atomic bomb. Los Alamos. Ever hear of it? Such a beautiful place." She stopped talking for a second and looked at both of us. "I am just so impolite, girls. I haven't introduced myself, now have I?" She smoothed down her dress. "I'm Mrs. Bustelo."

"Mustedo?" I asked, not sure.

"Bustelo," she repeated, "like the coffee. What are your names?"

She didn't look like she could hurt us, so I told her our names. Right then Mom walked on the bus and saw we were talking.

"Qué estás haciendo? Didn't I tell you not to talk to anyone?"

Boy, was she in a bad mood. "Mom, this is Miss Buñelo. She's going to see her son in Los Alamos where they make bombs."

Mom gave the lady her secret agent look, then finally said hi. She sat in a seat behind us and closed her eyes. Pretty soon the bus got going. There were only a few empty seats, most of them in the back. Mom acted like she was trying to sleep.

In a little while we were on the freeway on the way to Albuquerque, or wherever. I brought library books with me. Corin brought her books, but they were mostly for coloring.

I don't know why Mom wouldn't tell us where we were going. Miss Buñelo had a map with her, and after she was done looking at it, I asked if I could see it. I looked for the road to Albuquerque, then looked at the towns before it. Yup, Gallup was on the way. I gave the map back. Mom kept her eyes closed most of the time and didn't talk very much. I think she was nervous because she got up a few times to go in the back to smoke.

After we'd been riding a while, I asked Mom, "What about your job?" She said it was none of my business. She liked her work, so I bet she took a vacation. I looked out the window and thought about why Mom was doing this. She was mad at Eddie and was probably trying to teach him a lesson. She probably thought Eddie was gonna beg her back. Which he might, but I don't know if he would since he seemed to be having a lot of fun with that Wanda. Plus, we know he had fun with her before. Mom hates, hates, hates it when Eddie even *looks* at another girl. Maybe if Eddie wants Mom back he'll behave and will want to be just with her, but I doubt it. Why would he change? The only thing that's different now is how he hits us. Eddie won't change and Mom is stupid for thinking he will. But I can't tell her that because she has a broken record inside her brain. Before, when Mom would complain to Grandma Flor about Eddie, Grandma didn't say very much, but she'd tell me later, "Your mama sure loves his sorry ass." Then she'd pull her hair, twisting out one of the long purply-black curls, shake her head and say, "And I sure as hell don't know why."

The bus driver drove for a while, then stopped at a station in a town called Merced.

"Fifteen minute break," he said.

Mom asked if we were hungry. We said yes. She got us some Cokes and we ate ham and cheese sandwiches from our lunch bag that were so dry it took the whole can of Coke just to get them down. Then she said she'd be right back, and got off the bus. She looked at us through the window, and yelled, "Stay put." I watched her walk over to the telephones inside the station.

"Corin, Mom's calling someone. Come on. Let's go see who it is."

"What if she sees us?"

"She won't. Come on."

We got off the bus and went inside the station. Mom had her back to us talking to someone with her head bent over. There were two phones next to each other with a little wall in between. She didn't see us, so we snuck up behind her and stood where the other phone was. I pretended to call somebody so no one would take our place. This is what we heard:

"No. No—

Mama's house—

They're okay—

Mira, you need to tell me once and for all. La quieres a ella, o me quieres a mí?—

You do?—

How come you go out with her then?—

Yeah, you do. I know you do, Eddie. No soy pendeja—

No. No, Eddie, make up your mind—

No, now—

Now!—

Mira, tell me now, or we're staying at my mom's. It's up to you. I got no time for playing games anymore. Dígame—

You sure?—

You sure you're sure? 'Cause I ain't coming back there to that same pinche mierda. If you want her, tell me, because you ain't getting both of us. I mean it. You and me've been together a long time and, pues, te quiero, you know. But I ain't putting up with this shit anymore—

You better not be saying this to get me back there and then vas a hacer the same ol' shit again. I don't want her around, period—

Did you hear me? I said no more fooling around—

No, I don't believe you—

Why should I?—

Your word? Qué word? Where was your word when you had your arms wrapped around that Wanda the other night? Huh?—

Oh, so I got to believe you, now?—

No. I'm not fighting with you. I just need to know. You want me or her? 'Cause if you want me, then, it's just me. Not Wanda, or Shirley, or cualquier mujer que te gusta. It's just me, Eddie. Otherwise, forget it—

You sure?—

You sure you're sure?—

I guess so—

Yeah, I believe you. Pero—

I'll have to find out when the next one leaves—

Merced—

Well, what do you expect? I'm not playing, Eddie—

Yeah, okay. I miss you, too. I'll see you tonight—

I gotta go. The bus is leaving. Okay. Ba-bye."

I motioned for Corin to face the telephone until Mom walked away. After a few seconds, we followed her back to the bus. She got on and we waited in front, like we'd been there the whole time. In about two seconds she was back out with our books and the bag of food.

"I thought I told you two to stay on that bus!"

"We did, but we got tired of waiting so we've just been playing out here."

She came over and pinched us hard.

"Next time I tell you to do something you better do it. Entiendes?"

"Oww. You didn't have to pinch me."

She went over to talk to the driver who was almost ready to go. I saw her say something, then the driver let out a big breath and scratched his head. She walked with him over to where the bags were kept underneath the bus. She pointed to the ones that were ours and he took them out. She told us to get our bags.

"Now, I don't want to hear nothing from either of you, but we're going back."

"Why?" I asked. "How come were not going to Grandma Flor's?"

"Yeah, Mom," said Corin. "I thought you said you were mad at Eddie."

"I changed my mind. Now, vengan conmigo. And this time, don't go wandering around. We have to find out what time the bus home leaves."

✳

We got home in about three hours. Turned out Merced wasn't that far from where we lived. Eddie was waiting for us when we got there. He hugged Mom a long time and kissed her all over. He tried to hug me and Corin, but we wouldn't let him, and went into our room.

Mom called us out to eat the fried eggs she cooked for supper. After we finished eating, she told us to watch TV. Then her and Eddie went into the bedroom and shut the door.

We watched TV for a while, but I was tired, so I went to bed early. That night I don't know what it was, but I had nightmares. I woke up in the middle of the night after dreaming that I'd turned into a man but through the whole dream I only saw the back of me, never my face. I was happy I was a man because Raquel was in the dream and she was looking at me like she wanted me. This felt good until my face showed and when it did, it was Eddie! I had turned into Eddie! It was so awful I woke up panting like Tía Leti's dog Pepito when he gets too hot. Thank God Corin didn't hear me. I wish I could have been Superman in my dream, or someone besides Eddie. I would have even been George Reeves with his flat-butt and ham-head, anything besides Eddie. It made me mad that Raquel wanted the Eddie-me. I wish she would have wanted the me-me. I don't remember any other dreams that night. That was enough.

✳

After the bus ride to Merced, everything went back to normal. Well, except for two things: Mom didn't stop smoking and Eddie didn't stop seeing Wanda. We didn't know if Mom knew, but we did. We lived in a small town. So if you walked around, you could always see people you knew and the cars they drove. Like the Bel Air our neighbor, Miss Maestas drives to Fry's grocery store. Or Tía Leti's Plymouth at Flavio's Flaky Pastries. We'd walk by the bakery, look in the window, and see Tía Leti drinking coffee, talking a mile a minute with the other ladies in the place.

And that's how we found out Eddie was still seeing Wanda. We didn't know her car at first, but we figured it out because Tink's Tavern and Cha-Cha's were on our way home from school. Sort of. The bars were by the library. After we got back from Merced, I was walking home from the library and, wouldn't you know it, Eddie's car was in the parking lot at Cha-Cha's. Corin was with me. I looked at my watch. It was around 5:00. We had a bunch of books from the library so I told her to put the books down and sit between two cars where we'd be harder to see. I wanted to see what Eddie was up to.

We sat on the curb for about half an hour. Good thing we had our books because that's a long time to sit with nothing to do. I figured if Eddie was going to get home at his regular time he would need to leave around 5:30. Sure enough, at 5:30 he walked out with Wanda. She had on a blue dress, high heels and that same big hair. We scrunched down low so they wouldn't see us.

Eddie leaned against his car and Wanda put her arms around him and gave him a big kiss on the lips. Just like they do on TV. Eddie looked more expert at it than the people on TV. He sure was stupid, doing that in front of the bar where everyone, including his daughters, could see him. They talked some more and kissed one last time, then Eddie got in his car and drove away. Wanda walked back into the bar.

"I sure wish I had me a camera," I said, as we picked up our books and started walking home.

"Yeah, because Mom wouldn't believe us if we told her."

"We could try, but you're probably right." I stopped to think. "Well, what if we did get a camera?"

"From where? We can't use the one from our house, because they would know we took it." Corin shifted her books to the other arm.

"We can ask Uncle Tommy. I'll bet he has one he'll let us borrow."

"He'll ask what it's for."

"We'll tell him it's for a school project. He won't have to know what we're really doing."

"All right. Let's do it."

We got home and told Mom we were late because we were at the library. Eddie smelled like booze. He said he was a little late because he stopped off at Cha-Cha's to have a beer with some of the guys after work. Mom didn't say anything. She just looked at the books we brought home. Mine were mostly Hardy Boy stories, with a couple books on volcanoes. Ever since Miss Buck showed me that book about the guy changing into a girl, I never stopped thinking about it. But I never checked it out, because I'd have to sneak it in the house. It seemed weird that you can get an operation to change into a girl. That means there's gotta be operations to change into boys. I have to remember to ask her if any new books came in that talked about that. I didn't really want an operation. Even if I did, I'd have to wait a long time before I could get one and I wanted to be a boy *now*.

After supper, we called up Uncle Tommy and asked him if we could borrow his camera. He didn't even care. He said he got it used, but that it took good pictures. He even said he'd drop it by, but we told him no, that we'd pick it up after school the next day. So the next day when we got to Uncle Tommy's house, he gave us the camera. It was a Brownie. He showed us how to put the film in it.

"What kind of project are you doing for school, Marci?" he asked.

"My teacher wants us to take pictures of people we think are interesting."

"Oh yeah? You gonna come back and take a picture of your Uncle Tommy?"

"Sure." I looked over at Corin. "When we get some film we'll come back and take a picture of you and Auntie Arlene."

He smiled and we left to walk home. I hate lying, but I guess there are times when you just have to do it. We hid the camera in my sweater. We went into our room and counted the money in our piggy banks.

"How much do you have?" I asked Corin.

She took all the change from her bank and counted it.

"Not counting the $20.00 from Grandma Flor, I have thirty-five cents."

"I have two dollars and fifteen cents." Which is all I've

saved ever since I stopped putting nickels in the candles to pray to the Virgin Mary and Baby Jesus.

"We can use Grandma's money," she stacked the nickels and dimes on top of each other.

"No, we need to save that in case we really need it." I counted everything. "We have enough to buy film, but we're gonna have to get more to develop it."

"Where?"

"We'll collect Coke bottles."

So we did. We borrowed the MacCormacks' wagon and went to everybody's house asking them if they had any empty Coke bottles. Lots of people must have felt sorry for us, or just wanted to get rid of their bottles because when we were done, the wagon was full.

"We should do this more often," said Corin as she counted the bottles.

We went to Fry's, turned in the bottles, and got $1.80 for them.

"Okay," I said adding up the money again. "We got your thirty five, my $2.15, and the $1.80. So that makes $4.30. I think it's enough."

Across the street from Fry's was a drug store, where we knew they developed film. The guy behind the counter told us if we buy black and white and a roll of twelve, we'd have enough to buy the film and develop it. So we bought it, took it home, and put it in the camera. We were ready to spy.

Corin was scared. I told her to pretend that it was an adventure, a mystery, just like a Hardy Boy story. It didn't make her feel much better, I guess because she never reads Hardy Boy stories. Plus, we both knew it would be really bad for us if Eddie caught us taking pictures of him.

"One thing is on our side," I said. "Eddie doesn't know we know, so he'll never be looking for us. As long as we stay hidden we don't have to worry."

That still didn't make Corin feel better. She said she was

too scared to do it. She wondered if we could think of another way of letting Mom know about Wanda.

"We can try telling her and see what she says."

"We already talked about this," I said. "Mom won't believe us. She knows we don't like Eddie, and she'll think we're just making it up. It's the same as when we tell her he's hitting us. She always believes him and not us."

"I'm too scared, Marci." Corin squeezed her hands together and shrunk herself up into a little ball.

"All right. I'll do it myself."

"You will?"

"Yeah. You just have to help a little, but it won't be the spying part."

I didn't really know if I could do it, and I sure wanted Corin to come with me, but I was just going to have to pretend I was a detective. What would Joe Hardy do? He'd do it. So I'd be Joe Hardy. Better yet, I'd be the Secret Agent Man. I loved the Secret Agent Man.

"Daryn de daryn de daryn de daryn, de daryn de daryn de.—There's a man who leads a life of danger. Everyone he meets, he fears a stranger. With every move he makes, another chance he takes. Odds are he won't live to see tomorrow. —Secret—Agent Man! Secret—Agent Man! They're giving you a number, and taking away your name. Daryn de daryn de daryn de daryn de daryn de daryn de daryn.—Secret Agent Man!"

That song was so tough it made me feel like I could do anything. Use my karate to beat people up, take spy pictures, whatever. I could probably be a good secret agent when I grew up, too. This was just practice. All I had to do was think like Secret Agent Man and I wouldn't get caught. Look at that time I saw Uncle Tommy come out of the confessional with Father Chacón. Was that being a secret agent, or what? They never even knew I was there. Or how about the other day when we were in the bus station and I got us close enough to listen to Mom talking with Eddie? The more I thought about it, the more I felt I could do it. Besides, I'll bet Grandma Flor would probably think it was a good idea, as long as I didn't get caught.

So me and Corin made a plan. We didn't know when Eddie would be at the bar. And we didn't know if he'd go to Tink's or to Cha-Cha's. So on the days we decided to go looking for him, we had to make sure Corin was at the library checking out books. At 5:30, she had to meet me around the corner from the library so we could walk home together. That way when Mom checked on us, she would see we always had new books. The bars weren't very far from each other, maybe two or three blocks. And the library was almost across the street from Cha-Cha's. If I didn't find Eddie's car after I walked around, then I'd go back to the library and get Corin. It would be easy.

✳

How come things are always easier to plan than to do? We started on Thursday because that was a day close to the weekend and we thought Eddie might be there. But every time we went looking for him, we didn't see him. We went on Friday and still no Eddie. Miss Buck couldn't believe all the books Corin was reading.

"That librarian is weird," Corin said. "She said I must've taken an Eleven Wooded Reading Course."

I laughed. "It's the Evelyn Wood Speed Reading Course. She just thinks you read really fast." I looked at her stack of books. She did have a lot. "Maybe you should check out just three or four books." I looked over at the parking lot in front of Tink's. Eddie's car wasn't around. "I wonder where he is?"

"Maybe he meets Wanda at another bar."

"I don't know. He likes going to Tink's or Cha-Cha's. He could be going somewhere else to meet her. But let's keep trying and see what happens."

The whole next week we went looking for him. We

finally found his car at Tink's on Friday. Corin went to the library while I waited across the street, sitting between two parked cars. I quickly took a picture of his car in the lot. Since it was a busy street, lots of people walked by, and seeing me sitting there holding a camera, they always had something to say.

"What 'cha doin' thar, little lady?" asked a short, old man walking by with his cane. He bent over, leaning into my face. His nose was big and red, and the end of it had lots of veins. He reminded me of Mr. Magoo.

"It's for school. I have to take pictures of people." I didn't feel like saying more. It could blow my cover.

"What the devil kind of class project is that, takin' pictures of people?" He said it like he'd be the boss of whether I got to do it or not.

"It's our assignment. We take pictures of people doing the things they do." I stopped, then looked him straight in the eye. "Without their knowing it."

"Hmm. Doing the things they do. Sounds like some kind of rock song." Mr. Magoo stopped to think about it. He looked down the sidewalk, then turned back toward me. "Wait. Did you say you're taking pictures of people walkin' down sidewalks?"

"Sidewalks, stores, bars, whatever." I had to keep my eye on the bar in case Eddie came out.

"I sure as hell hope ya' don't piss anyone off with that photo shootin' you're doin'. It'd probably piss me off if ya' took my picture." He leaned both hands on his cane. "Ya' gonna take my picture?"

"No."

"What? I ain't good enough for ya' class project?"

"Sure," I said breathing hard, "You're good enough. You want me to take your picture?" This guy was driving me nuts.

"All right, I'll let you. But take it on my left side, heah." He pointed to his face.

I took his picture. "How's that?"

"I got one thing to tell ya', don't be takin' people's pictures without askin' 'em. Ya' might piss them off. Did I tell ya' that already?"

"Yeah."

"Well, who cares? When you get old like me ya' get a little forgetful." He pointed his cane at me when he talked. Then he gathered himself up, snorted, and walked away. "Damn kids," I heard him say.

And I had to waste a whole picture on him, too.

So far, the only people I saw were walking in the bar instead of out of it. It was 5:15. I tried to hide my camera between my feet so people passing by wouldn't notice what I was doing. I brought a book to read, but I couldn't read it because I had to keep an eye on the bar. So I just pretended.

Other people walked past me and didn't say anything. Most were in a hurry to do their shopping or go home. Everyone who passed me, though, stared at me like I was the weirdest person in the world.

More people kept going into the bar. Must be a fun place. I wondered what it looked like inside. Maybe I should go across the street and try to look in the window. It wouldn't be that hard since the windows are on the side and not in front. I decided to wait until Eddie was gone to do that. It was way too scary to walk across the street now, right when he might walk out.

So I sat some more. Waiting. Pretending to read. Waiting and waiting. At a quarter to six, Eddie still didn't come out, and I was beginning to get a little worried because now I knew Mom would start to wonder where we all were. All of a sudden there he was, walking out of the bar. And he wasn't alone, either. He was with Wanda, all right. I took my camera, framed them into the little square, and took a picture. They walked faster and it made it hard to follow them with the camera. Eddie had his arm around her and I think I got a picture of that. Next, Eddie leaned over to kiss her and I clicked the button again. I was feeling pretty good because I knew I had some proof to show Mom. Eddie got in his car and Wanda walked back inside.

I felt happy, because I finally got some pictures. I went over to the spot around the corner from the library to get Corin.

"Marci, where've you been? I thought you'd never get here." Corin was sitting on a bench looking like she was waiting to catch the bus. She had a bunch of books in a pile next to her.

"I got some pictures." I was really excited. "I got Eddie walking out with Wanda. Another of his arm around her, and I think I got one of them kissing."

"You did?"

"Yeah! I don't know how they'll come out, though, we'll have to see." I saw there were six pictures left in the roll. "We still have lots of film left. Maybe we should come back and take some more. Just in case these don't turn out."

"Okay. But I wish it didn't take you so long. It's really boring sitting here."

"God, Corin, read a book!" I looked at the books she checked out, *Briar Rabbit, Ramona, Pipi Longstockings.* All of them were either kids' books, or books I'd already read. "Corin, didn't you find any of the books I told you to get for me?"

"Nooo. I just went through and picked out ones I thought might be good. How am I supposed to know what books you like? You're too weird, anyway."

"Well, we don't have time to check out more. We gotta get home right away, or we'll be in big trouble."

We gathered up the books and walked home as fast as we could. It was funny, because Mom was worried about us being late, but when we told her we were at the library again and showed her our books, she didn't get mad. Eddie smelled like beer and didn't seem to care whether we were late or not. I was glad Eddie hadn't put two and two together about where the library was and where the bars were. We hid the books in our room and kept them there just so they wouldn't remind him of anything.

The next day I took my camera and rode my bike over to Tink's to try to look inside the windows. I knew Eddie was home working on his car, so I didn't worry about being there. It was really hard to see inside. The windows were painted a gold color and there were only two of them. Both windows were up high. I had to figure out how to get up there so I could look inside. I went around the back and found an old twin size mattress and a few boxes. A couple of the boxes were made of wood, kind of rickety, but I grabbed them anyway and dragged them over to where one of the windows was. I stacked them on top of each other, then climbed up one box and then the other. It was kind of shaky and both boxes jiggled the whole time I was on them. When I finally got high enough to see inside I was surprised because it looked just like a regular bar.

Inside was a TV, some tables, a juke box, and a pool table. I saw a few people drinking and smoking. The bartender was a tough-looking guy with a lot of hair cut short, kinda like Elvis Presley in one of his Army movies. I was going to take a picture, but of what? It didn't look no different than other bars I'd seen before. In fact, it was a lot like Grandma Flor's bar, but hers was nicer because she had deer heads, peanuts, jerky, and corn nuts that she sold from a little stand behind the bar. Tink's bar had posters of girls that looked a little like Mom standing next to cars with beer bottles all around. Grandma Flor didn't have posters like that. She said if you're going to have a poster to sell beer, then have a picture of the beer bottle, not a girl. She said "Why they put a girl standing next to a beer bottle? Except for Ruby Mejía and Cleo Abeyta, the ones who drink the most beer in my bar are los hombres. Pienso que they should put the mens next to the beer bottles, not the mujeres." Grandma Flor always said things that made a lot of sense.

I got down off the boxes and put them back behind the

bar. Then I jumped on my bike and rode home. I guess I thought there would be more inside. I couldn't tell what makes this place so special to Eddie and Wanda. Maybe after work everything changes. Who knows? All I know is that Eddie sure likes going there.

When I got home I looked for Corin and found her inside reading *Pipi Longstockings.*

"Corin, I went to Tink's and climbed up to look in the window and you know what?"

Corin pulled her eyes away from the book and looked at me. "What?"

"It looked just like a regular bar. It was no big deal. They had this bartender who looked like a mean Elvis Presley, and lots of dumb posters on the walls. There were tables, chairs, a TV, and a pool table. That's it."

"Nothing else?"

"Nope." I sat on my bed and put the camera back behind the headboard where I kept it hidden. "We have lots of pictures left. I was going to take one of inside the bar. Maybe I'll still do it when Eddie's in there. I don't think they can see me looking in."

"You're crazy if you do that," said Corin. "What if you did it, then him and Wanda go around the back to kiss? Then what? I wouldn't do it if I were you, Marci. It's stupid."

"I didn't say for sure I'd do it. I was just talking about maybe doing it. That's all."

"Well, if you do it, you better watch out, because it'd be really bad if you got caught."

"I'm not gonna get caught. But it'd be great if we could get a picture of him inside with Wanda, don't you think?"

Corin thought for a second, then smiled. "Yeah."

"Next time, when we go out to spy, I'm gonna try to get one of Eddie inside the bar."

"Okay, but—"

"Stop worrying. I won't get caught."

❋

The next week we went out looking for Eddie and Wanda again. We didn't see them until Friday. I guess that's their regular drinking time. They could be seeing each other someplace else, like her house, but we didn't know where she lived. Corin was at the library and I was in front of Tink's, waiting on the sidewalk between the parked cars, when the exact thing that I hoped wouldn't happen, happened. I was sitting with a book and the camera, when there—walking straight toward me—was Tía Leti. I thought she'd be home cooking supper, so I was shocked to see her. I wanted to crawl underneath one of the cars, but she saw me before I could do anything.

"O'ye, Marci. Qué 'stas haciendo?" She said it like *I* was the one fooling around with Wanda instead of Eddie.

"Oh, hi, Tía Leti. You mean me?" I looked at the book and held it up for her. "Reading." I glanced across the street. The worst that could happen was that Eddie would walk out right then and see her. Then he'd wonder who she was talking to, and see me, and then, oh boy. I had to get out of there. "Reading and doing my class project."

"Qué class project? What are you doing sitting there?"

"I have to take pictures of people doing things without their knowing." I held up my camera. She looked at me like I'd lost my mind.

"Does your mama know you're sitting out here on este dirty sidewalk taking pictures?"

"She might."

"You bad girl! Get out of there! Your mama finds out you're sitting there con all that mierda taking pictures, she's gonna spank you."

"Well, don't say nothing, okay?" I snuck a look across the street again. Then, as I was picking up my camera and book I saw the bar door open.

"Tía, come here." I motioned her to sit down next to me. "Quick. Get down here with me."

"Qué?"

"Get down here. I'm spying and I don't want anyone to see us." Maybe it was the way I said it, because she squatted down right away. Out of the doors walked Eddie and Wanda. Tía saw them and gasped.

"Ay, no!"

"Shhh. Don't say nothing. I have to take their picture."

I took my camera and framed their heads inside the square again. They weren't doing anything this time. Just talking. I took a picture anyway. Tía Leti started to stand up. Why, I don't know. I grabbed her shoulder and held her down.

"No, Tía. Stay down. I can't let them see us. Cálmate until they leave. Please!" I gave her the same look Jesus had on the cross. I practiced it during Mass when I was bored. Then I'd point to other statues in the church and do their faces to make Corin laugh. Boy, did it pay off now. Tía squatted back down and didn't say anything until they left. I got two more pictures of them saying good-bye. Then, like usual, Wanda walked back inside the bar and Eddie drove away.

"Okay, now we can get up." I helped Tía stand up.

"Marci, dígame, what do you think you're doing?" she said it police-man style as she brushed off her skirt.

"I'll tell you, but let's walk over to the library so we can get Corin. She's waiting for me."

"La Corin, también?"

"Yeah."

We walked over to where Corin was waiting. While we walked I tried to explain to Tía what our plan was. The whole time I talked, she didn't say a thing. Corin looked scared when she saw Tía Leti.

"Hi, Tía."

"You girls shouldn't be taking these pictures. Your daddy finds out what you're doing and he'll—" She put her fingers up to her forehead and closed her eyes. "Quién sabe what he'll do, but I know it won't be good."

"But Tía, we have to get pictures of him and Wanda together. Mom doesn't believe anything, so we have to have proof."

"Why you do this? Why? This is something between your mama and your daddy. You girls shouldn't be messing around with esta mierda. Is not for you to be sticking your nose where it don't belong."

I looked at my watch. It was a quarter to six.

"Tía, we have to go. Otherwise Mom's gonna get worried."

"No, no. I gonna take you home en mi carro. But first, we going to my house. I have to give you something."

"But—"

"Don't worry, I gonna call your mama and tell her you're with me."

"Okay," I said, worried about what she was going to say.

We got into Tía's Plymouth. It was old, but it ran smooth because Gordo was always working on it. Tía Leti drove, as Mom would say, "like a bat out of hell." When she was in that car it was like she was the only one on the road. She turned left right in front of cars coming our way and cut other cars off so close I thought she'd hit 'em. I must have had my eyes closed most of the way, just so I wouldn't see us crash, but we made it to her house in one piece.

Tía called Mom right away. She told her she saw us walking from the library and drove us to her house to give us some milk and cookies and would drive us home in a few minutes. When she hung up she went to the cabinet, brought out some Oreos and poured two glasses of milk.

"Don't eat too many. Your mama said not to spoil your supper." She lit a cigarette and sat down for a minute to smoke and watch us eat. Pepito ran up to her and hopped on her lap.

We were hungry and ate everything on the plate in about two seconds. Tía made some coffee in her percolator and walked out of the kitchen, saying she'd be right back. After a little while, she came back with a paper bag in her hands.

I looked around the house. No one else was home.

"Where's Gordo and Tío Agapo?"

"They went fishing today. They say it's the last day to go fishing so they went after work. They coming home pretty soon."

"What'cha got there, Tía?" asked Corin, pointing to the bag.

"Mira. I know why you want these pictures for your mama. I know how your daddy is. He can sometimes be muy, mmm—?"

"Chingón?" Corin said.

Tía laughed. "Sí—Chingón. Sí. I guess you could say that." She laughed again. "Pero, I think it's not good for you to be sitting on that sidewalk taking his picture. I want to give you este polvo I got from a friend of mine in San Francisco."

She took a red box with black writing on it out of the bag. The cover of the box had a man lying down all tied up like Gulliver, you know, with the ropes across him and little stakes all up and down each side. Next to the man were words that said, "Polvo Para Dominar a su Hombre."

"What's that, Tía?" I asked.

"Éste es polvo that you use to—como se dice—"

"Dominate?" I asked.

"Sí, dominate your man." She opened up the box, then went over to get a plastic bag. "Pero, you need just a little bit. Es muy fuerte. This stuff can do very special things. I never tell no one, not even tú mama, that I use this, but it works for me." She looked proudly at me as she spooned some into a bag. Tú conoces a tu tío, no?"

"Yeah." Tío Agapo was not my favorite uncle. Even though he never did anything to me, I could tell he was grouchy and spoiled, so I stayed away from him.

"Pues, how you think I keep him nice, eh? Con este

polvo. Es muy, muy, fuerte. You take just a little bit and put it into his comida. Poquito. Mira." She held up a tiny pinch of the polvo so we could see how much she was talking about. "Then you sprinkle it over his frijoles and mix it in so he doesn't see it. The only days you do this is on Tuesdays and Sundays. No lo pongas on any other day. Use this and after a while you gonna see a difference in your daddy."

"Like what?" I asked.

"Like him being at home more, and being nicer to you and your mama." She stopped to think for a second. "He gonna be a better man to have around the house. Try it, you'll see." She handed me the bag.

"How many times do we give him the polvo?" I asked.

"Try it maybe five or six times. See if you see anything different. If not, dale un otra. If your mama used it, it'd be mejor because he's her husband. But this is the best we can do for now."

"Okay, if you think it will work." I picked up the bag and looked at the powder. It was white, like baking powder mixed with salt.

"Mira, would I lie to you? Mi Agapíto es muy cariñoso ever since I give him éste," she said tapping her finger on the box. "He's nice, is good to me, and never yells anymore. I give him una touch-up once a month to keep him in line."

Tío Agapo didn't seem very cariñoso to me, but what do I know? I didn't live with him.

"Does this mean we're not going to show our pictures to Mom, Marci?" asked Corin.

"Ay Dios no! Why do you think I'm giving you este polvo?" Tía Leti practically choked on her own cigarette smoke. "Try this first before you show your mama pictures of your daddy con la gabacha fea he likes. This way you keep the peace. You show your mama those pictures and it's gonna be big trouble, and not just for your mama and daddy, but for both of you. I don't want nothing to happen to your mama and you guys. Your daddy le da mucha joda when he's mad.

Listen to me. Use the polvo. You'll be better off if you do." She blew out cigarette smoke. "Pero, take my picture before you go."

I took Tía's picture, with the cigarette and Pepito in her lap. We hopped in her car, did the sign of the cross when she wasn't looking, and headed home.

After we got back, we took the polvo and put it in under Corin's mattress. It was gonna be hard to put some in Eddie's food because Mom put the food in a bowl on the table and we served ourselves from there. But Corin solved the problem by sprinkling the powder over his plate and since the plates were white and it was such a tiny pinch, Eddie never saw it. We gave him the polvo this way about six times, then sat back to see if there were any changes.

✳

That Sunday, after Mass, I went to the chapel and knelt underneath the statue of the Virgin Mary holding Baby Jesus. I even put a nickel in the slot for the candle since it seemed that ever since I stopped putting in nickels Baby Jesus wasn't paying much attention to me.

The chapel was empty when I walked in. I sniffed hard so I could take in that smell I loved so much: wax and smoke. I knelt down and lit a candle. I looked up at Mary holding Baby Jesus and told them I really needed them to pay attention to me.

"Dear Jesus, you know, I've been praying to you, your father, and your mother every night for a long, long time and nothing, nothing I've wanted to happen, has happened. We had a chance to go to Grandma Flor's and instead we end up sitting on a bus for five hours because Mom thinks Eddie wants her back. Mary, if you can't get Eddie to go away, could you at least stick some sense into Mom's head? She hasn't acted like she's had any at all except for the time when Eddie left us and she had to work and be the boss of the house. I thought she'd see that Eddie is mean but she never does, not even when he hits us. Mary, you're supposed to help the helpless. Well, I'm not saying I'm helpless, but I sure could *use* some help. Know what I mean? Somebody's got to make Mom see. I don't know what's going to happen to us if she doesn't. Amen."

Then I looked up at the ceiling.

"God, I know you're here, too. I know you have lots of problems you have to think about like Vietnam and Biafra, but you need to take a little time to help me and Corin. We're sick and tired of getting hit by Eddie. We keep asking you to make him leave but he hasn't. We thought he'd go once he got another girlfriend, but he didn't, even though he sure seems to like that Wanda a lot.

"We're trying a polvo, a dominate powder that our Tía Leti gave us. It's supposed to change our dad into a nicer man. If you can help make this work, that would be great. If Eddie got nicer and didn't hit us anymore, that would be even better, because that's all we're really asking for. I guess it would be good if he brought us presents and was in a good mood all the time, too. Would that be asking too much? I don't think so. Please, God. Please help make the polvo work. Amen."

I checked around the chapel to see if anyone had walked in while I was talking. So far the coast was still clear. I looked up at Baby Jesus' little round head.

"Okay, Jesus," I whispered softly, looking at his marble blue eyes. "I know I ask you this every night, but you haven't changed me into a boy yet, and just in case you think I forgot about it, or that I don't want to be a boy anymore, you're wrong, because being a boy is what I want bad. I know you've probably heard me ask you this five million times and you probably thing I'm a broken record, but I haven't stopped liking girls. In fact, I can almost say I love them. Every time I turn around there's somebody new that I can't stop thinking about. On TV I see lots of girls I like, and I'd really like to be with them. Are you listening? You don't seem to be. You took Raquel away from me, and I was so sad I thought maybe you'd change me then. Instead, nothing's happened and all I did was get older. I believe in you Jesus, and I've prayed to you for a long time. I know lots of people pray to you. Everyone says you listen and answer our prayers. But where's *my* answer? Is it because I'm a kid? Sister 'Lizabeth says you listen to everyone, even us. I hope you do because I don't know what I'll do if you don't. Maybe you can give me some kind of sign. Okay? Amen."

✳

I got one. Eddie brought home a kitten. I don't know if it was a real sign or something that just happened. You know how it is when you can't tell? I guess I wanted to think of it as a sign, but I wasn't sure of what. The kitten was a boy with black fur, a white chest and white feet. Me and Corin had different names we wanted to call him. First I liked Pepito, but that was the name of Tía Leti's dog, and besides, it made me think of Pepe le Pew, which made me think of Mrs. Shaboom, or whatever her name was. So I decided I couldn't name him that. Corin wanted to name him Tube Socks because of his white feet, but I said it would be stupid to name your cat Tube Socks. Then I thought we should name him Black Beauty, but Corin said that was stupid, because he had too much white. She said we should name him Chewy because he liked to chew things a lot, but I said that was a little kid's name for a cat. Besides, Mom said we couldn't use that name because it was the nickname for Jesus, which I never even knew. Finally, we both liked the name Ringo, after Ringo Starr from the Beatles. I liked Paul, because I think he's cuter. But Corin likes Ringo, even though she should at least like John since he's cuter than Ringo, but Paul and John aren't good names for a cat. Ringo was, so that's what we named him.

We never found out where Eddie got the kitten. When I asked him he just smiled and said a friend of his had kittens and needed to give them away. When I asked "What friend?" he smiled again. I looked at Mom, who wasn't smiling. She hates animals so I know she wasn't happy. *We* were. We didn't care *where* Eddie got the kitten. Ringo got to sleep in our room where he had a cat box in the corner, behind the door. He played all the time and after just a little while, me and Corin said we loved him.

I kept thinking about why Eddie got us the kitten. Maybe that dominate powder was starting to work. Tía Leti said he would start acting nicer to us. He would never let us have a dog or a cat before and now we had one. And he didn't seem to be quite as mean as he normally was, either. Corin thought it was because he felt bad for what he'd done to us.

"Heck no," I said to her. "If Eddie was going to act nice because he felt bad for hitting us, he would have done that a long time ago." I thought maybe it was because he felt bad for having a girlfriend. All I could say was that I hoped he didn't change his mind about the kitten, because I sure didn't want to lose him.

Eddie was still seeing Wanda. We went to the library every Friday to check out books and spy on him. It didn't matter: rain or shine, they were always there. I wondered what other times he saw her. Maybe they only had drinks together. We really didn't know. We stopped off at at Tía Leti's for milk and cookies one day, and told her that Eddie was still seeing Wanda. She got a sad, worried look on her face.

"Maybe your dominate powder isn't working all the way," I said.

"Quién sabe?" Tía lifted up her shoulders. "It works on my husband." She looked away from us like she was thinking hard, but didn't say anything.

"Eddie's probably too mean for just a little bit of powder to change him," said Corin. "Maybe we should give him more."

"Yeah," I added. "Maybe we should make it gun powder instead."

Tía looked at me, shocked.

"Just kidding," I said. "Eddie probably needs more polvo than Tío Agapo."

"Yeah," said Corin. "Our dad is lots meaner than Tio Agapo and Tio's pretty mean."

Tía lit up a cigarette. "Pues, sí," she said thinking, but it sounded like she said, "poos-sy," which made me want to crack up but I couldn't, because, well, you know.

"Mira," she said, blowing out smoke from her cigarette. "Voy a pensar about this and I'll go back to the botánica to see if they have something más duro para su daddy."

"Okay," we said and kissed her good-bye. We told Tía we liked walking, which was a lie, but we couldn't stomach her driving.

"Well, we still have our film, Marci."

"Yeah, we do. Let's go get it developed and see what the pictures look like."

✳

We took our pictures to the drug store to get them developed. We'd spent some of the bottle money on candy, so we couldn't get the pictures developed right away. Plus, we weren't in a big hurry since Tía Leti made us promise to show her the pictures before we showed them to Mom and to give Eddie more polvo before we did anything else. We gave Eddie so much polvo that he complained to Mom about his beans tasting funny. After that, we cut back a little bit so we wouldn't get caught. We didn't notice any big changes except he was a little nicer, which I guess is what the polvo was for.

But deep down, we knew Eddie could always get mad and turn into someone the devil brought back. This always made me scared because I never knew what he would do. Besides, just because someone's nice for a little while doesn't mean he always will be. Corin thought Eddie would be nice only while Wanda was around and, I hate to say it, but I thought so, too. Me and Corin talked and thought we should let Eddie keep seeing Wanda instead of trying to break them up. We both thought it wouldn't hurt to have the pictures of him and Wanda, as long as Mom didn't see them. It was good to have two plans. If plan A didn't work (which used to be telling Mom about Eddie and Wanda, but was now was switched to letting Eddie stay with Wanda), there was always plan B. This plan was to show Mom the pictures and hope that it made her want to break up with Eddie.

The other day Uncle Tommy gave me and Corin some money. Why? Who knows? He felt like it, I guess. We said thanks, took the money home and added everything up. It was enough. So on Wednesday we took the film to the drugstore, where they said the pictures would be ready by Saturday.

I started getting more and more excited. Saturday was taking forever to get here. Finally it came, and me and Corin walked to the store to pick up our pictures. We gave the man our name. It wasn't our real name since we made one up just in case anyone came snooping after us. If we were gonna be spies, we had to make sure no one knew it.

Finally we got the pictures, paid the man, bought some Red Hots and Sweet Tarts with the money we had left over, and walked out of the store. We walked normal until we passed the window, then we ran until we got to Flavio's Flaky Pastries and hid behind the building. We opened the envelope and pulled out all twelve of the black and white shots. The first one was a picture of my feet that I must have accidentally taken when I loaded the camera. Then there was a picture of Tink's bar with Eddie's car in the parking lot. After that one came that dumb Mr. Magoo. His eyes were closed and he was standing there with his cane. He looked more like Mr. Magoo than the cartoon did. The next picture was of Eddie walking out of the bar with Wanda. After that, was one of

Eddie walking with his arm around her. The next was of Eddie and Wanda kissing good-bye. Then there was one of Eddie and Wanda talking and the two of them saying good-bye. Tía Leti's picture was funny because she was blowing out smoke from her cigarette with Pepito on her lap. She was petting Pepito with one hand, holding the cigarette with the other, and blowing the smoke towards the ceiling. On the kitchen table was the little red box of "Polvo Para Dominar a su Hombre," except you couldn't really tell that from the picture. *We* knew what was in the box. Then there was a picture of Ringo sitting on Corin's lap. Last of all was another picture of Ringo sitting on the porch.

Well, we finally got the proof we wanted. There was only one problem.

"They're too tiny," said Corin.

The camera wasn't very good, and when I took the pictures, I didn't think I was that far away, but I guess I was, because the ones of Eddie and Wanda looked more like gray, blurry squirrels.

"If you were looking at these for the first time, would you be able to tell who it was?"

Corin studied the pictures for a long time. Then she gave them back to me. "I guess if I saw the people first in real life, I might think they were the same, but only if I saw them before."

"Then we don't have to worry."

"Why not?"

"Because Mom knows them. Plus you can totally tell it's Eddie's car, and even though you can't see their faces very good, Mom'll still know it's them."

"I guess so," Corin said, taking the pictures and looking at them again.

"I know, let's show them to Uncle Tommy. We won't tell him who they are and we'll see if he can tell." I was happy with my idea.

Corin scratched her head and thought about it for a second.

"Okay, but do you think Uncle Tommy will tell Mom?"

"We'll just have to make him take a code of silence like the spies do in the movies. I think Uncle Tommy will keep things secret if we ask him." I thought about the time I saw Uncle Tommy and Father Chacón in the confessional. "Yeah, I think he will. Let's go show him."

"But what about the class project?"

"Corin, remember, our project is to take pictures of people we think are interesting." Isn't that what we did? I smiled and she started laughing.

After we went to the library to check out a few books so Mom wouldn't know what we were up to, we walked over to Uncle Tommy's and found him down in the basement lifting weights.

"Hi, Uncle Tommy," I said, looking at his chest with the giant muscles that were so big they reminded me of chiches, except they were flatter and harder.

"Hi, girls," he grunted, as he put a barbell with what looked like 5,000 pounds back on those little holders on the bench. He looked surprised to see us. "How are my two little princesses?"

"Fine," said Corin.

"I'm not a princess," I said. "I can be a prince or a knight, but not a princess."

"Hijo, Marci. Okay, okay. What brings you guys here?"

He looked at both of us, checking, it seemed, for signs of our father, then he reached down and gave us a hug and kiss on the cheek.

"We have something we want to ask you," I said as I pulled the pictures out of the envelope.

"Yeah, Uncle Tommy, we want to know if you can tell who's in these," said Corin as I gave them to him. He took the pictures, sat down on the bench, and started looking at them.

"Well this here's Tía Leti and that mean little dog of hers. What's his name?" he asked, looking at Corin.

"Pepito."

"Right, Pepito." He stared hard at the next picture. "Hmm, I don't know this old guy, who is he?"

I grabbed the picture from him. "Oh, him. Don't pay any attention to him. He was just walking down the street and wanted me to take his picture. Look at the other ones and see if you can tell who they are," I commanded.

Uncle Tommy looked at me and smiled. "Okay. Boy, you're bossy today."

Then he saw the pictures of Eddie and Wanda and stared at them a long time. He didn't say anything. Finally he let out a big breath.

"Where'd you get these?" he said, his face looking worried.

"We got them—"

"We'll tell you after you tell us who you think they are," I said, interrupting Corin.

"Come on, Marci. You don't live in the same house with a guy for sixteen years and not know your own brother, even if he's just a blur in a picture. Who's the girl with him?"

"Her? Her name is Wanda."

"Wanda, Wanda. Wanda Pickett who lives over on Second Avenue?"

"I don't know," I said.

"We don't know where she lives. We just know her name is Wanda," Corin said as she took the pictures back.

"I know it's your daddy and that floozy, Wanda Pickett. So," he said, nodding toward the pictures, "Where'd you get these?"

"I took 'em," I said.

"Yeah, since they're not very good we wanted to see if you could tell who they were."

"It's not that hard," he said.

"But you have to swear not to tell anyone, not Auntie Arlene and especially not Mom or Eddie," I demanded.

"Okay, but why did you take these pictures if nobody can see them?"

"We took them because we—" Corin looked over at me.

"We took them because we, uh—"

"We took them because we *had* to. That's why," Corin said matter of factly.

"Uncle Tommy, we need you to promise not to say anything," I said.

"But why? Why shouldn't your mom know what your dad is up to? She never believes anything and here's proof plain as day."

"Then it's good you can tell, which is why we showed 'em to you," I said. "We'll show them to Mom, but not until it's the right time. That's why we don't want you to say anything. Okay, Uncle Tommy?"

He looked down at all his weights lying across the floor.

"Okay?" added Corin, asking again to make sure.

"Okay," he finally said. "That's why you wanted to borrow my camera, huh?"

We nodded.

"All right. I won't say anything. But I sure as heck hope these pictures never end up in the wrong hands. It ain't gonna be good for the both of you if your dad ever sees these." He stopped and looked at us with sad puppy-dog eyes. No wonder Auntie Arlene and Father Chacón liked him. He was so cute. "So, what's the plan? What are you gonna do with these, blackmail your dad?" he said, trying to make a joke.

"No, but that's a good idea," I said.

"What's blackmail?" asked Corin.

"Never mind. I'll tell you later," I said. "Remember, Uncle Tommy, you can't say anything."

"Yeah, you have to be a secret agent just like us."

Uncle Tommy looked worried and shook his head.

217

"Well, you two little secret agents better keep this stuff away from your James Bond father, and his Sherlock Holmes wife, or the both of you might be in big trouble." He stopped to think for a second. "Maybe I should keep them. That way, your mom and dad won't find them by accident. And if you want 'em, all you got to do is tell me and I'll bring 'em right over." He looked at us both. "What d'you think?"

"Uh, I don't know, Uncle Tommy." I looked over at Corin. "How do we know you won't get rid of them? It was hard taking these pictures. Spying isn't easy, you know. You have to be super sneaky, can't tell the truth, and you always have to say you're doing something you're really not."

Uncle Tommy started laughing.

"Why are you laughing?" asked Corin.

"I don't know. I think I know a little bit about having to do some of those things." He kept laughing. "You know, there are some people who have to do those things just to get through the day, much less being a spy." He looked like he was thinking about something that bothered him.

Corin reached down fast and grabbed her cuca. "Marci, I gotta go to the bathroom."

"Go 'head," Uncle Tommy said. "You know where it is."

Corin set the pictures on the bench and went to the bathroom down the hall.

"Uncle Tommy, I think you know I don't like to lie or hide things from Mom and Eddie." I paused for a second. "Well, not from Mom, but right now that's what we have to do. If we need these pictures, we'll use them, but right now, we're gonna hang on to them."

"Well, I still think I should keep 'em. If you girls keep 'em, I wouldn't rest thinking what would happen if your mom or dad gets a hold of 'em. People don't like having other people know their secrets."

"Even you, huh Uncle Tommy?" I couldn't believe I'd said it. It was as if something had taken over my mouth.

He looked at me with such a scary face that it made me

think of Eddie for a second. "Yeah? What secrets do you know about me?"

"Never mind. I was just kidding." Boy, did I wish I could lie better.

He grabbed both of my arms and pulled me up to his face.

"Marci, tell me what you know about me."

He was holding me tight and seemed nervous. Either that, or I was. I was so scared and mad at myself for saying what I just said that I didn't know what to do. It was the same thing that happened to me when I was trying to lie in confession to Father Chacón.

"I don't know...I was just playing with you, Uncle Tommy." I was afraid that if I did tell him the secret, he'd get really mad.

"Come on, tell me! What do you know?"

He was holding me so tight I knew I was going to have to tell him something.

"Nothing."

"Don't lie to me, Marci. What is it?"

"Nothing." I looked around hoping Corin would come back.

"I know you know something, so you better tell me." His eyes were hard. "Either that, or I'll tear up your pictures."

"No!" I said, trying to squirm away.

"Then you better tell me."

"Okay," I said breathing fast. "Well, one time I saw you and, and—"

"And who?"

I wanted to get out of there. I was breathing harder now, and his hands felt like a vice that could hold me forever.

"Well, one time I saw you and Father Chacón come out of the same confessional booth." I was so scared that the words barely trickled out of me.

Uncle Tommy slumped forward like someone punched him in the stomach. He let go of me and I picked up the books that I'd dropped. I went over to the bench to get the pictures.

"Uh-uh. No, you don't. You're not taking these with you," he said, as he grabbed the pictures and held them in his hand. Right then, Corin walked into the room.

"What're you guys doing?" she asked.

"Nothing," I said. "What took you so long?"

"I had to go number two."

"We have to go now, Uncle Tommy. If you keep the pictures, you have to promise us you won't show them to no one, not even Auntie Arlene. And you have to give them back when we want them."

He was looking down at the floor and then glanced at me for a second while I talked.

"Okay. I promise." His face looked sad, like all the air was let out of it.

"Uncle Tommy," I said.

He didn't answer.

"Uncle Tommy."

"Just go on. Go." He bent over and put his hands on two dumbbells.

I got up close to him. "Uncle Tommy, don't worry," I said. "I won't tell."

For the first time, his eyes had a sliver of a light in them. "No?"

"No. There's always gonna be secrets. Everyone has one." I turned and headed out the door. "Even me."

❊

Grandma Flor never forgot about us. After we wrote her, she called every Friday to ask how we were doing and what we were up to. We didn't say much because Mom was usually listening. So we couldn't say anything about being spies and taking pictures of Eddie and Wanda. It seemed like Grandma mostly wanted to know if Eddie was still hitting us. And you know, the funny thing was, that ever since Eddie started seeing Wanda again, he didn't hit us as much. On top of that, he wasn't as mean. I know I said this before, but it was hard to believe. Grandma Flor always said Eddie wasn't gonna change because "he's too much of a sonnavabitch." I told Grandma he seemed nicer and even got us a kitten, but she said not to trust him. Grandma asked me why I thought Eddie was different.

"I don't know," I said to her.

"Mira, hija, tu papá es muy cabrone. He not gonna change for no reason. What he doing? Eh? Qué está haciendo? Come on, dígame."

"I don't know Grandma, he drinks at a bar," I said hoping, she wouldn't keep asking.

"Ya sí, I know. Y qué más?"

"Nothing."

"He probably has una güisa. Hmmm, ya sí, es eso, qué no?" she asked almost talking to herself. "Marci, your daddy have a girlfriend?"

"That? No, I don't think so."

"Hmpfh! I thought so. Let me talk to your mama."

"No, Grandma, don't! It would be really bad if you said anything." Mom wasn't in the room, thank God, but I knew she could come back any second.

There wasn't any sound coming from the other end of the phone for a long time except breathing in a way that I guess was her puffing on a cigarette.

"Okay, hija. I no gonna say nothing, but I want you and Corin to take the money I sent you and come stay with me. Why don't you come out here for Christmas? That way I can see you and you can have a little vacation. What do think?"

"Okay, Grandma, that would be fun. I'll ask my mom. Then we can get our tickets. We can come right when Christmas break starts."

"Bueno. Let me talk to your mama, now. Cuídate con todo. And if something bad happens, I want you to call up your Tío Tomás and go over his house, then call me right away. Okay?"

"Okay. We will."

"Cuídate."

"Okay, Grandma. Don't worry."

"Bye-bye, mijita."

"Bye Grandma."

❋

I'm starting to think that God is just the air. Sister 'Lizabeth says that God isn't the air because he makes it. But I don't know who God really is anymore. The reason is that I haven't gotten any proof that God is around like everyone says he is. The war's still happening, more people are starving in Biafra, Danny's dead, Raquel's gone, Eddie lives with us, and I'm still a girl. On top of that I think things might've happened in this world more like how my science books said. Here's why. I just turned twelve and that means only one thing: I'm getting older. And even though I asked God to change me into a boy by the time I turned twelve, I had a funny feeling it wasn't going to happen. You kinda think if it was gonna happen he would have changed me by now so that everyone, including me, could've gotten used to it.

I look at the sky and follow the clouds moving across it. Where are you God? If you can read my mind, do it and show me you're real. Talk to me! Light up a bush like you did for Moses. Make it snow, lightening, hail, *something* to prove you're here.

I wait a long time and watch for any sign he's listening. I study rocks for water, trees for fire, darkness for light; anything to show me proof. And I pray. I pray and pray and pray some more.

Nothing.

The cars drive by. The MacCormacks play kickball down the street. Everything is the same.

All of a sudden it hits me. I'm never gonna be a boy. No matter how hard I pray, or how good I try to be, I'll always be a girl.

I look at my cuca, then back at the sky. What do you do, God? What do you do with people like me? I stand up and throw a rock as far as I can. I watch it fall in the neighbor's yard making a soft thunk in the dirt. I don't know if God does anything for people like me, or anyone else who asks. I pick up another rock. This time, I throw it even farther. If I'm gonna stay a girl I'd better figure out what to do. Problem is, is what?

✳

Christmas vacation came a little early. It was right after I talked with Grandma Flor. I remember it being a cold, rainy day, the kind of day where we wore our rain boots and jackets. We were taking off our boots outside when we heard loud crying from inside the house. I could tell it was Mom. She sounded bad. It was a little after five. Mom still worked at Woolworth's but now she worked from eight to five every day so there wouldn't be fights anymore over my cooking and her not being there when Eddie got home.

We listened and heard more screaming and crying. I was scared because I never heard Mom sound so sad.

"Think we should go in?" Corin asked. She looked scared, too.

I didn't see Eddie's car anywhere, so I put my ear to the door and listened for a few seconds.

"We probably should." I said, then took a deep breath and slowly opened the door.

Mom saw us and stopped crying.

"You kids vengan aquí," she said, pointing her finger on the dining room table where she was sitting. "Come over here, because I have a few things I need to ask you." Her hair was messed up, her eyes were watery, and her nose was red and snotty. I don't think I'd ever seen her this way before. She was holding something in her hand, and that's when I saw them. The pictures. I was instantly mad at Uncle Tommy, but couldn't think about it right then. Mom was holding the pictures so tight they were almost crumbled together.

Corin walked behind me, then slowly sat down on the same chair. I wish we'd never walked into the house, that we'd have gone over Tía Leti's instead. I looked at Mom and knew it was too late to wish for anything.

"Now I want you to tell me where the hell you got these!" Mom was yelling and crying at the same time. She took the pictures and threw them across the table at us. Her eyes were big and puffy, like Pepíto's. The little black dots in the middle zipped back and forth between me and Corin like mad black bugs. After a few seconds she gathered up the pictures with both hands like a little kid picking up the pieces of a game.

"I don't know anything about those pictures." Corin said glancing at me. "What're they of?"

Mom shoved them into my hands. "No me digas that shit. You both know they're yours. Your Auntie Arlene me dijo that she found them and sent them to me. She says she asked your tío where he got them, and he said you guys took 'em. Now tell me when! When did you take these?"

I guess she had no trouble figuring out who was in the pictures. I wondered why Uncle Tommy busted on us to Auntie Arlene. I picked up a picture and saw there wasn't a date on it. I tried to remember what day it was when Eddie left us after that fight with Grandma Flor. I felt I had to lie. I didn't know what else to do.

"We took them that time when Eddie and Grandma Flor got into a fight. Eddie wasn't living with us, remember? And I told you he had a girlfriend. Remember? We told you he was with Wanda and you didn't believe us. We borrowed a camera and took these pictures so you could see we were telling the truth." I stopped for a second to gather my breath. "No matter what we said, you never believed us. Eddie lies all the time, and you always think he's telling the truth. Then, when he has a girlfriend, you still didn't want to believe it. This was the only way we could prove it."

"Then how come you didn't give me these pictures before? If you wanted me to believe Eddie had a girlfriend, how come you didn't show me these back then?" She pointed to the pictures. "Huh? How come?" She grabbed the picture out of my hands. "No, you two are pinche mustedas. I think you're both lying to me." She looked at each of us. "I think you two took these when he came back to live with us and you didn't want to tell me. What kind of daughters are you? Huh? What kind of daughter would keep this secret from her own mother? Huh? Huh? Dígame, Marci. Why didn't you tell me about this before? Huh? Why?!"

Bam! She slapped me across my face. Bam! Bam! Bam! She slapped me again and again.

"Cut it out!" I put up my hands as I tried to block her from hitting me. "I didn't tell you because of what you're doing right now! I knew you'd go crazy."

"Sí? Well I'll show you what happens when you lie to me."

She ran to the bedroom and came out with one of Eddie's belts. She walked over, folded it in half and lifted it up to hit me. Just then, Eddie walked through the door.

"Hey, hey! Hold on. Hold on. What's going on here?"

Mom looked over at Eddie. Her eyes were slits of hot metal. She still held the belt up ready to hit me.

"Delia, what the hell's goin' on?" He went over to Mom and grabbed the belt out of her hand. "Now, goddammit, settle down and tell me what's happening!"

He took the belt, then carefully laid it on the table.

Mom grabbed the pictures, shoved them into Eddie's chest, and started screaming at him.

"You lying sonavabitch! You tell *me* what's happening! I come home to find estos in the mail from Arlene who says it was your own damn kids who took 'em!" She gathered the pictures which had fallen to the floor, and threw them at him. "Now you tell me, cabrón, who the hell this is and what the hell were you were doing with her!"

Eddie arranged each picture carefully in his hands. I was so scared I couldn't move.

He took each of them and looked at every one of 'em fast. Then he smiled and threw them on the table.

"Bueno, these," he put his fingers down on top of them like he was cutting a deal, "these pictures, ain't shit." He didn't even blink. "I was just having a drink at Tink's, y la Wanda was there, and you know how friendly and everything she is, so she was just giving me a hug and a peck good-bye. That's all. You're making a big deal out of nothing." He glanced at Corin and me. "When'd the kids do this?" he asked Mom, pointing to the pictures.

"'A hug and a peck' my ass,'" Mom copied the way he was talking. "Don't be trying to pull the wool over my eyes, Eddie. Soy 'stúpida but I wasn't born yesterday, cabrón! You're still seeing that bitch and not only is this proof of it, but you've got the nerve to stand there and lie to me! What the hell kind of idiot do you take me for?" She was yelling in his face with both of her hands clenched into fists. I don't remember ever seeing her so mad.

Eddie didn't back down. In fact he was standing about two inches from Mom and started yelling back. "Mira, Delia, I told you those pictures ain't shit! All we was doing was having a drink. You're getting bent out of shape over nothing. I'm telling you there ain't nothing going on. So calm down or I'm gonna do something you'll really regret." I saw his hand curling up into a fist.

You could tell Eddie was mad. His eyes always told you so. But this time his face got white, and his lips lifted up in a way that reminded me of Pepito, right before he bit you. I've seen Eddie mad hundreds of times, but I never saw him like this. I got scared just looking at him.

"Qué dices? Did you say to calm down? I don't need to

do nothing you say. In fact, I don't need your sorry ass around here anymore. No te quiero! I don't ever want to see your gringa-loving midget-ass self around here ever again! So why don't you just leave!"

Wham! He slapped her right across the face. She grabbed her face in surprise and started crying.

"Now goddammit shut up, Delia. I ain't never hit you before, but I'll hit you again if you ever disrespect me like that! Especially in front of the kids."

Since when does he care about us? I grabbed Corin and slowly moved us away from the table to the couch. It still felt too close. I was scared because I didn't know what was gonna happen. I started to feel sick to my stomach.

"Since when do *you* care about the kids?" Mom must have read my mind. "You're always kicking them around like perros. They already know what kind of asshole their daddy is, and now they know how much he cats around, too. You ain't nothing but a lying sonavabitching cheat."

His hands were in tight fists and I knew if she pushed him too far he'd really give it to her.

"Delia! I'm warning you—"

"You ain't warning shit. If you're such a gran chingón, then why don't you just haul off and hit me? You seem to like it so much. Go ahead. Hit me!"

"I don't need to put up with this shit." He started to turn away but she caught him by the arm.

"Where the hell you think you're going, cabrón! I ain't finished talking to you yet!"

Bam! That was it. He hit her across the face with his free hand. Bam! Bam! Bam! He hit her over and over. She put her hands up and screamed for him to stop as she tried to cover her face. I knew doing that would only make him madder. It was funny because just a few minutes ago I was doing the same thing, but getting it from her.

Corin slipped off the couch and ran down the hallway. Mom begged Eddie to stop, but he wouldn't. Her face was getting redder and redder. Even though I was mad at Mom, I was madder at Eddie. I couldn't let him do that to her, so I jumped in without thinking, trying to hit him and grab his arms.

"Leave her alone! Leave her alone!" I said punching him as hard as I could, but it was like slapping a tire. He kept hitting Mom and even though I was punching him hard, he didn't even know I was there until he looked down for a second, saw me, then backhanded me across the room. I must have slammed into the coffee table because I felt dizzy and my head hurt.

I searched around for something to hit Eddie with, but before I could get off the floor, I saw Corin standing in the hallway with Eddie's rifle. Her eyes were almost closed, like she was sleepwalking. Eddie was still hitting Mom so neither of them saw Corin. In a heartbeat Corin had the gun pointed at both of them.

"Corin, no!" I yelled.

She pulled the trigger. The shot rang out and Eddie went down. I looked at Eddie, then at Corin. She was still pointing the gun at Eddie.

"Corin, no! Put it down! Put it down, mija," Mom was on her knees next to Eddie. She held his head up with one hand and waved at Corin with the other. "Corin, please! Por favor, put the gun down. Marci!" she yelled at me, "get the gun from Corin!"

Corin had shot Eddie in the back, but he was still alive. I got up slowly and walked over to her.

"Corin," I said so soft it was almost a whisper. "Give me the gun."

She didn't do anything. Her eyes tore themselves between Eddie, Mom, then back at me. I slowly moved toward the rifle until I finally got my hand on it. Then I grabbed it even though her finger was still on the trigger.

"Corin," I begged. "Give me the gun. Come on. Give it to me."

Her eyes snapped open like she just woke up from a trance. She stared at the gun, then handed it over like she was giving me the bat for my turn at the plate. I let out my breath, took the gun, put the safety on, and took out the bullets. We'd seen Eddie bring that gun out so many times that loading it was scorched like a pattern in our heads. I put the gun down and went over to where Eddie was lying. He was on his stomach and blood was pouring out of his back. Mom was practically on top of him crying. Her face was a bloody mess.

"Mensa, don't just stand there! Call the police, and tell them we need an ambulance."

I started to walk toward the phone but I already heard the sirens. The blood under Eddie was making a puddle on the floor.

"Mom, the police are coming now."

She listened. The sirens were getting louder and louder. Satisfied, I guess, she stroked Eddie's head.

"You think he's gonna live?" I asked, wondering if my real wish was gonna come true.

"No sé, no sé," she answered, still crying. "Eduardo, pobrecito. Don't die, mi amor. Don't die."

I leaned in closer to Eddie's face and checked his eyes. They were still open but he wasn't moving. Eddie might be dead even though his eyes were open. I know people can sometimes die that way. But he was still breathing. I don't know what I was feeling right then. It was hard to say. Mom looked bad. There were bruises all over her face, her nose was bleeding, and one of her eyes was puffed up and swollen. I felt bad for even thinking it, but for a split second I wished Corin had fired twice.

Even though Eddie was bleeding like crazy, he wasn't going to die. Eddie was too tough; too mean to die. Mom was still wailing for me to do something, but I didn't listen to her. I looked for Corin and found her sunk down against the wall.

"Corin!" I grabbed her arm and shook it. "Come on," I whispered. "We gotta go."

She didn't seem to understand what I was saying. "What?"

"We got to get out of here. We can't stay."

Someone was pounding at the door. "Open up! This is the police!"

"Go get our stuff from under the mattresses. Pack some clothes in the Barbie case, and get the money Grandma Flor sent us." She looked like she didn't believe me. "Go on! We can't stay. We got to go to Grandma's, now!"

Bam! Bam! Bam! "Open up!"

"Marci, la puerta. Open it." Mom was still lying next to Eddie stroking his face.

"Okay," I said to Mom, but looked at Corin. "Go on!"

Corin got up and walked to the bedroom. I opened the door. Two big, red-faced cops were standing there with their guns drawn. They seemed surprised to see me.

"He's over there," I jerked my head to where Eddie was lying. "You better call an ambulance. He's been shot."

They kept their guns out until they saw that no one else had one, then put them back in their holsters. One of them went over to Eddie and pressed on his neck to see if he was still alive. The other cop saw the rifle and picked it up. The cop next to Eddie told the other cop to call an ambulance. As the rifle cop picked up the phone, the other cop tried to talk to Mom to see what happened. I slipped into the hallway and ran into our bedroom. Corin was sitting on the bed with some clothes packed into the Barbie case. She was almost crying, but not quite.

"Did you get the money?" I asked her.

She showed me the two twenties. I took them and put 'em in my pocket.

"Okay, get your coat and I want you to pay attention to everything I say." I checked the Barbie doll case, saw there was room left, and took some of my underwear, socks and a couple tee shirts, and shoved them inside.

"Come on, let's go," I said, grabbing my coat.

I peeked into the hallway. The hard part was that the hallway meets the dining room and we had to go that way if we were gonna get out of the house. I saw both the cops kneeling next to Eddie. Mom was crying as if he was already dead. One of the cops kept trying to calm her down. He put his hand on her shoulder and said, "Calm down Mrs. Cruz, an ambulance is coming." We heard a siren getting closer and closer. Suddenly the siren stopped and I knew the ambulance was right outside our house. One of the cops went toward the door and the other cop was doing something to Eddie, but I couldn't figure out what. None of them seemed to be paying any attention to Corin or me.

"Corin, now! Let's go! Follow me and keep quiet." I looked at her and she seemed like she'd be able to do what I said. "Come on!"

Either I'd been watching *Combat* too much, or those cops and our mom were way too worried about Eddie to pay any attention to us. We walked through the dining room and into the kitchen without them saying a word. We slipped out the back door.

It was already dark. There were people standing on our front lawn. I saw the ambulance and two more cop cars. I knew we had to sneak past everybody if we were going to make it, but there were too many people in front of the house.

"Come on," I whispered, "We'll have to go out the back way." We turned around and ran toward the back where I gave Corin a boost and helped her over the fence. Then I handed her the Barbie case, found a small piece of leftover wood from my garden, set it against the fence, and used it to get my own boost over. It's a good thing it was dark, otherwise someone would have seen us. We were now in the Petersons' backyard. The Petersons were retired so their yard was always perfect. "Good thing they hate dogs," I thought. We landed in some soft bushes. I didn't know if anyone was home and hoped they wouldn't see us if they were. We ran up to their gate, unlatched it and tore out of the yard.

At the end of the block we stopped and checked for cops. We didn't see any, so we crossed the street. We came back around the corner, and when we got to our street, we looked over and saw them loading Eddie into the ambulance. I knew it'd be just a few minutes before they'd start wondering where we were. There were lots of people standing in front of our house. I saw the MacCormacks, Randy, even Raquel's mom.

"Good-bye everyone," I thought. I turned to Corin. Her face was as white as a zombie.

"Come on, let's go," I said. "If a cop stops us, we'll just tell him our names are Sally and Cindy Alvarez and that we're going over to Ana Marie Dominguez's to spend the night." Yeah sure, I thought, but I had to say something for poor Corin. She seemed to be fading fast.

I grabbed the suitcase and we hurried away. I knew as soon as everyone figured out we were missing, there'd be cops all over the place searching for us. We walked toward the bus station. I took us on the quieter streets where there was less of a chance of people seeing us.

"Where we going?" Corin asked, her first words in a long time. She stopped for a second and took one last look behind her.

"We're going to Grandma Flor's. It'll be better if we stay with her. If we stay here, the cops will come and take us away and probably put us in jail. Then it'll be really awful. This way, Grandma Flor can take care of us and won't let anyone come and get us."

Corin nodded, "Uncle Tommy would probably take care of us."

"I don't know what Uncle Tommy would do." I said, switching the suitcase to the other hand. "Someday I'll ask him how Auntie Arlene got hold of those pictures."

We walked for a long time without saying anything. Pretty soon we heard a car coming down the street. I grabbed Corin and pulled her behind some bushes. The car drove slowly past us. Even in the dark, we could tell it was a cop.

"Stay here till he's gone," I commanded.

We knelt behind the bushes watching the car drive slowly away. My heart felt like it was going to bust through my chest.

"Okay, coast is clear. Let's go."

I don't know how long we walked. The bus station was pretty far from our house, but we were lucky and didn't see any more cops. The suitcase was light and easy to carry. After a while we came around a corner and saw the station lit up like a Christmas tree.

"Corin, there might be cops there looking for us, so we have to watch out."

I checked the parking lot and didn't see any police cars. Maybe Mom told the cops to go over Uncle Tommy's or Tía Leti's. We walked right into the station. There were lots of people around, which was good, since it would be harder to see us. We got in line at the ticket booth and we waited a few minutes until it was our turn. I kept an eye out for cops.

"Next!" The ticket person was an older lady with pink puffy eyes and lips so red they looked like she'd smeared red finger-paint on them. She had a cigarette burning in an ashtray next to her. The smoke from it kept going into her eyes making her blink. Maybe that's why they were puffy.

"We'd like two tickets to Gallup, New Mexico, please," I said as normal sounding as I could.

She was counting something behind the counter so she didn't even look at me when I asked for the tickets.

"That'll be fifteen apiece." She picked up the cigarette and sucked in a big gulp of smoke. She turned her face up as she blew it out. I handed her the twenties. "Ten dollar's your change," she said as she laid the money on the counter and gave me the tickets. "Door thirteen." She looked at me out of the corner of the less smoky eye. "You girls are lucky tonight.

The bus leaves at seven-twenty." She jerked her head in the direction of door 13.

"Thanks," I said. It was a little before seven. I took the tickets and put them in my back pocket. Then we turned and walked toward the waiting area.

"Corin, let's go over to a corner just in case someone comes looking for us." I grabbed her arm and led her to the far end where I saw two empty seats. "We have about a half hour before the bus leaves." I saw a snack bar in the corner. There was plenty of money left. "You hungry?"

She shook her head.

"How about a Coke?"

This time she nodded.

"Okay. Stay right here and watch our bag. I'll be right back."

She sat down slowly, looked at me, then looked at the bag. I walked over to the snack bar and ordered two Cokes. They cost ninety cents, so that left us with about eight dollars. I checked for cops again, didn't see any, and walked back to our seats and gave Corin the Coke. She drank it fast.

"Thirsty, huh?"

She nodded again.

We didn't talk. We sat there drinking our Cokes while I kept an eye out for cops. Finally our bus number was called. They said a whole bunch of cities that were on the way there, or past Gallup, I guessed. I picked up the suitcase and we walked toward the bus. It was a good thing we did this with Mom the last time she was mad at Eddie. Even though we didn't go all the way to Grandma Flor's, it still made everything easier.

We handed the bus driver our suitcase. He gave us back a little card and winked at us. Then we got on the bus, picked two empty seats in the middle, and sat down.

In a few minutes, the driver climbed into his seat, and started the engine. A couple more people got on, but no one sat close to us. I was glad because I didn't feel like talking. I thought about Ringo and felt bad, but knew I'd just have to come back later and get him. Finally, the driver closed the doors, let the brakes go with a big hiss, and pressed on the gas. We left the station, stopped at a light, then made a right turn onto the highway. It was only then that I let out the breath I must've been holding inside forever. Corin was sitting next to the window looking through it like she was trying hard to see something. I couldn't figure out what it was though, since it was pitch dark.

"Tomorrow we'll be in Gallup," I said. "Then we'll call Grandma Flor to come get us." Corin didn't say anything. I couldn't tell if she heard me or not.

Finally, with her hands held together like she was praying, she turned to me and asked the question that was probably on her mind ever since she pulled the trigger.

"Think Eddie's going to die?"

I didn't say anything for a second, then I grabbed her hand and answered, "No."

She looked away, then nodded her head, just a little bit.

✳

Grandma Flor plants flowers outside her bar. It's the funniest thing to see because it doesn't look like she ever stops to sniff them. But she does. Grandma likes to keep The Coronado pretty on the outside almost as much as on the inside. Me and Corin help her with everything, just like our mom used to. We clean, fill up the jerky and potato chip racks, and get beer from the back. Grandma doesn't let us work nights, though. We have to go home with Tío Fonso and do our homework while he watches wrestling. She wants us to go to college, not end up working in a bar like her all her life.

"You know, en este lugar hay mucho trabajo," she said taking a puff from her cigarette and looking around the bar. "Either that, or I'm just getting old."

I think Grandma's just tired of worrying about things, especially me and Corin. After the accident, which is what everyone calls it, Corin didn't sleep through the night for about a year. I asked her what she was afraid of, but she wouldn't tell me. She'd just wake up screaming from some kind of nightmare, then call out to Grandma who came and sat with her till she fell back asleep. Now she sleeps all the way through, but I still wonder about her.

Mom never told the truth about what happened that day. She said Dad was cleaning the gun and Corin started playing with it when he got up to get a beer. The police asked her how come it was loaded and she told them "I don't know. Maybe my husband forgot to take the bullets out the last time he went hunting." I guess they believed her because they didn't bother Mom or Eddie anymore after that. Mom even tried to tell Grandma the made-up story, but me and Corin told her what really happened. Grandma shook her head and hugged us when we told her.

"Mira hijas, your mama...well, I don't know," she said, still holding us. "She just don't want to do what's right." Grandma let us go but hung on to each of our hands. "From now on, you don't worry, 'cause I'm gonna take care of you."

"What if Mom comes back to get us?" I asked.

"She won't," she said shaking her head. "I won't let her."

"Eddie, either?" asked Corin.

"Eddie, either," she said, gently touching Corin's face. "Especially not him." She lit a cigarette, puffed on it and blew out the smoke. "Es muy importante que te recuerdes," she said pointing at us, "that your mama loves you. But she can't think straight when it comes to your daddy." She stopped and took another puff. "Though I sure as hell don't know why."

Mom calls us once a week to see how we're doing, but not Eddie. I can't even remember what he looks like anymore—but that's okay with me. He's probably still feeling sorry for himself for getting shot in the back, just like the time he pouted for a month when Corin kicked him in the huevos.

When we came to Grandma's, we didn't know what would happen. Was she going to keep us or send us back to Mom and Eddie, like Uncle Tommy did? Lucky for us we got to stay. I miss my mom. Corin does, too, though she never says it. She's different than she used to be. More quiet. But both of us know we can't live in that house anymore, not with Eddie there. I wish Mom would come and see us, but so far, she hasn't. She says she has to work all the time, but I know she gets vacation. Corin says it doesn't matter, that she's happy here with Grandma. I feel mad, but there's nothing I can do about it.

Grandma never talks much about Mom and Eddie. She hardly says anything when Mom calls. Just "hello," and "cómo le va?" Then she hands the phone over to me. I talk for a little while, then give the phone to Corin who talks even less.

After we got here, Uncle Tommy called to see if we were okay. I told him we were, but I was mad at him for giving the pictures to Auntie Arlene. He said she found them and sent them to our mom without him knowing. "Sure," I said. But he said it was the truth. "I'm sorry, Marci," he told me. "I'm sorry about everything." I didn't know what to say, so I said "okay." He calls once in a while, then sends protein powder and chocolate. Last week Mom told me him and Auntie Arlene were getting a divorce. I wonder what he'll do now?

When we got here I met this girl named Robbie. It's short for Roberta. Her mom named her after her dad, Roberto. Guess she didn't want to wait for a boy. Anyway, I got to know this girl because she always rode through the neighborhood on a bike that was too big for her. She rode that bike all the time, and since mine was still in California, I asked her if I could ride it.

"Okay, but don't wreck it," she said, hopping off at the curb.

It felt great riding around since I missed my own bike so much. Robbie was nice and let me ride it anytime I wanted. To pay her back I gave her gum and chips from Grandma's bar.

Robbie's dad works driving a forklift and her mom works at Lutie's, which is a grocery store on Prospero Ave. Her mom is pretty. She smiles every time I walk in, even if I'm not buying anything. Robbie looks like her—clear down to the gold specks in her eyes.

Me and Robbie hang out every day. We go to the same school, and we're in the same class. School's easy, but Corin doesn't do as good as she used to. She says it's 'cause her teacher's mean. Robbie said she *is* mean, but told Corin she'll be luckier next year because Miss López, the fifth grade teacher, is nice. Corin made friends with a girl named Terri who's part Navajo. It took a while for her to make friends after we got here because she was so quiet. I made lots of friends, but my favorite is Robbie.

The only time I don't see Robbie is on Sundays when she goes to church. That's one thing I don't do anymore. First, because Grandma gave up on God a long time ago, which is a big secret no one is supposed to know. Second, because I hate our priest. Father Pedrota came from San Diego. He's old, and too big to fit in a car, so he drives a truck that you'd think a macho with boots and a gun would be driving. It's really funny watching him climb into that truck. When he talks in Mass he says whatever he wants and tries to makes us think like him—except I can't because he talks to us like we're stuck in the first grade. Everyone gets mad but they don't say nothing because it's hard to get a priest to come to a church like ours. On top of that, he's got a head even bigger than George Reeves'. It reminds me of a basketball, so I call him Father Pelota, which makes Grandma laugh.

I don't go to church anymore, but I still think about God. It's not like I've given up on him, like Grandma. I think he's here. I just don't think he's going to do what I asked him. He didn't change me into a boy, and he didn't make Eddie go away. Plus, Danny died, which happened, I think, because of him being in Vietnam. Sister 'Lizabeth would say it was because I didn't have enough faith, but I did. All I lived for was to be good so I could get my wishes. Grandma Flor says God doesn't grant wishes. She said *you* have to be the one to make things happen. She thinks God himself is just a wish. I don't know if all that's true, but the more I think about it, the more I think she might be right.

Last Friday me and Robbie got to see their dog have puppies. Her name is Beauty. She's part Chow and part no sé qué. Me and Robbie watched all six puppies get born but it looked like one was dead. Beauty kept licking it. In fact, she licked all of them.

"How can she do that?" I asked, crinkling up my nose.

"My dad says it's in stink," said Robbie, watching Beauty trying to make the puppy move.

"In stink?"

"Yeah. He says dogs don't learn to do those things. They just know what to do." It looked like she was trying not to cry.

Me and Robbie watched Beauty lick the puppy for a while but it just laid there. I felt sad, and glanced at Robbie who had tears she kept trying to wipe away.

"Poor thing is dead," I said.

Robbie nodded, then left to go get her Dad. "I'll be right back."

Her dad came over looking worried. "Qúe pasó con la perra?

"I think one of her puppies is dead, Daddy."

"Oooh, yah. Let's see." He reached in to grab the puppy. Beauty watched him take her, but didn't do nothing. He walked to the room at the back of the house and told Robbie to get a paper bag and lay it on the floor. Robbie did, and her dad put the dead puppy on the bag. He spent a minute looking at her.

"Pobrecita," he said shaking his head. "Shall we bury it?"

We both nodded and followed her dad who was carrying the puppy in both his hands like it was something special. I started crying along with Robbie. We dug a hole under the big cottonwood tree in the backyard and put the puppy in it. It looked so little and grey.

"You two want to say anything?" asked her dad.

"So long, little girl," I said.

"Just a sec—" Robbie went and got a couple of her mom's daisies and some of Beauty's dog biscuits and put them around the puppy like a picture frame. "There," she said, wiping the dirt from her hands.

"Están listas?" asked her dad, his foot on the shovel.

"Yeah," she said, still crying. "Bye-bye, perrita."

Then her dad took the shovel, scooped up some dirt and started covering up the puppy. That's when it was saddest to me, I don't know why. When he finished, he made a little cross out of popsicle sticks and stuck it in the ground. "That way we'll always remember her," he said. We walked back to the garage where Beauty was with the five other puppies making little mewing noises. We smiled when we saw them.

After that, me and Robbie decided to be blood sisters. We took a knife, cut ourselves, then rubbed our fingers together. Blood sisters could tell secrets, and that's what we did. Secrets we promised never to tell. I told her about liking girls. I said I think I was born that way since that's all I thought about for as long as I could remember. I told her my biggest secret was that I wanted to turn into a boy so I could be with girls, and how I prayed to God every night to change me.

"Nothing happened, right?" she asked.

"Nope." I looked down at the ground. We were sitting outside underneath the tree where the puppy was buried. For the longest time Robbie didn't say anything. I started getting scared since I never told anyone before.

"You think that's a big secret? Well, it's not, because you know what?"

"What?" I asked.

"I like 'em, too."

I could hardly talk. "Y-You do?"

"Uh-huh," she said, not looking at me.

"Really?"

She nodded.

"What do *you* do about it?"

"Think and wish."

"Like what?"

"Oh, you know, think about girls and wish I could kiss one."

"Me, too!" I said. I couldn't believe she felt the same as me.

"Does your mom and dad know you like girls?" I asked.

"I don't think so," she said with a soft laugh.

I spotted a lizard skittering under some plants. "Well, you're the first I ever told."

"Yeah, you too." She dug a stick into the dirt. "You think it's a sin?" she asked, finally looking at me.

"No," I said. "I don't."

"Me neither," she said, smiling.

We were quiet again. Then slowly, softly, she reached out and touched my hand. It felt good. Really good, like an electric wire running from the tips of my fingers to the end of my spine.

I looked at Robbie's hand, taking in how it felt to have her touch me. Then I carefully moved my fingers into hers. For the first time ever, I was holding hands with a girl.

We sat underneath that tree without saying anything and watched the sun go down. As it grew dark I knew I had to go home.

"I gotta get going," I said squeezing her hand tight.

"Okay," she said. "See you tomorrow?"

"Yeah," I said, smiling.

Then, without a word, she leaned in and kissed me.

And you know, I didn't know what to do or think. But for once I could say I felt so good it didn't matter.

~

CARLA TRUJILLO was born to a working class family in Las Vegas, New Mexico, and grew up in Northern California. She attended U.C. Davis, where she got a B.S. in human development, then went to graduate school at the University of Wisconsin where she earned a PhD in educational psychology. She works as an administrator in diversity education at the University of California, Berkeley.

Carla Trujillo is the editor of *Chicana Lesbians: The Girls Our Mothers Warned Us About* (Third Woman Press, 1991) which won the LAMBDA Book Award for Best Lesbian Anthology and the Out/Write Vanguard Award for Best Pioneering Contribution to the field of Gay/Lesbian Lifestyle Literature. In addition to editing *Living Chicana Theory* (Third Woman Press, 1998), she is also the author of various articles on identity, sexuality, and higher education as well as several short stories.

Excerpts from the early manuscript for *What Night Brings* received a Runner-up award from the Astraea Lesbian Writers Fund, and Honorable Mention for the Writers at Work 2000 competition.

CURBSTONE PRESS, INC.

is a non-profit publishing house dedicated to literature that reflects a commitment to social change, with an emphasis on contemporary writing from Latino, Latin American and Vietnamese cultures. Curbstone presents writers who give voice to the unheard in a language that goes beyond denunciation to celebrate, honor and teach. Curbstone builds bridges between its writers and the public – from inner-city to rural areas, colleges to community centers, children to adults. Curbstone seeks out the highest aesthetic expression of the dedication to human rights and intercultural understanding: poetry, testimonies, novels, stories, and children's books.

This mission requires more than just producing books. It requires ensuring that as many people as possible learn about these books and read them. To achieve this, a large portion of Curbstone's schedule is dedicated to arranging tours and programs for its authors, working with public school and university teachers to enrich curricula, reaching out to underserved audiences by donating books and conducting readings and community programs, and promoting discussion in the media. It is only through these combined efforts that literature can truly make a difference.

Curbstone Press, like all non-profit presses, depends on the support of individuals, foundations, and government agencies to bring you, the reader, works of literary merit and social significance which might not find a place in profit-driven publishing channels, and to bring the authors and their books into communities across the country. Our sincere thanks to the many individuals, foundations, and government agencies who support this endeavor: J. Walton Bissell Foundation, Connecticut Commission on the Arts, Connecticut Humanities Council, Fisher Foundation, Greater Hartford Arts Council, Hartford Courant Foundation, J. M. Kaplan Fund, Eric Mathieu King Fund, John D. and Catherine T. MacArthur Foundation, National Endowment for the Arts, Open Society Institute, and the Woodrow Wilson National Fellowship Foundation.

Please help to support Curbstone's efforts to present the diverse voices and views that make our culture richer. Tax-deductible donations can be made by check or credit card to:
Curbstone Press, 321 Jackson Street, Willimantic, CT 06226
phone: (860) 423-5110   fax: (860) 423-9242
www.curbstone.org

IF YOU WOULD LIKE TO BE A MAJOR SPONSOR OF A
CURBSTONE BOOK, PLEASE CONTACT US.